Epoch

THE HOURGLASS SAGA
BOOK ONE

SAMANTHA GAIL

DSTAR PUBLISHING LLC

For all the little girls who wanted Belle to kick ass.

Author's Note

Extensive research went into the history, characters, and settings for this book. There are several Easter eggs for any history buffs. I tried my best to maintain authentic, historical integrity as much as possible while also serving the requirements of the plot.

Many characters are inspired by real people. I encourage all readers to learn their true stories so that the past can never truly be forgotten.

-SG

I slammed my hands over my ears as I hid under the kitchen sink and the crashing sounds echoed outside. One of Mommy's boyfriends was here and he was yelling so loud it made my ears hurt. I hated all of Mommy's boyfriends, but this one was the worst. He only came to see her once a week, but he screamed and broke things every time. Mommy said he was a bad man and that I needed to hide when he was around.

My knees were jutting into my chin as I crouched in the cabinet. At six-years-old, I was growing a little too big to fit under the sink, but there was no other place to hide. Mommy and I shared a bedroom, but most of the time she slept out on the couch. The doors had been ripped off the bedroom closet a while ago and there was nowhere else I could fit anymore. My muscles were cramping in the small space, and I desperately wished Mommy would make him leave so I could go visit Mr. Cooper down the hall.

Mommy's piercing wail made me jump in the small space,

tasting blood from where I bit my tongue. Mommy had never screamed like that before. I needed to check on her. When I pushed open the cabinet door and unfolded myself from the inside, I could see Mommy lying on the floor in the living room. The coffee table had been pushed to the side, the ashtray upended on the carpet. There was a needle hanging out of her arm and her mean boyfriend was straddling her, pummeling her face with his hand. Blood poured from her nose, mixing in with the heavy mascara and eyeliner that ran down her face.

Without thinking, I rushed towards the bad man and smacked his shoulder. "Get away from my mommy!" I yelled.

He grabbed the collar of my shirt to yank me forward only to shove me backwards. I landed hard on my butt and began to cry.

"Get this little shit out of here, Aimee," he growled at Mommy.

She sat up, wailing again, and yanked the needle from her arm. "Don't hurt her!" she cried. She looked at me and tried to wipe the tears from her face.

"Get out, Mirielle," she snapped. Her voice made me wonder if I had done something wrong. She sounded angry with me. "You ruin everything! Just get out!" Mommy fell back on the floor, sniffling, throwing an arm across her eyes. Her skirt was hiked up around her waist and her shirt was torn. She would be really angry tomorrow.

Her boyfriend gleamed maliciously at me. "You heard her, you little brat. Leave!"

My eyes were blurring from the tears now. I didn't want him to hurt her, but my mommy made me think I was being bad. She made me leave our apartment whenever I was being punished. Hastily, I wiped the snot on my arm and ran out the door, letting it slam behind me. Mr. Cooper, my only friend, was already peeking out his door at the end of the hall.

"Come here, sweet girl," he said tenderly, his Armenian accent thick.

I rushed into his open arms and allowed him to envelope me in a bear hug. He smelled like tobacco and peppermint, and it was my favorite smell in the world. Mr. Cooper always made me feel safe whenever Mommy was upset or one of Mommy's boyfriends showed up. He would hug me and let me stay in his apartment until Mommy was okay again.

After a few minutes I felt my tears drying up and I pulled away. His apartment was as cramped as ours but felt cozier with his oversized chair and stacks of books everywhere. Mommy never got me books. I loved it here.

"There, now, that's better," he said, using a tissue to wipe my face. "I was hoping you'd come see me today. I have a new book for us!"

I sniffled one last time, his distraction working. "Really?" I whimpered.

He nodded. "Go ahead and grab yourself a juice box, and we can start it now." He held up a worn paperback with a little girl on the cover, surrounded by books. I was going to like this story, I could already tell.

Settling into the armchair, Mr. Cooper huffed and adjusted his glasses. Just as I had dozens of times before, I turned off all the other lights except for the lamp beside him and wrapped myself in a worn blanket before sitting on his lap. He always read to me when I came to visit, his deep voice pulling me away from the terrors at home.

"This is called 'Matilda' by an author named Roald Dahl," he explained. "And she likes to read as much as you do!"

Before long I was lost in the words, hating Matilda's horrible family, and cheering for her friends as they battled the evil Miss

Trunchbull. I fell asleep on Mr. Cooper's chest, feeling safe for the first time all day. Mr. Cooper would always protect me, of that I was absolutely sure.

CHAPTER 1

The Phone Call

Holding my breath, I leaned further over the vellum document spread on the table before me and grazed the first mark lightly with a Q-tip. The chemical solvent reacted instantly, making the T appear clearly on the document, eliminating hundreds of years' worth of grime and decay. One letter down, only four hundred more to go. Restoring historical documents was time consuming, but it was one of my favorite parts of my job as an archivist at the Museum of Natural History. It was like a mystery to be solved, one layer of dirt at a time.

My cell phone rang on the desk behind me and I started in surprise. The phone was more of a watch and calendar than anything else since I did not really have anyone to talk to. If it was ringing now, it had to be urgent. I quickly pulled my gloves off and exited the vacuum-sealed space where documents had to be preserved lest the particles in the air destroy the ink or ancient paper. I smiled, however, when I read the caller ID.

"Good morning, Mr. Cooper," I said. "To what do I owe this pleasure?"

His voice sounded gruffer than my early childhood memories after another twenty years of smoking a pack a day and I could tell he was fighting back another coughing fit as he greeted me. His health had been steadily declining for years, but he refused to see a doctor because "they just want to give you medicine in America." Despite immigrating to New York City in 1962 and changing his name from the Armenian 'Choolijyan' to the American 'Cooper,' he never lost his distrust of the country. I waited patiently for him to collect himself.

"Sweet girl, I need you to come see me tonight," he finally rasped out. It was odd for him to make such a request outside of our normal schedule and I immediately felt a slither of trepidation run down my spine.

"Is something wrong?" I hedged.

He hacked out a cough. "Do I need a reason to see the only person who brings me joy?"

That made me roll my eyes. He had been using that excuse a lot lately to guilt me into staying longer when I visited.

Sighing heavily, I tried to think of an acceptable excuse. Telling Mr. Cooper I had a new project at work that demanded my attention would only upset him. His favorite complaint was that I worked too hard and never had time for a life anymore. He blasted me constantly for not having more friends or, god forbid, dating. It was not natural, he said, to focus all of my time on the past. "Has my mom been around lately?" I asked instead, certain the subject would derail him.

He snarled into the phone. "You know your mother won't show her face around here again. I would never allow it now!"

I believed him. After years of watching my mother's clientele rotate in and out of our apartment in the projects, bringing drugs, weapons, and all sorts of illegal activity, Mr. Cooper had finally snapped and reported her the day that I moved into my own place. She had been evicted and warrants were issued for her arrest, but she still frequented the area, selling her body to other neighbors in the surrounding buildings and businesses. He threatened her every time, determined to protect me even now that I was an adult doing well for myself.

Since I could not think of an excuse he would find acceptable, I agreed to swing by before I went home for the evening. It sounded like he was coughing hard enough to bring up phlegm as he thanked me for brightening his day. There was nothing I wouldn't do for this man.

Mr. Cooper remained the best part of my childhood. He always kept his bedroom clean for my use, preferring to sleep upright in his comfy chair any time my mother kicked me out. He was the one who insisted I start tae kwon do as a child to protect myself from my mother's "boyfriends" and walked me to the community center every week for my class. I had graduated with my black belt and moved on to things like krav maga and jiu jitsu, all thanks to him.

He filled my spare time with books and puzzles, encouraging me to focus on my studies. "Your mind," he used to say, "is something they will never take from you." It was solely due to his support that I applied to college.

The day I received my acceptance letter with a full scholarship to Princeton was one of the happiest days of my life. He cried tears of joy at my side and insisted on buying me an expensive dinner all the way uptown to celebrate. In many ways, Mr. Cooper was the grandfather I never had. He was certainly the only person I considered family, having parted ways with my mother the same day I received my Princeton letter. If he needed me to stop by today, then I would do so with a smile on my face.

The day passed far too quickly. I had to set an alarm to remind myself to leave at a decent hour. I only made it through three lines on the document, but I was able to determine it was written in Occitan, an old French dialect, and estimated the date to be early 1400s. My colleagues often badgered me about going out in the field to help locate and identify the artifacts sent back to the museum, but I was happiest by myself in the farthest recess of the basement archives. Field life was not for me. I preferred working alone, my own thoughts to keep me company, and the idea of seeing a piece of history battered, torn, and potentially destroyed as I dug it out of the earth or pried it free from a small hole in a cave gave me tremendous anxiety. I knew my limits.

Emerging on the street outside the museum, the cold air swirled around me, nipping my nose and ears. Snow was falling softly, coating the trees across the street in Central Park. It was picturesque without yet turning into dangerous. The snow wasn't sticking to the roads and thanks to the heavy foot traffic, ice hadn't had a chance to form on the sidewalk. Steering towards the subway, I decided to save some money rather than hail a taxi. Growing up with nothing taught me to be frugal as an adult. Taking the train to the Bronx was the responsible choice.

That was how I chose to live my life. Responsible. Careful. Predictable. I knew Mr. Cooper wanted something to thrill me, something to remind me that I was a single, 26-year-old woman, but I was content. Seeing my mother turn to drugs and prostitution was enough excitement to last me a lifetime. My life felt safe, each day bringing quiet challenges in my archive room, with occasional evenings spent at the dojo a few blocks from my apartment. There were no complications, no stressors from my mother, nothing to keep me up at night anymore, and it felt divine. I had recently entertained the idea of adopting a cat, an idea that Mr.

Cooper vehemently shot down at our weekly Sunday dinner. "You'll turn into a spinster," he spat out in his thick accent.

The memory of that conversation brought a smile to my face. Mr. Cooper had started swearing in Armenian, something he did when my arguments made too much sense. Whenever I reminded him that having more of a social life would mean less time with him, he would smile and mutter, "God willing," but there would be a twinkle in his eye that let me know how little sentiment there was behind the statement.

As I rounded the corner to Mr. Cooper's block flashing blue and red lights momentarily blinded me. There were four squad cars and a fire truck haphazardly parked in front of the building. I could see several of my former neighbors outside, huddled together for warmth. My heart dropped to my stomach and I dashed underneath the police tape blocking off the door of the building, racing up three flights of stairs to my old floor.

I could not hear the voices around me as I zeroed in on Mr. Cooper's open door at the opposite end of the hall. An officer was standing in the doorway taking photographs of the interior of the apartment. I shoved him out of the way and choked down a sob.

The apartment looked as though it had been ransacked. All of Mr. Cooper's books were torn, with pieces of the pages on every surface. His beloved armchair was ripped open and the feathers coated the floor. The lone window in the living room was shattered and snow was blowing in. A detective in a tie came around the corner, barking an order at the officer I pushed out of the way. My stomach bottomed out at the sight of Barrett Collins, NYPD.

"Ma'am, you can't be in here!" he snapped at me. Barrett finally made eye contact with me and I saw the recognition dawn in his eyes. "Mirielle...how are you?"

Barrett Collins was the bane of my existence from 6th grade

through my senior year of high school. He was more than popular —he was a school legend—varsity in wrestling, tennis, and football, and more than half the girls in my graduating class had slept with him, earning him a reputation as a player. For some reason, I seemed to be the only one immune to his charms, a fact that must have rankled him to his core because he never stopped pressuring me to go out with him. Once, he even went so far as to blackmail me by threatening to tell the school about my mother's nightly activities, but Mr. Cooper intervened and contacted the principal. Barrett was suspended, but it only served to add fuel to the fire. He pursued me relentlessly; it was the biggest blessing when I crossed the auditorium stage for that diploma and never had to see him again. Until now, at least.

"Where is Mr. Cooper?" I asked. "Is he okay?"

"What are you doing here?" Barrett countered.

I shook my head as I tried to fight back the tears. Barrett would make me do a song and dance for him before he would give me any information. It was at this moment I caught sight of a framed photograph on the floor near the window, Mr. Cooper and me at my undergraduate graduation ceremony. The image steeled my resolve and I squared my shoulders to glare at him. "Where is Mr. Cooper, Barrett?"

For once Barrett's pale blue eyes held pity. "We have not been able to locate a body," he finally said.

I could never have anticipated that response. "You haven't located a body?" I repeated. "You haven't seen him?" My hands started shaking and I sank into the desecrated sofa before my knees followed suit.

He shook his head. "Were you supposed to meet him or did Mrs. Vandermire alert you, too?"

"He called me this morning and asked me to come see him

tonight. We usually have dinner together a few times a week, but he's been wanting to spend more time with me lately as his health has gotten worse. Tell me what's going on!"

I watched Barrett war with himself over what information to divulge. I wasn't above flirting or flaunting my bodily assets at this point if it meant he shared what he knew. Everyone in the area knew how important Mr. Cooper was to me. Barrett was certainly no exception.

"Mrs. Vandermire said she could hear screams coming from the apartment and an unidentified man yelling before what sounded like an explosion."

"An explosion?" I echoed. It was then that I noticed the walls had a charred look to them as if a ring of fire had gone around the room. "But there's no fire damage?"

"None. Fire alarms never went off. By the time we arrived, the apartment was empty," Barrett explained.

It didn't make any sense. Mr. Cooper did not have enemies. Other than the few older neighbors in the building and the bridge group at the community center, he did not socialize with many people. I had no idea what man would have been in his apartment, especially if he was expecting me for dinner.

"Why did you say you didn't find a body?" I asked. "Is there a reason you should have?"

Barrett shifted the weight on his other foot and dropped his gaze to the floor. I could sense the inner conflict rolling off him in waves. He began absentmindedly rubbing his thumb over his badge as if covering it up would free him of guilt. "We found a large pool of blood in the bedroom," he finally said, his head snapping up to gaze fiercely at my face. "We have no way of knowing yet if the blood belongs to Mr. Cooper," he added, eyes softening slightly.

I did not bother to respond as I once again pushed past the officer taking crime scene photos into Mr. Cooper's bedroom. It was just as disheveled as the rest of the apartment, but the crimson splotches on the floor had my stomach churning. I could not hold in my fear any longer as I sank against the doorway and allowed my sobs to break free. I sensed my nemesis' presence behind me, but he made no move to stop me or offer comfort of any kind. I was well and truly alone.

CHAPTER 2

The Search Begins

It took several minutes for me to collect myself. I could not imagine someone hurting dear Mr. Cooper, who was so kind to everyone. I needed him to be okay. I needed to find him.

"Do you have any idea where he is?" I asked him, my voice raspy.

"I was hoping you might be able to tell me something," Barrett admitted. "Did you know of anyone else meeting you here tonight?"

Shaking my head, I rose from the ground and brushed the fly away feathers from my leggings. I did not trust myself to keep my composure if I looked up and saw pity in Barrett's face. It was already bleeding into his tone and that was too much for me. Having Barrett Collins, asshole extraordinaire, see me weak and vulnerable was about as bad as dangling raw meat in front of a tiger.

"Do you know who the other man could be? The neighbor seemed to think he may have had an accent. She couldn't make out what he was saying."

I shook my head again. "He rarely had anyone in his apartment. He would meet his friends at the community center for Bridge Club on Tuesday evenings, but most of the time, he was here alone, to my knowledge."

Before I could stop them, my shoulders began to rack with sobs. It was difficult to breathe, the pain in my chest acute, and my pulse skyrocketed. I hugged both arms around my waist to try and hold myself together, but in only a moment, Barrett was there, gently guiding me to sit on the ground and then forcing my head between my knees. He ordered me to take a few deep breaths. His touch was soothing as he slowly but firmly drew circles over my shoulder blades, quietly instructing me when to hold and when to release my breath. After a few tense minutes with him squatting beside me, he pulled my hair back from my face, and I felt the rush of air as the panic attack abated.

Shock emerged as I considered Barrett's kindness. I couldn't imagine him helping anyone like that back in high school. When I turned to face him, his eyes only radiated concern. He scrutinized my features, assessing my reaction. It was the first time I could recall him ever touching me where I did not draw back in disgust, but now his hands were gentle on my face. My face grew warm as he continued to stare into my eyes and I felt my cheeks flush.

"Thank you," I whispered.

He offered me the briefest of smiles, gone in an instant. "Mirielle Townsend," he purred. "How you've grown." There was a hint of something more in his expression, as if he wanted to say something else, but caution held him back. A family of butterflies suddenly took residence in my stomach and I registered how close our bodies were. Softly, he pushed my bangs from my face and gripped me tighter around my lower back as he prepared to push us to our feet.

I couldn't help but notice how his silky brown hair fell into his eyes as he studied me, sizing me up. He was still very attractive, with piercing gray-blue eyes and high cheekbones. Although he could never be considered tall, there was something about the way he carried himself that came across as arrogant, the real OG swagger before that was a thing. Now, though, time had improved his physique; his shoulders were broader, his waist slimmer, and he was able to pull my entire body up with only one arm. Whereas in high school Barrett was too much of a player for me, this new version prompted me to glance down and check for a wedding ring. Did he still chase after women left and right or was monogamy more his speed?

It was several moments before I realized we were standing in the middle of a crime scene with one of his strong arms holding my waist and the other clutching my bicep. I blinked rapidly, breaking the spell, and pulling myself back into the present moment. *Was I seriously checking out Barrett frickin' Collins?! While Mr. Cooper was missing?!*

Suddenly, his stare turned sharp, like a veil had been drawn, and it changed his features. This was the Barrett I remembered, the bully with the giant ego.

"I don't suppose making Mr. Cooper's case my number one priority will finally get you to come over to my place." His smirk twisted along his stubbled jawline, but did not reach his eyes.

I rolled my eyes and shoved him away. "Just as despicable as ever, I see," I muttered.

He raked his eyes down my entire frame, leaving me feeling dirty and exposed to him before dismissing me. "Like I said, if you think of anything else, give me a call." He abruptly turned to another police officer who was taking samples of the charred remnants on the wall.

My knees were shaking as I wobbled down the stairs. I spotted Mrs. Vandermire out of the corner of my eye, but I wasn't ready to hear what poor Mr. Cooper experienced. Although his declining health had been on the forefront of my mind, I had never considered a world where he was no longer a train ride away. Mr. Cooper was the only true presence in my life and I wasn't ready to give him up.

Mechanically I took the train back towards Hell's Kitchen, exiting on the stop near my apartment, right on the border to Chelsea. It was located on the sixth floor in a building above a Chinese restaurant, but I loved how different it felt from the apartment of my childhood. It was a completely open concept--white bookcases covered two walls and three large windows let in plenty of light. I kept the colors soft and relaxing, the exact opposite of the broken, mismatched furniture where I grew up.

As proud as I was of my little oasis, I preferred to make the journey to Mr. Cooper's tiny apartment whenever we got together. He never made me feel embarrassed about my success, but I felt a keen sting of guilt whenever I discussed my finances with him. It seemed trivial now, though once again I felt angry with myself for not insisting on the two bedroom apartment when I bought my own place. If Mr. Cooper had been here with me, where I knew he belonged, maybe this would not have happened. My building was certainly more secure than the broken locks and dilapidated walls where he lived.

My apartment did little now to block out the chill crawling up my spine. I did not even bother to take the steps to my lofted bed. Expecting to stay up half the night overanalyzing the evening's events, I plopped down on the sofa with an Afghan and soon fell into a fitful sleep.

A shrill bell woke me up the next morning and it took me a

moment to remember why I was downstairs rather than in my own bed. The alarm on my cell signaled it was time to get my day started, but for once the thought of going to work repulsed me. I needed answers. I needed to find Mr. Cooper.

Thankfully my supervisor at the museum was very understanding. I had never taken any time off before, so he didn't really have grounds to deny my request. As I rushed through a quick shower, I decided the best course of action would be to return to the neighborhood and find out more on my own. People living in that area often had reason to be mistrustful of the police, let alone an officer with a reputation like Detective Barrett Collins, so there was a good chance they would open up to me rather than him.

I threw my long red hair into a messy bun on top of my head and pulled on my favorite pair of skinny jeans. Wanting to keep my look neutral and unimposing, I paired it with a black crop sweater and plain black thigh high boots. No sense in ruffling feathers by reminding the neighbors that I got out and made a good living now, which is all they would see if I showed up in anything name brand.

It seemed too early to head that way and risk waking everyone up, but I knew myself well enough to know that I would never be able to sit still in my apartment under the circumstances. Perhaps I could poke around Mr. Cooper's place now that the police weren't swarming the area. They didn't know him as well as I did, so they could have easily missed something that I wouldn't overlook. I would stall long enough to caffeinate at Starbucks. That was about as reasonable as I could be at the moment.

The sun bore down on me by the time I made it through Starbucks and took the train out to the Bronx. The police tape over the front door had been removed, but the building sounded eerily quiet. Usually televisions and crying babies could be heard at all hours through the paper thin walls, yet as I climbed up to the third floor towards Mr. Cooper's, I did not encounter any signs of life. The dirty yellow floor creaked beneath me as I approached his door and I felt the hair on the back of my neck rise with apprehension. Something did not feel right.

"Mirielle, is that you?!" The squeak of a voice came from behind me, making me jump a foot in the air.

It was Mrs. Vandermire; she propped her door open enough for one beady eye to glance down the hall, but I was positive she had a firm grip on the baseball bat she kept by the door as her "alarm system." She had lived in the building longer than Mr. Cooper had and kept watch over everyone.

I held a hand over my furiously beating heart to steady myself and nodded. She closed her door with a snap to unlock the many chains on the door, then opened it wider to welcome me in. Sure enough, I caught her placing the bat in the corner next to the door as I closed it behind me and stifled my laugh. Some things never changed.

"Oh, sweetheart, I was hoping you would come back. All this business has me so flustered!" she cried.

Mrs. Vandermire could not have been a hair over five feet tall and weighed no more than 90 pounds soaking wet. She was a tiny thing with the voice of a mouse, but her eyes held the knowledge of the ages. The late Mr. Vandermire had squandered their family fortune, leaving her high and dry at the ripe old age of 45. Too proud to ask her grown children for help, she had instead moved into the tiny apartment and earned her living by watching the babies of all the residents. Most of my high school class only graduated because she took care of their children.

She politely steered me towards the miniscule table and began bustling around the kitchen to make a pot of tea. The hum of the stove kicking to life calmed me somewhat. It was a familiar sound, much like the stove in Mr. Cooper's.

I paused, unsure of where to begin. "Mrs. Vandermire, can you tell me what happened?"

Scowling, she pulled a box of cookies out of the cabinet and shook her head. "Something strange is goin' on here," she said. "I don't even know how to explain it."

"The police said you heard screams from Mr. Cooper's apartment?" I prompted her.

"Is that what they told you?" Mrs. Vandermire snorted. "Sounded more like witchcraft. Like someone was casting spells, speakin' in tongues or something. I didn't recognize the voice. It sounded like a younger man, but kind of like a British accent. European, at the very least." She placed a cup of tea in front of me and sat down.

My mind was reeling from this information. It ruled out every acquaintance I knew of for Mr. Cooper. Most of the members of his bridge club were older Armenian men like himself. Speaking in tongues? Mr. Cooper identified as an "unorthodox Christian" and only attended church at Christmas and Easter. He certainly never expressed an interest in speaking in tongues. Who would visit him and do such a thing?

"Had you ever heard this man before?" I asked.

"Nope," she replied quickly. "You know ol' Coop never had anyone visit 'cept you. Kept to himself, that ol' man."

I agreed but felt a trickle of relief at hearing my impressions confirmed. It would have made it worse, somehow, to find out that I didn't know Mr. Cooper the way I believed I did. If Mrs. Vandermire, the building gossip, did not recognize the man, he certainly must be a mystery.

"And what of the explosion?" I inquired.

Mrs. Vandermire shifted in her seat, seeming to choose her next words with care. "It didn't...feel like an explosion. Felt a ripple of something pass through the place. But there was a loud sound. Nothin' I ever heard before." Her eyes glazed over, lost in her memory. I involuntarily shuddered at the haunted look on her face.

I chugged the last remnants of my tea and stood up. "I'm going to go look around. See if I can find anything the police might've missed," I announced.

She nodded. "That's a good idea. You know they ain't gonna take this seriously. You're his only hope."

Tears threatened as I considered how accurate her words were. Crime was so rampant in this part of the city, it's a wonder the police even showed at all. The likelihood of them investigating Mr. Cooper's disappearance was slim to none. Who cared about an elderly immigrant who lived alone? Unless Barrett returned to old habits and used it to manipulate me. I couldn't put it past him.

As I slid under the caution tape over Mr. Cooper's door, the hair on the back of my neck stood up again. An eerie feeling as though someone was breathing on me made me whip my head around. There was no one in sight, not even Mrs. Vandermire, but I could not shake the feeling that I was not alone. The building still maintained the unnatural quiet as if all sound had been snuffed out.

It did not look like anything had been touched since I left yesterday. All of Mr. Cooper's beloved books were in tattered shreds around the small apartment. I dropped to my knees next to a pile that used to house his favorites. He would weep if he saw the state of things. Normally he kept them in stacks on the floor as well as teetering on a rickety bookshelf beside the kitchen table, too many to place anywhere else. To this day, I had no idea how he accumulated so many on his tiny pension. He must have scouted bookstores for sales like coaches scouted star athletes.

The floors creaking behind me had me whipping around for the second time. Barrett was standing in the doorway, observing me with an unreadable look on his face. There was a heat to it that I could not place, but apprehension bloomed fresh. Slowly, I rose from the crouched position on the floor and turned to face him. His eyes roamed my body in a way that made me draw my coat over my chest. It made me uncomfortable to have that kind of attention, no matter how much I was attracted to him. Socially awkward was more my wheelhouse.

He cleared his throat audibly. "What are you doing here, Miri?" He must remember how much I despised that nickname when we were kids. Without breaking eye contact, he closed the gap between us, all but pinning me back against the wall. Our chests were practically touching, and the temperature in the room was rapidly climbing. I suddenly wanted him to look at my body again. We had both changed a lot since high school.

"I-I.." I stammered, trying to think of a feasible excuse. It was hard to do under the intensity of his stare. I shook my bangs out of my eyes and that drew his attention to my hair. As a freshman in college I had dyed it a bright red on a dare, but found it suited my complexion and had maintained the red ever since. He pulled a loose strand out of my face and my heart skipped a beat.

Barrett leaned in close to my ear as he whispered, "I like the red, Miri. You've always been a feisty one." His tone was seductive and brought back the butterflies in my stomach from the day before.

His words, however, transported me back to a similar situation our sophomore year where he tried to corner me in an alcove after school. I had been working on a solar power battery meant to operate the robotic car our Science Olympiad team built when he accosted me after using the gym with the wrestling team. He had been shirtless and sweaty, with gray sweatpants loosely tied on his hips. Even then he had the chiseled body of an athlete, using those muscles to cage me in and proposition me again. I had kneed him in the groin area before pushing past him to run like hell down the hall and out of the building. He had used the word "feisty" then, too.

"This is a crime scene," he said, drawing me back to the present. "You're not supposed to be here."

It was not the time for me to notice how light the blue in his eyes were, crystalline, like they had been forged from starlight. They made my knees quiver, out of fear or arousal, I was not sure. Barrett Collins had never had this kind of effect on me before.

"I was just, um, checking to see if Mr. Cooper came back," I offered weakly.

My answer must have amused him because the corners of his mouth tilted up. "You are too beautiful to be roaming around here on your own," he replied. His statement held the promise of so much more, and it made me want to scrub my body clean in a piping hot shower.

Trying to gather my bearings, I glanced around the room and noted a patch of what looked to be parchment--brown, faded, and torn--on the floor behind the armchair. It did not belong there. Mr. Cooper didn't collect books old enough to use that kind of paper.

Not wanting to draw the detective's eyes to my discovery, I looked back at him and smiled shyly. "I'll just be going, then."

I casually slipped to my left, bumping into the armchair intentionally and dropping my bag to the floor. I barely breathed as I tried to nonchalantly gather my bag while scooping up the heavy parchment that laid underneath it, clutching both to my chest as I swept from the room.

"Oh, Miri?" Barrett called when I was halfway to the stairs at the far end of the hall.

I did not say anything to him as I peered back over my shoulder, but the tension in my jaw would require use of a retainer again. His entire figure was highlighted by the winter sun pouring in from the window behind him, big enough to fill the doorway from this angle.

"You work at the museum, right? That's what I heard through the grapevine. I will be in touch with you *very* soon," he said. The heat that laced his words set off warning bells in my head.

I nodded. "Yes, sir."

He smiled wickedly, clearly believing he had won.

Not trusting myself to say anything else, I ran down the stairs and out onto the street, just like that day in high school. I wanted as much distance between us as possible. History did not need to repeat itself for me to already know--no good ever came from catching attention from a man like Barrett Collins.

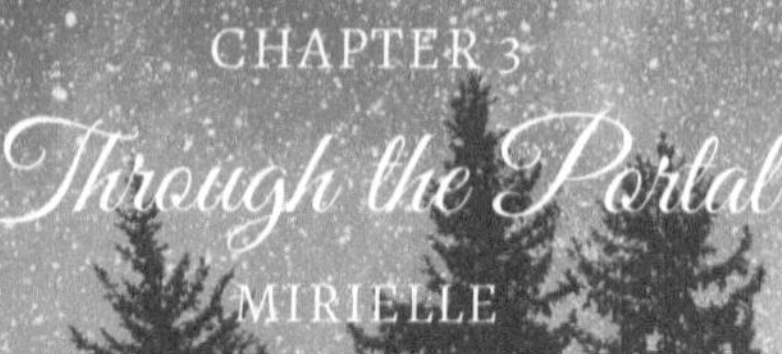

City blocks blurred as I raced from Mr. Cooper's apartment without any sense of direction or purpose. I merely wanted to get away from Barrett's oily gaze as fast as possible. By the time I allowed myself to slow down and catch my breath, the sun was high overhead and sweat was pouring down my face. Quickly, I hailed a cab to my office. I needed to examine this parchment.

The underground labyrinth that is the Museum of Natural History can be quite daunting the first time you enter. As the museum grew and expanded since it first opened its doors in 1874, the new additions had led to subterranean tunnels to allow easier access for employees. It also provided much needed space for the restoration and preservation of artifacts and an archival library. It was a dream come true when I was offered a position here fresh out of graduate school, and I have thanked my lucky stars every day since.

I was fortunate enough not to encounter anyone when I entered the tunnels through an obscure office building near W.

86th St. and followed the corridor down without bothering to turn on the light. Darkness didn't scare you when you have already encountered the worst sort of monsters in the daylight. The entire time I had to shake the feeling that there was a presence watching me, but now that the adrenaline stopped flowing, I was probably being overly paranoid. Something about the whole encounter with Barrett felt off. Did he return to the crime scene because of me? Would the police actually take it seriously or was this yet another way for my high school enemy to torture me? None of it added up.

My lab was situated on the second floor of the subterranean level in the back of a giant warehouse. It was where the collection of museums in New York stored their artifacts when they were not on display, so although to the untrained eye it all appeared chaotic and random, everything was actually carefully catalogued. The museum had been updating everything to a digital tracking system in order to optimize the process and monitor security, pinpointing the exact location of any artifact at any time. An item could not move so much as five feet without triggering an alarm that only authorized personnel had the code to turn off. The museum had to nearly triple security to track everything, but accidents and "misplacements"--the official word for losing an artifact--had been drastically reduced. Walking through the maze of bones, treasure, and excavation remnants everyday always gave me a thrill of excitement. Preserving history for future generations was an under appreciated responsibility.

My lab was empty, though I rarely saw my co-workers anymore as we all worked odd hours. The museum did not necessarily require standard office hours so long as the work was done, and most of my colleagues enjoyed the New York City nightlife too much to keep themselves on that kind of schedule. I sent a prayer of thanks to whatever gods would listen that I wouldn't have to explain what I found to any other prying eyes.

Donning my nitrile gloves and protective glasses, I gingerly pulled the scrap out of my bag. It was brown and heavy, thick enough for me to need all five fingers to hold properly. The fibers were woven unevenly and at first glance, the writing appeared to be written by hand rather than printed. It was a curving scrawl, a language I did not recognize. There was no way this came from one of Mr. Cooper's books. It could not have even come from Mr. Cooper himself.

Goosebumps erupted down my arms as the creepy feeling of being watched returned. Snapping my head up, I observed the office to be empty, a soft white glow emanating around the room from the lamp over my table. None of the other workstations were on since my colleagues were gone, but it was unusual for all the other lights to be out. Were they on when I arrived? I couldn't remember.

My breath began to fog in front of me as my heart rate accelerated. The temperature in the room was always cooler, which was standard for document preservation, but it seemed to be dropping rapidly as the seconds ticked by. I rubbed my hands up and down the opposing arm for warmth and slowly backed away from the table. The clock was no longer ticking above the door, like time had frozen, and the same unnatural quiet from Mr. Cooper's apartment enveloped me.

"H-hello?" I stuttered. There was no one there that I could see, but my gut instinct told me I was not alone. "Is anyone here?"

BAM! Boxes of old files stacked on shelves along the far wall shot out, papers flying all over the room. A boom echoed throughout the room as an ethereal green glow circled in front of me. My survival instincts kicked in and I dove behind my desk several feet away. The papers continued to fly about the room as though we were caught in a tornado. Daring myself to be brave, I peeked above my desk to see the greenish glow had expanded into an oval from the floor to the ceiling and a shadowy figure was stepping out.

I ducked back down behind my desk, breathing heavily. They didn't teach you *this* in grad school! All of my training from my dojo reminded me that I need a weapon, but I left my bottle of pepper spray in my messenger bag at the table...the table that was now placed directly behind the green portal of doom several feet away.

Heavy footsteps alerted me that the figure was now here in the room with me. I refused to succumb to whatever the fuck was going on, so offense it would be. Bracing my feet firmly beneath me, I took a deep breath before launching myself over the desk, my right leg kicking out. My boot connected with the jawline of a creature that should have terrified me. He stumbled backwards, clearly caught off guard.

Years of training had me in a fighting stance, fists hovering in front of my face, body angled towards the threat, but it never prepared me for this kind of opponent. The creature had gold hair that shimmered down below his shoulders, but most of the rest of his features were animalistic. He stood well over six feet and had a sharp beak where a nose and mouth should be. His eyes were human, the most stunning emerald color I had ever seen, glowing with the same sort of ethereal light as the portal. His body resembled that of a man's, including feet with golden boots, but instead of hands, there were sharp talons. The most astonishing feature of all was the pair of iridescent wings fanning out behind him. Their wingspan had to be close to nine feet as they rippled with light upon movement. He did not have on what I would call clothing, but something akin to body paint, also a shimmery gold, plated scales along his torso, arms, and legs. His beauty would be breathtaking if I was not fighting for my life.

"I mean you no harm, mortal," the creature said. His voice…it could have been composed from music, it was so harmonious. The accent was vaguely British, but certainly not American. The scientist in me wondered how a beak-like mouth was able to speak so articulately.

"And yet you destroyed my lab," I replied coolly. I did not so much as blink. Danger radiated from this thing in waves.

He merely cocked his head to the side as if studying me. While he did not openly engage in aggression, I noted that he shifted his stance ever so slightly to have a more even distribution of weight. His shoulders rolled back enough to tell me that he was bracing himself for a fight.

"I have come for what is mine," he stated in the same melodious voice. It was like a balm to ease my anxiety, much the same way venomous snakes often release a paralytic with their bites to subdue their prey. This predator wasn't going to subdue me; I grew up in the Bronx.

My fists tightened in return. "Did you take Mr. Cooper?"

He rolled his eyes and began to survey the room rather than answer me. I used his nonchalance as an opportunity and struck his jaw with my left fist. Although he was not looking in my direction, he swept an arm up and caught my wrist in an iron grip as I pulled back. The razor sharp edges of his talons threatened to puncture my skin.

"Never do that again, mortal," he warned me in an icy whisper. His hold loosened just enough that I snapped my fist back. He did not bother to look at me as he turned about the room.

"What is this 'lab' that you speak of?"

I did not provide an answer, just continued to angle my body away from his movements, my fists up and ready. With this, I was able to position myself closer to my worktable, my messenger bag and the parchment just behind me.

His eyes tracked the movement and zeroed in on the brown document behind me. "It calls to me," he said, nodding towards the parchment. "There's nowhere you can go where I won't find it."

My nerves were stretched to their breaking point, my fear and anxiety ready to snap. All of the muscles in my body were on high alert. "Then you better come get it!" I yelled before lunging at him. As if on autopilot, my head ducked to avoid the swipe of his talons and I kicked out into his torso. He did not anticipate the impact of the kick and doubled over. Using the brief height differential, I drove both my elbows into the back of his head while my left knee connected with his face. I heard the satisfying crunch of his beaklike nose breaking.

With a roar of rage he barreled towards me, catching me around the middle and tackling me to the ground. I grunted as the wind left my body. He straddled my waist, pinning both my arms above my head, but leaving my legs completely free. Blood dripped from a beak that was slowly morphing into a human-shaped nose, which is the only reason I attributed to my hesitation for not breaking his hold immediately. The extra few seconds were all he needed to snatch the parchment off the table.

"You're coming with me, mortal!" he bellowed. Yanking both my wrists up so that I was sitting upright, he snarled into my face. The emerald in his eyes looked like a whirling vortex, growing with intensity until the room plummeted into darkness and I began what felt like a free fall into nothingness. The air was sucked out of my lungs as I hurtled through a black vacuum, void of light and sound. I could not have provided a sense of direction if my life depended on it, which, at the moment, it did.

A moment later I collapsed onto icy, gray stone while the creature slammed onto his feet beside me. Without even putting my hands to my face I could already feel the bruise forming on my left cheek. As I slowly rose on all fours and blew my bangs out of my eyes, I gasped in shock at the sight before me.

The man smirked, now entirely human. "Welcome," he sneered, "to Aeternitas."

CHAPTER 4

An Aeternitas Welcome

The behemoth before me would probably be classified as a castle, but it looked massive enough to encompass an entire city. Steely gray turrets rose into a dense fog-filled sky, so tall that I had to crane my neck to see the top. Gargoyles the size of children decorated the roof line, and I could barely stop the shudder that began to creep out at their homely, distorted faces. An ornate iron gate large enough to fit two double decker busses side by side was the only entry point of a stone wall surrounding the monstrosity on both sides. The windows were sporadic, tall and thin, but black as night. There couldn't have been any glass. Given the frost coating every surface, that did not bode well for the possibility of warmth to come. This was not a place that welcomed outsiders.

Turning around to look behind me, I could only see more thick fog. I had no sense of time or place, which unnerved me more than I cared to admit. What kind of Harry Potter shit was this?

I sprang to my feet, ready to burst into attack mode, but the man simply held up a hand. A wave of power swept over me, locking my limbs in place to halt my movement. My muscles strained to fight the control his effortless gesture had over me.

"That sort of thing will not be tolerated here, mortal," the man said. He turned to face me and thank whatever gods existed my body no longer moved because there was no way I could have prevented my jaw from hitting the ground. "Beauty" was an absurd summarization of the blatant sex-appeal oozing from this man. Gone were the beak, talons, and wings, but their disappearance led me to notice his chiseled jaw line, sculpted abs leading to a deep V cut above his pant line, and protruding biceps that looked strong enough to bench press a Buick. The body paint style cover up was still painted in gold over his lower body, leaving his torso naked, but the paint left little to the imagination as to the muscular build of his legs. It took sincere effort on my part not to glance between them. His eyes maintained their ethereal emerald coloring, but here they sizzled with power that left me slightly intimidated.

My brain finally snapped to attention as I felt his power wash away. "'Eternity'?" I translated from his earlier welcome. It had been several years since I took Latin but given the number of archaic languages I encountered at work, it was hard to keep track. This answer, however, seemed to please him.

"Come," he ordered. "We have much to discuss."

I shook my head and took a large step back from him. "No, I'm not going anywhere with you! Who are you? Where am I?"

His smirk grew wider. "I will explain everything inside."

"Nope, not gonna work for me, buddy. I'm not the kind of girl who blindly takes orders from *things* that kidnap people." I hurtled the word at him as if it would demean him to point out that he was so different from me. Childish, I knew.

Golden brows furrowed as he sized me up. Did my insult actually work? Before I had time to ponder that, he snapped his fingers and I felt the same sort of free fall as I had minutes before.

Landing solidly on my ass this time, he stood before me in what looked like a dungeon from medieval times. One wall was iron lattice work, showing only a dark, stone corridor beyond. The other three walls were the same stone as the exterior of the castle, however, the temperature was significantly colder. Everything was coated in thick ice, making my breath appear in huffs. Just as I suspected, the window did not have any glass, though it looked to be too narrow for a human body to crawl through. I scrambled to it anyway and felt my stomach drop out. We were in one of the tallest towers, the ground so far below that the wall was barely visible.

"We do things my way, mortal, or there will be drastic conse-quences," he stated flatly. His tone had a hint of warning to it.

"I'm not doing shit until you tell me where I am and what the hell is going on!" I cried.

"Your questions will all be answered in due time, as I see fit," he replied.

I snorted, flipping my long hair over my shoulder now that it had fallen out of the bun. "You're in for a rude awakening then, psycho," I snapped back. "You can go fuck yourself."

Faster than I could blink, he had me pinned against the wall, arms above my head, exposing more of my stomach to the frigid air. Damn crop tops for always riding up!

He gazed at me with an intensity that left me panting, and there was a distinct clenching in my lower belly. My traitorous nipples peaked as he pushed his entire body against mine. He threw me for a loop as he leaned in and inhaled deeply along the top of my head. A chest that could have been carved from stone pressed harshly against me. I was acutely aware of the frigid stone wall scraping against my back, but it was almost titillating to have the pain mixed with the pleasure blossoming in the apex of my thighs. Glowing emerald was all I could see as I bit my lip and dared to look up at him.

I caught his eyes in mine, questioning his actions, and found the same sort of surprise mirroring back at me. "It does not matter how beautiful you are, temptress, nor will you ever win against me in a battle of wills," he whispered seductively in my ear. "I have had millennia to build my patience. But you are a guest here, and I will not permit you to speak to me in such a manner. Consider this your only warning."

So quickly I almost wondered if I imagined it, he softly brushed the knuckles from his free hand along my cheek, murmuring something in another language I did not have the chance to decipher.

Abruptly he dropped my hands from the hold above my head and disappeared.

Attempting to leave this cell was proving to be a lesson in futility. The bars would not budge no matter how hard I pushed and pulled, which resulted in me slipping on the ice underfoot and landing squarely on my ass again. I didn't need a mirror to know how bruised my backside must be. It also belatedly occurred to me as I braced myself to get back up that the bars did not have a door. Clearly, I needed the golden stranger to get me in or out of this cell. Despite being several stories high, I tried to squeeze myself through the window, but let's face it, with a shapely rear and thick thighs like mine, that was never going to happen.

Finally, after extracting myself from the opening, I slid down the wall to sit on the floor and stared forlornly into the foggy abyss. I had not been this powerless in years, probably not since I first started toddling over to Mr. Cooper's. At least then I had him to help protect me.

And let's not begin to talk about the freak with a beak who walked through a damn *portal* to bring me here before pinning me to a wall to sniff me. What were the odds that in roughly the span of a few hours, two different men had me writhing beneath their holds? It was hard enough to wrap my head around my sudden attraction to Barrett Collins, but my visceral reaction to the golden haired stranger was a true mystery. My mind was flashing bright red warning flags to my lady bits to remind them to keep it in check.

I must have fallen asleep because a firm hand jerked me awake. It was dark outside and only a lone torch in the creature's hand cast any light about the room. He crouched down over me, eyeing me warily with a cock of his head. I pushed my bangs out of my eyes and forced myself to sit up.

"You were muttering in your sleep," he said.

My eyebrow rose in challenge. "Is that a crime here?" I asked.

He rolled his eyes and stood, backing away to the other side of the cell. His hair had been pulled back into a bun and he now donned a simple linen shirt and dark pants with black boots. Authority radiated off him and I instinctually knew this was not a man who could be crossed. The threat of violence oozed from his very pores.

"Have you not yet grown weary of this exchange?" he inquired in his melodious voice.

Nothing else that I could see would get me out of this cell and I needed that freedom before I could figure out a way to get back to New York. I was fairly certain this was the same man Mrs. Vandermire heard in Mr. Cooper's apartment, but there was no indication he would ever provide me with the information I needed to locate Mr. Cooper, so I might as well make it back to the safety of my own world to conduct my investigation.

Subjecting myself to whatever magical sort of adventure lay on the other side of the iron bars was not exactly appealing, either. Still, I squared my shoulders back before simply nodding, steeling myself against another free fall into the void. He nodded as well and we were off.

This time I managed to land on my feet, although I stumbled a bit before righting myself. I glanced at the man long enough to catch his smirk, but quickly got distracted by the splendor of the room. White marble floors led to 12 foot walls coated in emerald and gold filigree silk. Rich tapestries decorated the two walls encasing one half of the room while the other two opened onto a stone balcony overlooking a gloomy mountainside of evergreen trees that faded into the same thick fog as I saw upon arrival. There was snow on the trees and balcony, yet it no longer felt chilly. A roaring fire in a fireplace that stretched at least six feet could have been the reason my breath no longer appeared before me.

Dominating the room was a monstrous canopy bed, far bigger than anything I had ever seen. My entire apartment could have fit inside the chamber. I wondered idly if I looked like a dwarf inside such a space. I turned about the room, not bothering to stop my mouth from hanging open as I gawked.

The man leaned against the gold bed post, arms crossed in front of his chest as he observed me. He did not comment as I gingerly ran my hand along the white marble mantel or gently rubbed the green brocade curtain ensconcing the doorway to the balcony. The great height intimidated me too much to go further; I was not a fan of heights.

"Am I staying here?" I whispered. It made no sense to do so, but the sheer size and grandeur of the room had my inferiority complex rearing its ugly head. Suddenly I was the awkward daughter of an addict wearing clothes found in the dumpster all over again.

The creature nodded. "As long as you follow the rules, this will be yours for the duration of your stay. There is a bathing chamber behind that tapestry." He gestured behind me to the depiction of a willow tree on the bank of a lake. A few feet to the left was a wooden door carved with roses. "I will send Darda in to tend to you."

"Darda?" I echoed.

He nodded. "My housekeeper. She will assist you in bathing."

My eyebrows receded to my hairline. "I don't need help with showering!"

His emerald eyes blazed as he approached me, stopping only an inch away. If I took a deep breath, we would have been chest to chest. The man towered over me, so much so I craned my head back to glare at him, determined to stand my ground as much as possible. A small voice in my head reminded me that he had already demonstrated he had the upper hand, but I ignored it. This may have been a man used to obedience, but I was nobody's submissive.

As our gazes locked, heated no doubt by our battle of wills, the familiar clench in my abdomen tightened. I could faintly smell a hint of roses about him. Satisfaction took over as I noted the tense lock of his chiseled jaw, surely a sign that he was about to give in to my demand. I could feel his muscles tensing as he fought to control his anger.

More gently than I could have anticipated, he tenderly brushed the bangs out of my eyes, tucking my hair behind my ear. His gaze roamed my face and down my body, and I flushed with arousal at the primitive urge to flaunt what nature gave me. It wasn't much, but I certainly wasn't ashamed either.

"I will have her bring you something for your nerves, then," he offered in a whisper. His hand still lingered near my ear, pulling the red locks through his fingers. The intensity of his gaze nearly knocked me off my feet when I smiled in triumph. He looked at me as though he did not recognize happiness.

"You will find the castle to be quite hospitable. As soon as you bathe, merely snap your fingers. You will join me for dinner." There was a finality to his order that I did not question.

Showering without an audience was enough of a win for me at the moment. "Yes, sir," I replied quietly.

He smirked at that and finally dropped his hand from my hair. Taking a step back, he broke the spell between us. "You may call me Gryphon," was all he said before he snapped his fingers and vanished into thin air.

CHAPTER 5

Gryphon. I rolled the name around on my tongue as I mulled in the bathwater. The "bathing chamber," as he called it, was the approximate size of my apartment and featured a soaking tub set in stone that had a short staircase to enter. A long, open window to my left provided more stunning views of the mountainous peaks beyond that blended into the smothering fog, which had yet to dissipate.

More than a dozen taps of various shapes and sizes stood at either end of the tub, and to my delight, each one pumped out a different soap, bath salt, scented bubble, or hot water. The fragrant smell of roses clouded the air in the room as a result of all the luxuries I now soaked in, and I leaned back with a contented sigh against a velvet pillow just above the water line. Steam cloaked the room, plastering my hair to my face, but it had been so long since I indulged in a bath that I could not bring myself to care.

The opposite wall featured a floor to ceiling mirror along with a vanity and sink big enough to bathe a toddler. To my surprise, the drawers in the vanity had been filled with hairbrushes of different sizes and thickness, hair straighteners, curling wands, and more makeup than an Atlantic City drag club. When I had pulled out one of the curling wands and pondered aloud where to plug it in, the light on the handle simply sprang on before a faint curl of steam issued from the ceramic rod. I nearly burned my foot after I dropped it in shock. There was a small water closet in the back that featured a toilet and bidet.

Perhaps I had hit my head after I slipped on the icy stairs heading down to the subway platform. Or one of those pesky bike messengers all over Manhattan had finally clipped me and I busted my skull on the sidewalk. This entire situation had to be a fabrication my mind made up after some sort of extreme trauma, right? The only other alternative would be something ridiculous like magic.

Magic did not actually exist, so the logical part of my brain warred with the rest of me that yearned for this to be a fantasy fit for a book. The scientist in me refused to believe in things I could not see or discover for myself, but five-year-old Mirielle would have squealed in delight at the prospect of an enchanted castle. Mr. Cooper and I had read endless fairytales when I was a child and although reality had set in fairly quickly, the dream of far off places, princesses, dragons, and knights had never quite gone away. In a way, that was what drove me into the classics and litera-ture at university, because a romantic heart could never fully embrace the pragmatism the world demanded. It was impossible to grow up reading the fanciful stories Mr. Cooper provided without wondering in the back of my mind if maybe someday I was meant for a grand adventure, too.

But at what cost? I still had no clue where I was or how to get home. I needed to find Mr. Cooper before my anxiety crippled me. And what of my job? My vandalized lab? No one would even question to look for me for several days since I did not maintain relationships with any of my co-workers and I did not regularly keep in contact with any of my school friends. I could be stuck here forever and no one would even realize it. Aeternitas...the irony was not lost on me.

The muffled sounds of a door slamming echoed from behind the tapestry and I bolted to my feet. Water sloshed around the rim of the tub, soaking into the stone, as I searched frantically for a towel. I groaned in frustration and muttered in vexation, "Why isn't there a fucking towel?!" when a fluffy green bathing sheet appeared beside me, folded into thirds. Apparently, I could just speak things into existence in here.

"Channing Tatum!" I called out. Nothing happened, but it never hurt to check.

"Is that you, dearie?" a cheerful voice called from the bedroom. There were muted sounds like something heavy was being dragged across the marble floor.

I wrapped the bathing sheet tightly around my body before pushing the tapestry up to enter the bedroom. The only source of light in the dim room was from the fireplace, but I could not see a person anywhere.

"Hello?" I uttered.

"Oh my, but you're a pretty one!" came the same cheerful voice. It had an Irish accent belonging to a woman I would assume to be older, but there was no one visible in the room.

"A-are y-you a ghost-t?" I stammered. There were far too many scientists who swore a belief in the occult for me to deny its existence. I could not battle a poltergeist and maintain my sanity imprisoned in a castle accessed through a magic portal, I just couldn't.

The disembodied voice belted out a loud peal of laughter to

my right, a high pitched sound that made me think of a rosy grandmother. "Dearie, no! My name is Darda. I'm the housekeeper, you could say."

Had I gone mad while in the bathtub? Were there hallucinogenic powers in the water? There was no one else in the room with me. I even spun around to check.

"Ah, I see the Master did not warn you yet," Darda's voice sighed heavily.

I whipped my head back towards the door, the direction where I heard the voice. An antique writing desk engraved with gold filigree was against the wall closest to the door, but there was no chair for anyone to sit at to use the desk. The room was entirely empty, save for me.

"I think it best you speak with the Master, dearie," Darda said gently. "He requested you wear the garment in the desk here."

Scanning the corners of the room for hidden cameras and speakers, I quickly opened the heavy lid and snatched the contents therein. It was a billowy black dress that looked at least four sizes too big for my muscular frame. A tulle petticoat large enough for a circus tumbled out as I held the dress closer to the light.

I snorted. "You can tell your *Master* that I will do no such thing. I will put my own clothes back on or go naked before I wear something that silly." To prove my point I returned to the bathroom to find my discarded jeans and shirt, but all of my clothing was gone. I even opened all of the cabinets and drawers along the vanity and under the sink. Nothing. What the hell?

"Darda, where are my clothes?!" I shrieked. The voice did not answer, but the same muffled scraping sound as before reverberated through the tapestry. I yanked it back to reveal a still empty bedroom. This time she did not answer. When I went to try the door, I realized there was no doorknob. I had no way out of this room unless someone opened the door from the outside.

Sighing in defeat, I snatched the damned black tent off the floor. The entire thing sank right back to the floor as the neckline bypassed my body completely. "I guess I'm not meeting him for dinner," I muttered to myself, only belatedly realizing that talking to myself was not a promising sign.

CHAPTER 6

Vexations Galore

GRYPHON

I released a heavy sigh of annoyance as Darda, my housekeeper for all intents and purposes, berated me for not warning our latest guest about the inner workings of the castle. I tuned her out the same way I had every other time we had similar conversations. Only I could determine what to reveal to my unwilling subjects. This human was no different.

Darda had been a member of my household from the beginning and recognized when my attention waned. Her exasperation was only outweighed by her dedication to me, but I could feel her impatience saturating the air. It truly was unjust that she suffered for my shortcomings and she had every right to turn her back on me, yet she remained as steadfastly devoted as she had since I first began toddling about the castle. Somehow, I could not even force myself to give her enough respect to listen now.

I pushed myself away from the large worktable centered in my private office and turned my back on Darda, focusing instead on the fog outside the window. This room featured a gallery in the second story above, all of which faced the massive two-story window and stone balcony. It was the largest balcony in the palace, stretching beyond the office to include my bed and bathing chambers, almost entirely encompassing the west wing. It jutted out so far that it passed the edge of the cliffside on which the castle had been built, and there was a point where one could stand on the balcony and only see the black void into the endless valley below. The sight used to take my breath away when I had been a lad still impressed by size and grandeur, and I longed for the days when it was possible for me to feel a sense of wonder and excitement as I had then. Now it was next to impossible for me to feel much of anything.

Nothing was visible anymore because of the thick fog, so dense it even blocked out the light. Stars no longer shone in the sky at night, the sun never penetrated during the day, and without checking a clock, you never had a sense of either. Time basically stood still, which was no doubt intentional. I hated it, the feeling of being stuck--of nothingness. It made me desperate for answers, answers that I believed the woman could give to me.

Darda finally caught my attention with her next line of questioning. "Why is the young missy receiving special treatment, my lord?"

I rolled my shoulders to ease some of the tension. I had anticipated this from the moment I provided the mortal her own bed chamber. "There is no special treatment. She is simply used to different accommodations."

"'Different accommodations?'" repeated Darda. "D'you mean to tell me that you think the other humans *liked* the cell you kept them in?"

Her judgmental tone irked me, which was the only reason my frayed nerves finally snapped. "We are not discussing my past failures! She is to have her own room and you are not to say a word to her beyond that of a servant! Mind your place!"

The tension in the space mounted as my anger ebbed and shame filtered in. Despite my current predicament, it had been through no fault of Darda's. My own shortcomings had led me to this moment and her faithfulness was a debt I would never be able to repay.

"I have minded my place more than you ever deserved, my lord," Darda spat out angrily. I could hear the tears in her voice and more guilt slithered its way into my heart. "Had I learned years ago to not 'mind my place' perhaps we would all be in different circumstances now! However, I yield to you now not as your servant, but as the only friend you have in the world. I take my leave of you now, my lord."

Too ashamed to look back at her, I continued glaring at the gray abyss before me until I flinched at the slam of the door. Her words pierced the deepest recesses of my heart, but pride prevented me from ever letting her know that. While Darda was only a servant, she had spent millennia trapped inside this castle with me and had been the only real caretaker I had ever known. It pained me to hear the reproach in her voice.

Yet I could not deny it as unwarranted. There was something about this woman that transfixed me, certainly more so than any other mortal had. She could be either the key to my salvation or the executor of my ruin. Allowing someone, especially a human woman at that, to have such power over me could not be tolerated, yet I found myself unwilling to stop. There was something in her eyes, a sort of empty despair guarding a flaming flicker of hope that entranced me. I could already tell that faint flicker had the capacity to light the torch that would ignite the world. She was special—unique--and Destiny had intervened on my behalf. Her beauty only enhanced my attraction to her.

I recalled her battle stance in what she called her lab. Though I had smelled her fear and watched her recoil from the monster I became outside the castle walls, she had not run away. Using my powers against her would have been an affront to Nature itself and though her blows to my jaw and nose hurt, it had also been refreshing to have someone challenge me. I only hoped her determination would not be her downfall in Aeternitas. None of the other mortals had been successful in the query I was about to pose to her, but I expected her to outright fight me over the information I would reveal.

Stubborn pride was not a virtue, I had come to learn.

CHAPTER 7

Dinner Gone Wrong

After I requested another bathing sheet from the bathing chamber, I rolled myself tightly in them both and sat on the floor before the fire. The exhausting events of the day were catching up to me, despite my brief nap in the tower cell earlier, and I could feel my eyelids beginning to droop. Missing dinner with *the Master* was probably not the smartest decision I had ever made, but if they did not provide me with clothing, I would not summon him to me while I was naked and vulnerable. Since I was uncertain of the repercussions of that decision, the floor was a more appropriate place to wait than the soft bed that would probably lull me to sleep instantly.

The only light came from the fire and I could not locate any other lamps or candles throughout the room. My mind whirled as I tried to make sense of my predicament, but it only worsened the tightening in my chest. A gilded cage was still a cage, and I was just as much a prisoner here now as I had been in that icy cell. Now I not only needed to find out what happened to Mr. Cooper, but to find my way back to the city when I had no idea where I was or how I got here. Given the circumstances, I sincerely doubted I was in a place that existed on Earth. Aeternitas was something else entirely.

"Do you no longer understand the English language?" came Gryphon's voice from behind me, a musical cadence that would have charmed me had it not sent me into panic.

I scrambled to my feet while trying to maintain my dignity in the bathing sheets.

He stood a few feet away on the edge of the shadows, which made his expression impossible to read. I clutched the green material tighter to my body and did not respond.

A sigh escaped him. "Why are you not dressed for dinner?" he snarled impatiently.

I rolled my eyes. "Your magic bathroom stole my clothes and you provided the dress of a woolly mammoth instead. What else was I supposed to do?" I turned away from him, facing the fireplace.

Gryphon came to my side and jerked my elbow, pulling me to him. "You should have notified Darda or me so the mistake could be rectified. Do humans no longer problem solve?" The corners of his mouth curled up at his own humor.

His sarcasm irked me. I turned to him with a glare that should have incinerated him on the spot. "Relying on someone else to solve the problem *isn't* problem solving!" I snapped.

My response must have surprised him because he lessened his grip on my elbow. His eyebrows rose as he contemplated my answer with a cock of his head. "Have you ever relied on anyone?"

I barked out a bitter laugh. "No, definitely not. You can't depend on anyone except yourself." I pulled my elbow from his hand and pulled the bathing sheets tighter around my body. For the first time in a long time, discussing how alone I really was embarrassed me, and I did not want him to recognize my weakness. However, the look he gave me was not one of pity, but more curious than anything. I turned back to face the fire before I commanded, "You'll return my clothes if I'm gonna leave this room."

Even from the corner of my eye I could see his smirk widen. He snapped his fingers and a simple black dress that looked much closer to my size appeared in his hand. Angrily, I snatched it from his hand and stomped towards the bathroom. Why did I have to wear a dress of all things?

As I pulled the tapestry back, his melodious chuckle stopped me in my tracks. "Have you no need for undergarments?" he teased. I caught the gleam in his eye as I lasered him with another glare.

Two could play this game. "I'll get by just fine without them," I replied sweetly. That dropped his playful smirk immediately.

This dress was definitely an improvement from the first, however, it was a bit more revealing than my usual taste. The neckline was a deeper V-neck than I had ever worn before and hugged the curves of my breasts in a way that made me self-conscious. I never could have pulled off a bra with a getup like this! After quickly running a brush through my thick hair, now curly from the steam in the bath earlier, I roped it into a long braid over one shoulder and emerged into the bedroom.

Gryphon had been pacing in front of the fire and he stopped now, his eyes widening in surprise as he took in my appearance. A flush crept up his cheeks as he perused my body and turned his attention to my face. The intensity of his stare nearly had me whimpering, and I had to stop myself from folding my arms across my chest. It was only a dress. I had nothing to be ashamed of.

He approached me slowly, keeping his eyes trained on my

face, his powerful gaze never wavering. We stood nearly chest to chest, mine starting to rise and fall more rapidly as his glowing green eyes set my heart aflutter. It was like a spell thickened the air between us, and I was sure that if I touched him the electricity would shock us both. He gave no indication of his thoughts, simply considered my face with his silent scrutiny.

After several long moments Gryphon gave me a small smile. "What is your name, mortal?"

I swallowed hard, too caught up in the heat of his gaze to function properly. "Mirielle," I finally whispered. "Mirielle Townsend."

"Such a French name for an American woman," he muttered, more to himself than to me. He had not yet blinked.

Still maintaining eye contact, I shrugged. "My mother was high when she filled out my birth certificate. 'Mirielle' was the closest guess they could make at the hospital." It was not a pretty story with any sentimental value like the stories I read about all through my childhood, but still. I had always liked how unique my name was. There were never any other girls with that name in my classes.

My backstory seemed to bother him, however, because his eyebrows furrowed at my explanation. It broke whatever was developing between us and he took several steps away from me. Cold air rushed in to bring me back to my senses. He no longer could maintain eye contact and instead spoke next to the floor.

"Now you will dine with me."

I vehemently shook my head. "No, now I will have answers!"

He snorted and snapped his fingers.

The same free fall of teleportation had me flailing into a black void before landing on all fours at his feet, something that appeared to greatly amuse him. I huffed the bangs out of my eyes as I clambered to my feet. The frilly skirt clung with static to my legs and I all but moaned in longing for pants. It had been years since I last wore a dress or skirt.

Righting myself, my jaw dropped open in awe at the dining room before me. There was enough food on the table to feed a hundred sumo wrestlers and the steam from several dishes was sizzling in the air, but there were only two place settings next to one another. The table was round, built to accommodate ten people, and the wood gleamed as though it had been freshly polished. I glanced about the room and observed the same grandeur as the bed chamber. A marble fireplace with a gilded mirror stood at one end with a decorative wooden door opposite. The room was smaller than I expected and gave a sense of intimacy.

The view outside the windows made me startle in surprise. Two large windows flanked one wall with a small serving table in between, and although these did not contain any glass either, there was a warm breeze blowing inside. Dense fog still coated the land-scape, but there were palm trees and sand. It was brighter than the area outside my bedroom or even the tower cell from earlier. The air smelled faintly of saltwater, making me wonder if there was an ocean or lake nearby.

"Are we still in the castle?" I marveled. I longed to climb through the window and wrap myself in the warmth.

Gryphon did not comment, merely sat down at a place setting and began to serve food to his plate.

I allowed myself another moment to stare before sinking into the chair to his left. He began piling food in front of me, never asking what I would like or identifying any of the dishes. My appetite was all but gone and a disappointed sigh escaped me when I found the gold goblet at my chair to contain a deep red wine. Alcohol would only lower my inhibitions, which sounded like a recipe for disaster at this point.

After several minutes where the only sounds were the scraping of his knife and fork, Gryphon slammed down his cutlery and fixed me with a glare. "You will eat or I will force it down your throat, human!"

"Please just explain to me what the hell is going on!" I pleaded. "I can't eat when my anxiety is through the roof!" To prove my point, I shoved my still full plate away from me and crossed my arms over my chest.

Gryphon let out a heavy sigh and stood up. He resumed his pacing from before and stated quietly, "I am not sure where to begin. I cannot answer all of your questions."

My windpipe constricted. This had to be a nightmare. I only needed to force myself to wake up. The alternative, that I was truly a prisoner in a fantastical place with someone who was part beast, part human, was too outrageous to comprehend.

I needed to coax more information from him. "Why don't you start by telling me what you can and we'll go from there?" I suggested. Hopefully he could not hear my heart beating frantically in my chest.

He seemed to reflect on this before responding. Finally, he clasped his hands behind his back and stood still to face me, his expression grim. "Aeternitas is a very special place. One that your world needs in order to survive. Everything here is...different." Gryphon's musical voice caught and he swallowed rapidly before continuing,

"Many years ago, Aeternitas found itself at the mercy of a foe, a very powerful enemy. It was unexpected and I was blindsided. This enemy was once someone I believed to care about me. A curse was cast that turned me into the beast you met in your lab. I need your help to break the curse and free my realm."

I could not help it--I laughed. The kind of deep belly laugh that leaves your shoulders shaking, your stomach cramping, and sends tears streaming down your cheeks. My arms wrapped around my middle, clutching my sides, as my entire body convulsed with the absurdity over his explanation. A magical curse? His *realm*? It sounded like a twisted fairy tale, and now I knew I had to be dreaming.

Gryphon did not appreciate my reaction. He leaned down on the table, flexing the muscles in his arms and making his veins pop. There was venom in his eyes as he swore, "This is not a joke!"

My eyes widened at his aggression, but I could not stop the peal of mirth that escaped. "This *has* to be a joke!" I countered. "There is no way this can be real!"

His face hardened. "This is very much real, and the consequences for us both will be deadly if you do not heed my words."

That brought me up short. No one mentioned this was life or death.

"How am I supposed to help?" I asked.

"You will assist me as I search for what I need to break the curse. It is an object, but I do not know what it is or where I will find it."

"But that could be anything!" I sputtered, too stunned to say anything else,

He simply nodded.

It was not enough of an explanation, and my reasoning skills were in a frenzy as I tried to make sense of what he was saying. In my craze, I stood up and began pacing the room, too. "So I'm stuck here until you find some random object in whatever random place you find it?! And what about Mr. Cooper?!" My arms flung wide to emphasize how distraught I was.

Gryphon did not have any idea what I was talking about. I could tell from the way he cocked his head and how his gaze softened. "Is that your lover?"

Gag me! How mortifying! "Mr. Cooper is the only family I have," I grit out through my teeth. There was an edge to my voice that should have warned him from pursuing this topic any further, but Gryphon either didn't notice or didn't care.

"Family is overrated." Gryphon waved his hand impatiently in front of his face as if this subject was an annoying fly. "My uncle Vulcan is one of my realm's biggest enemies. Family ties mean nothing."

Anger flooded my system at his audacity. "I suppose that's easy to say when you have none! Clearly no one ever cared about you!" I snapped. My fingernails dug into my palms as I clenched my fists. This man, beast, or whatever the hell he was, was insufferable.

This response struck a nerve, however, because he rounded the table in two great strides and snatched me to him by my biceps. My eyes widened in alarm as he shook me.

"You know nothing! Never discuss my family again if you want to keep your tongue in your mouth!" snarled Gryphon. His entire face was flushed with rage.

Intimidation kept me locked in place. So much for two decades worth of martial arts training. A brief whimper sounded from my lips and I nodded infinitesimally. He shoved me away with a look that said he was sickened with the sight of me.

"We will begin at another time. You will retire for the evening," Gryphon said flatly. Before I could respond, there was a snap of his fingers, and I crashed into a heap on the floor of the bedchamber. I let the tears run freely as I hugged my knees to my chest and sobbed away my fear.

CHAPTER 8

Pure Rage

GRYPHON

The smash of the vase against the rough stone wall of my bedchamber did little to relieve my fury and I grabbed the next closest object without a second glance. The resulting sound of glass shattering from the candlestick I threw meeting the mirror did nothing either. Pretty soon my quarters would be destroyed. Again.

"I take it dinner did not go well," Darda stated from behind.

My labored breathing was the only response before I chucked a stray piece of a chair leg against the wall. It landed on top of the remnants of the vase and the thought that haunted me since the start of the curse ran through my mind on repeat. *You ruin everything you touch.*

She sighed heavily. "I shall go tend to her, the poor dearie."

I whipped my head around, roaring in anger. "You'll do no such thing!"

It still caught me off guard in these instances not to see Darda as her natural self. I bristled indignantly at the visual reminder of why I needed this curse to lift. While I may have deserved the fall-out, Darda did not.

"Go to her," I ground out before I could change my mind.

I heard the telltale shuffle on the stone floor and the thud of the heavy door as she made her exit. My rooms occupied the oldest part of the castle, and I maintained the original look of medieval stone. I liked the darkness, welcomed the cold, a mindful penance for my many gaffes that brought me here. Here, relying on a mortal to help me in breaking the bonds of this infernal curse.

Mirielle could not have known how deeply her cutting remarks about family would slice me, but it was a wound to my very core. It had been my mother, in all her supernatural glory, who had set the curse in motion, and that act of betrayal still burned to this day. My father was another victim, imprisoned somewhere beyond my reach. Her curse was meant to separate us as my mother felt my allegiance to him was too strong and there-fore caused too much influence in the way I ruled Aeternitas. While my mother believed my father to be cruel and barbaric, so too, did he believe that my mother's vicious sense of justice was the wrong example for me to follow. My mother was ruthless, always calculating her next move even though she was likely three steps ahead anyway.

This was how Darda came to be my primary caretaker as both of them were intent on sowing seeds of division between me and the other parent, yet both failed to care for me in the interim. Darda did not allow a cross word about either of them in her pres-ence, but as I grew into manhood, I yearned for the male guidance my father offered. Jealousy led my mother to act and well...the equivalent of thousands of years had passed as I sought relief, although time stood still here.

As soon as she cast her curse, my mother had disappeared. I searched for her whenever I entered another realm on a quest, but so far it yielded nothing. She had vanished without a trace. I could feel her presence hovering just beyond my reach. My desperation had even led me to enter my uncle's kingdom, that of the Elementals, and ask to search for her there. Dear Uncle Vulcan, my mother's brother, seized the opportunity to glean as much information as possible about my kingdom and the curse, his ugly ambition to rule outright practically tangible during our meeting. If I knew my mother, she would lie in wait, watching me struggle and gleeful of the divide between myself and my father. And now it was only a matter of time before my uncle led the Elementals into Aeternitas for battle.

Time, however, was running out. I needed Mirielle to be the one to break the curse or all was lost. Unlike others I had encountered, she was not afraid of me and peppered me with questions. It was unnerving as I wanted someone who would blindly follow orders, like a servant, and a servant Mirielle Townsend most certainly was not. She did not have a submissive bone in her body.

That intriguing fact gave me pause. I *liked* her defiance, how spirited she became when her emotions took hold. Up until she made her snide commentary on my family, her accurate description hitting a little too close to home for my tolerance, her outburst in my private dining room had been entertaining. Although her strength bled through every movement she made and every word she uttered, it was refreshing to be around someone who felt so...*alive*. Mirielle represented what I wanted my life to be.

Perhaps I had buggered the exchange over dinner. It was not her fault that she demanded answers. She must be some kind of scientist since I found her in a lab. It was in her nature to question everything. Clearly, I would have to approach her differently than I had others in the past. She was not like the other humans.

I could almost hear Darda's snickering in my head. She had already accused me of giving the girl special treatment because I provided her a bed chamber. Calming my unpredictable temper would most certainly be preferential treatment, but what more could I do? Desperation led people to do crazy things.

As much as it would humble me, Mirielle deserved an apology. Hopefully I could keep whatever the current of electricity was between us at bay as it was proving more and more difficult to keep my distance from her whenever we were in the same room. I found myself visualizing reasons to touch her again, and I grimaced as I recalled the way I yanked her to me while she was cloaked in only a bathing sheet. She must think I'm a brute. There was something that drew me to her and made my heart race, and now I was acting like a lovestruck mortal in her presence. I needed to redirect this energy into the search for the object.

My feet automatically carried me out to my balcony against the stone railing, just as I had done every night since the start of the curse. It was blacker than shadow here, literally where realm turned into nothingness. This part of the palace was left in its original form for a purpose as it served as the edge of everything, both mortal and magical alike.

I could not keep the despair from my voice as I commanded, "Show me the rose."

The magic I used to shield the rose fell away and the flower materialized in the ether just out of my reach. My mother had held the crimson blossom in her hand when she cast her curse and altered the course of my life, warning me that time was limited right before she disappeared. She never explained what was supposed to change or why she had destroyed my future, but I clung to the rose as my only sign of hope. As the centuries passed with no end in sight, the rose's petals began to fall, mocking my resolve. Now the rose wilted and its petals turned black. We were nearing the end and I was no closer to breaking the curse than I was to locating my parents. Time was not on my side, but Mirielle would be the key. I could feel it.

CHAPTER 9

A Prophecy Foretold

The floor was cold beneath my cheek as pilfered light seeped through the windows. The fire had long since died out, and my muscles cried in protest as I stretched. Everything felt stiff, no doubt cramping from the position I slept in on the marble. After I had bawled my eyes out, I must have fallen into a deep sleep right there on the hearth.

I wanted nothing more than to scrub away the memories of the previous day, however, it dawned on me as I entered the bathroom that there was no shower. Bathing was about to be a nightmare. It took far longer than necessary to get ready, but afterwards I was left with the same conundrum as yesterday: I had no other clothing to wear.

Hesitantly, I asked the ceiling, "Can I have pants and a shirt?" It sounded so stupid to request anything of an empty room, but to my delight, dark gray trousers and a long sleeve white shirt materialized on the vanity counter. They were probably handmade, judging by the coarse stitching, but the material felt soft as butter and molded to my body in a way that oozed comfort. I could get used to this.

"Are you up yet, dearie?" Darda called through the tapestry.

I gulped and hoped she wouldn't be the same invisible phantom as yesterday. If she was, I at least needed coffee first.

Inside the bedroom, the writing desk from yesterday stood in the center of the room. I noted quickly that the bedroom door was open, showing a hallway beyond that was decked in dark blue cloth and more marble flooring.

"Where are you?" I called, still not seeing anyone. Why would she move the writing desk to such an odd location?

The writing desk lid opened on its own. "I'm here, dearie," it said.

My neck hair stood on end as I screamed. "A ghost!" I ran to the doorway and heard scraping on the floor behind me.

"No, young miss, it's Darda!"

I turned back in time to see the writing desk lid move up and down, like it was waving to me. Blinking rapidly, my brain tried to make sense of what I was seeing.

You're a desk?!" was all I came up with.

Darda chuckled. The desk inched closer to me, making the same scraping sound on the floor. "The Master missed a few key things at dinner last night."

All I could do was nod. A fucking desk was talking to me! Of course it was.

"Follow me to the library, dearie," Darda instructed. "The Master will meet you there and explain a bit more."

I stepped out of the way as the desk pushed through the doorway and wondered in the back of my mind if all desks would move so swiftly as I rushed to keep up. We traveled so quickly that

I barely had time to register any of my surroundings. It was like walking through a maze.

"What is this place?" I asked incredulously.

She chuckled again. "This castle is the center of our realm. Aeternitas, you could say, is the place where time and space meet. Most of our inhabitants are hidden by the fog, but we are home to many souls."

Her wording caught me off guard. Souls, not people. "And is everything here in the castle alive like you?"

"Dearie, *nobody* in this castle is like me!" There was an edge to her voice that told me while she found my question amusing, she was trying to shut down my line of questioning as politely as possible. Although perhaps my question was rude. Was there proper etiquette when discussing the existence of an animate piece of furniture?

We finally emerged on a wide landing. A grand staircase of gold and marble led down to an entry way lined with chiseled statues and suits of armor. I estimated them to be around 14th century based on the chest plate, rerebrace, and poleyns, although all of these suits were a bronze color, not the dull gray usually found in that time period. A dark blue banner with a gold coat of arms hung over the door. It looked to be a crest of some kind, an hourglass with thick roses circling the base and stars outlined at the top. I did not recognize the symbol, but catalogued it away in my mind for further scrutiny.

"How are you going to get down the stairs?" I asked Darda quizzically.

In the next instant, the desk was on the main floor. "Like this," she replied simply.

I stifled another scream and mechanically descended the stairs on foot. There was no way I would ever understand this experience.

"Does Gryphon live here alone? Does he have a wife? Children?" Part of me didn't want her to answer, but given the primal attraction I felt any time I was in the same vicinity, I needed to know. If he were married or had a family, I would do better to maintain my distance and respect those boundaries.

At this question, the desk stopped, slowly scraping around to face me. "The Master has been alone for a very long time, young miss. You mustn't blame him, for loneliness is only one small step away from despair."

I wanted the time to process her words and the veiled warning lacing them, but she abruptly turned so we were off again. For being a household object, I definitely admired her stamina.

We proceeded to the right, keeping the same fast pace as before, but this time I would be able to repeat my movements because we stayed in the same hallway. Blue silk still coated the walls, but every so often the crest from the entryway hung over a table. More coats of armor lined the way. They all looked dilapidated, like they had actually seen battle and were left for safekeeping rather than decorative display. If I had been alone, I would have stopped to examine them and see if I could approximate the real time period and country of origin.

A set of double doors to the right suddenly sprung open and Darda hurried inside. The library, as she called it, was stunning. It was the first room I had seen in the castle to feature wood floors, a rich oak, that matched the floor to ceiling shelves. It stretched into three stories above, with books tightly packed on all four walls. There were no windows, but the entire ceiling was one massive skylight. The gray fog was all that could be seen, yet I imagined how beautiful the stars would be at night, if they were ever visible.

An oversized desk of a darker wood sat in the center of the room with a plush green chair. Across from the desk were two plump armchairs of the same green velvet. In the farthest corner sat a globe in an ornate golden stand guarding a circular staircase to the open galley above. A round table made of the same dark wood was closest to the door, four chairs tucked in underneath. Globes of soft yellow light hovered in the air, each swaying slightly as though a breeze filtered through. The shelves on all four walls were filled with leather volumes, some of the spines too faded to read. At first glance, the titles closest were not written in any language I recognized.

I entered the room slowly, turning in a full 360 to observe it all, before sinking into one of the armchairs. I was suddenly overwhelmed. Every room in the castle was so lush and lavish, and I had never felt more out of place. This was not my world and it challenged every belief I had, which left me drained and vulnerable.

"The Master will join you shortly, young miss," Darda said gently. There was kindness in her voice, but it fell on deaf ears.

Almost as soon as the door closed behind her, Gryphon appeared in the chair behind the desk. His ring finger grazed his bottom lip and his legs were crossed, a student of contemplation. I let him make his observations because I was far too flustered to care. I wanted to go home.

"Ms. Townsend, we did not begin on the right foot," he said carefully. "I would like to start over."

He paused, waiting for my response. He was left with disappointment as I remained silent, my lips firmly pressed in a hard line.

"My realm is in trouble and I have spent millennia searching for a particular object that can break the spell. It is very rare and very valuable, I believe. It is my hope that you will join me in my search."

Curiosity finally set in. "Why me? What could I possibly do for you that all your magic powers couldn't?" I pulled my knees to my chest and wrapped my arms around my legs.

This did not seem to be an easy answer for Gryphon cocked his head and stared at the desk before answering. He would not meet my eyes as he said, "There is a prophecy that foretold it."

A prophecy? It was on the tip of my tongue to ask if Bigfoot made it, but I shook my head, hair falling into my eyes as I scoffed. "I highly doubt that. I'm nobody."

"You are *not* nobody." Gryphon's deep emerald eyes glowed with passion at my words. "The prophecy did not identify you by name, but I believe you may be the person to which it refers."

I snorted and rolled my eyes. "Let me see it, then," I goaded him. "Show me the prophecy."

His face hardened, but I did not expect what happened next. With a wave of his hand a hologram hung in the air between us. It reminded me of Princess Leia's call for help in *A New Hope*, grainy and glitchy. A woman in a dark dress stood with her hands in the air. A blood red rose was clutched in her left hand. Her hood was drawn down over her eyes and the poor quality of the image did not reveal any distinct facial features, but her wild blonde curls fell in long tresses over her breasts. At first, I thought it was nonsensical chanting, but then I began to make out the words.

The sands of time begin to slow,
Reaping, evil and ugly, grow.
A curse upon this land forever,
Until a mortal pairing together.
All who fail share in sorrow,
Bid farewell to known tomorrow.
Seek out that which all shall covet,
The wicked are still worthy of it.
Sacrifice the past for this treasure,
To gain a future in eternal measure.

I asked him to repeat the hologram twice more before I had it memorized, though it contained very few clues that Gryphon had not already deciphered. He waited patiently, chin propped on his hand, as my mind began to whirl like a rolodex. There were all kinds of lost and hidden treasures throughout the world. Which one could possibly be the answer? And most importantly, if the treasure really was lost, how were we to find it? Did the prophecy really mean that if I failed, I would die?

A shudder rippled down my spine as I considered the implications. It sounded as though this truly was a matter of life and death. Yet I had no idea where to even begin.

Gryphon abruptly stood up and approached me, cautiously holding up his hands in surrender to signify he meant me no harm. He sat in the armchair next to me, angling his body so that our knees intwined, and gingerly took my hands in his. His mannerisms told me how hard he was trying to be gentle and I smiled inwardly as I recalled Mr. Cooper's lesson that actions always show people's true intentions.

"Ms. Townsend, time is running out for me and for my realm.

You are my last hope." Sincerity laced every word and despite my fear, I felt compassion flood my system.

Still, I stood up, desperate for air that was not saturated with his presence, and crossed to the other side of the room, closer to the fireplace. "I have never been in the field," I explained. "I merely restore artifacts to their original state. I don't know how to look for them or extract them."

Confusion laced his features. "'Restore artifacts?'" he repeated. "My apologies, but I do not know what you mean."

It was my turn to be puzzled. "Isn't that why you took me from the museum? You want me to help you find this lost treasure or something?"

He frowned and I had the ridiculous thought that I wanted to smooth the crease along his brow line. I liked it so much better when he smiled.

"The parchment you carried is what drew me to you," he explained. "I do not know what a museum is or why you were in such a place. I thought you called it a lab?"

My eyebrows rose in surprise. "I am an archivist for the Museum of Natural History in New York City. I specialize in restoring historical documents, but I also have a background in ancient languages."

It was his turn to act surprised. "Is this a means of employment in the mortal realm? You clean paper as a livelihood?"

My temper sparked at his comment. "It's a very well regarded museum! I was hand selected after excellent recommendations from my professors at Princeton and Harvard! Millions of people travel there to see all of the history we've collected and repaired."

I could tell from his blank facial expression that my words had no impact. Gryphon continued to stare at me expectantly, as if there was more to my explanation.

I sighed in exasperation. "How have you not heard of a museum? Any idiot has at least heard of a museum!" It stung a little to have my hard work so easily disregarded. Most people were impressed by my education, and it was my one source of pride to have earned degrees at such prestigious schools.

"You try my patience, human," he cautioned. I could practically hear his jaw clenching.

Like a lady does when irritated, I flipped him off. "This should show you how much I give a shit," I retorted.

Faster than I could blink he crossed the room to me, pinning both my wrists behind my back with a single hand. His other hand grabbed me by the throat and squeezed, allowing just enough air to keep me conscious while still incapacitating me. The more I struggled against his hold, the more he yanked down on my wrists until my entire front was pressed against him, leaning my body backwards. My breath came out in ragged gulps and I tried to ignore the surge of pleasure from the friction against my nipples. The planes of his chest were hard, pressing down my stomach to remind me of his muscular frame. It was frightening and erotic at the same time.

The faint smell of roses still permeated the air around him as I watched the anger in his eyes fade to arousal. Further proof could be found in the solid cock pressing against my waist. The glowing emerald light was back in his eyes. I was utterly transfixed, unwilling to yield but incapable of leaving. My body craved more, and my tongue darted out to wet my lips in preparation.

His eyes tracked the movement to my mouth. "Trust me, Ms. Townsend, when I say your stay here can be pleasurable or agony. The choice is yours. But if you continue to disrespect me in my own home, torture would be pleasant in comparison to what I will inflict upon you."

Gryphon's threat awoke the fighter in me. He was a bully, no different than the many "boyfriends" my mother paraded in and out of our apartment. Ever so slightly I shifted my weight back to my dominant foot. I maintained eye contact for a moment, allowing the trepidation to show in hopes of catching him off guard. Evidently, I succeeded because in the next second I swung my knee up into his brawny thigh, using his momentum forward to catch him across my shoulder blades in a fireman's hold.

His surprise forced him to let go of my wrists, but I grabbed his shirt as I heaved my body headfirst to the ground from his weight. Since I was prepared for the tumble, I managed to tuck my neck in and roll out of the movement like a child doing a somersault, but Gryphon landed hard on his side with a grunt. My tumble landed me on my feet and I leapt out of his arm's reach, my fists locked in my defensive stance in front of my face.

The look of astonishment on his face was worth the soreness lacing my trapezius muscles. His hair formed a golden halo around his head as he lay sprawled out on the floor. Judging by the way he gulped in air, the fall might have knocked the wind out of him.

"Listen up, Gryphon, because I will only say this once. NEVER touch me like that again, you got that?" My voice carried far more force than I thought myself capable of. I backed away another few paces. A sinking feeling told me I just bought myself a one way ticket to the ice tower cell.

CHAPTER 10

Something New

GRYPHON

I could barely breathe. Inconveniently, I was also rock hard and so aroused that the power of speech left my body. How she had managed to throw me off like that after *centuries* worth of training as a warrior was incomprehensible. She exhibited total control over her body and its movements at all times, and despite my bruised ego, I yearned to set her free and watch her throw caution to the wind. Preferably while riding on top of me.

Yet the idea also repulsed me, and my father's voice echoed in the recesses of my mind that she was unworthy of the Crowned Prince of his kingdom. She was a human, completely mortal and destined to die, whereas I was doomed to remain frozen in time. Even without my mother's curse I would never age. My role in Aeternitas was absolute and never ending as the keeper of souls on Earth. Destiny, therefore, had all but eradicated any hopes I once harbored of finding a mate.

Perhaps my sexual thoughts stemmed from the lack of social interactions. Once the curse fell, all of my realm's subjects disappeared and it had been some time since I had been able to exercise my needs in that manner. A hand could only do so much...

I glanced up at her from my position on the floor, her perfect breasts heaving, her fists bared at her sides, and my desire only escalated. Bright red tendrils of hair wisped about her face, and her hazel eyes zeroed in on me with caution and disdain, a look that I was not used to seeing from the opposite sex. Yep, it was definitely my attraction to her, then.

Ever so slowly I returned to a standing position and faced her. She stayed in a fighting stance, her feet staggered, body angled towards me. She did not so much as blink, though her facial expression betrayed her fear. My rage was acute, the desire to punish her strong enough to make me clench my fists and take two strides towards her, battling with my arousal that wanted to punish her in other ways. But for once a nagging thought in the back of my mind pushed to the forefront--*she could be the key to ending the curse.*

She did not cower or flinch, merely braced herself for the fight she anticipated. I could tell from the rigid flex in her arms that she was prepared to fight until the bitter end. However, it no longer felt right to exact my anger on her. Not when I needed her compliance.

Although the words felt bitter on my tongue, I ground out an apology. Never in my working memory could I recall such a statement leaving my lips, but it caught her by surprise. Her eyebrows rose to her hairline and she lowered her fists a fraction of an inch.

"That's it?" she asked incredulously.

I was still far too enraged to continue this line of questioning. "That apology will have to suffice for now!" I snarled.

She shook her head, making her gorgeous red hair spill across her shoulders. "No, I meant, you're not going to punish me?"

I sighed heavily. How were we ever to start over if we kept repeating the same fight? "There will be no more punishments and no more fighting as long as there is no more swearing on your part. Do not insult me as I will not stand for it. Can we agree?"

Her eyes were wary, but she lowered her fists and resumed a more relaxed posture. "I'm sorry for insulting you. I will try to do better next time." She smirked, the hint of sarcasm clear.

The admission that she expected there to be a next time was not lost on me and I chuckled despite myself. She offered a wide smile at my laughter, which eliminated all my pent up frustration. There truly could not be a more beautiful woman. I realized I was probably giving her emotional whiplash because I could barely handle the sudden shift in my feelings myself, but damn it, she shouldn't be so intoxicating!

Since we had landed on a shaky truce, I retreated back to the desk and sat behind it in a vain hope that farther proximity would make it easier for us to finalize our discussion. Her explanation of what a museum was and the conditions of her employment there ignited my dream that she really was the mortal who could break my dreadful mother's curse. Without realizing it, I had been curating a museum of my own.

This revelation made me smile, an action that stifled her banter immediately.

"What is it?" Mirielle asked.

I steepled my fingers in front of me. "Ms. Townsend, I do not go to ancient battlefields and temples as they stand in your time," I clarified. "I travel to the moment items are lost and take them from their own time."

Her face scrunched in concentration as she considered my words, their meaning puzzling her. "You're talking about time travel."

I nodded once. "That is what mortals call it, yes. Even without the curse, time operates differently here in my realm. It is possible for me to move from moment to moment between time and space because neither have any meaning for me. Aeternitas is the point of the universe where the two meet."

Her eyes were puzzled, but intrigued. I could practically see the gears in her head working to decipher my explanation, and there were questions ready to burst from her. I held up a hand to stop her.

"There are certain questions I cannot answer, for your own safety," I explained. "Some things you may learn in time if we are successful."

Mirielle's eyebrows disappeared under her bangs, but she nodded her acceptance. She sat down in an armchair across from me and folded her hands over her right knee. "What sort of objects have you already collected? How many are there?"

"Let me show you," I offered instead.

CHAPTER 11

Warehouse of Dreams

MIRIELLE

My heart stopped beating in my chest and my feet were locked to the floor. It felt as though sand was coating my throat and my tongue had turned to lead. The sight before me would have been every historian's wet dream, but I could not so much as move beyond the doorway as the implications of the room before me left me awestruck.

Gryphon had led me deeper into the castle than I would have believed possible. The journey to this room must have taken over an hour. There was only one door and Gryphon withdrew a heavy bronze key hanging from a string around his neck to unlock it for me. He told me that no one else was allowed access and until I had proven myself, I would not be allowed to enter this room again.

"Room" was probably not the most appropriate term, but then again, "warehouse" would hardly fit the bill either. It was massive, spanning longer and wider than five football fields end to end. In truth, from the doorway I could not see another corner in sight, like the room simply extended into eternity. Which, I belatedly reminded myself, it probably did. It housed the greatest display of human history that ever existed.

To my right were white stone columns stretching up to the dark shadows of an immeasurable ceiling, holding row upon row of shelves packed with scrolls. Small tags hung from a few of the scrolls, swaying from an unknown breeze. A small sign hung on the first column that read, "Alexandria, 346 A.D." The columns and shelves continued beyond my line of vision, with occasional signs as they went on.

Countless mounds of gold coins, rubies, diamonds, sapphires, and other precious gemstones lay in various piles along the floor. A stone dais fifteen feet in front of me housed a gilded chest with two poles parallel to one another on opposite sides. Stones jutted in a circle from the lid, and unless my eyes were playing tricks on my brain, it matched descriptions of the Ark of the Covenant, a treasure that was lost from King Solomon's temple in approximately 587 B.C. It had disappeared after the Babylonians invaded and ransacked the temple's contents.

Next to the door hung a large painting that I instantly recognized. Several people rode on horseback in the forefront with rolling hills in the skyline of the background along with a distant castle.

"Is this the Just Judges panel?!" I cried in a panic. The panel was part of an art piece commissioned in 15th century Belgium and had not been seen anywhere since it was stolen in the 1930's, although periodic tips kept the investigation open with law enforcement.

Gryphon's lips curled at the corners, but he gave no other response.

Further beyond the Just Judges art was an oil painting, a Rembrandt entitled "A Lady and Gentleman in Black." The scene depicted a woman sitting on a chair in the bottom right corner while a man stood in the center background, both dressed in black clothing fit for the time period. Although originally painted in 1633, it was famously stolen from a museum in 1990, along with several other works of art, and never recovered. Police had been searching for it ever since.

It was all like this. Every piece of this collection was missing or lost from the real world. This was a treasure trove of lost history.

I could not form coherent sentences. Seeing the Rembrandt painting was too much for me to process and I sank to my knees, zoning out into nothing as I tried to get a handle on my feelings. This room contained miles worth of lost treasure and history! Relics and artifacts that people spent *lifetimes* searching for...and I had only stepped into the doorway!

After a few minutes of my statue-like reaction, Gryphon squatted down in front of me. My eyes were so lost in thought and unfocused that he gently tilted my chin up to meet his gaze. For once, his eyes were soft and full of compassion. Had I not been in shock, I might have appreciated his concern.

"Please say something," he finally said.

Numbly, I shook my head. "What is there to say?" I whispered. "You have collected the world's treasures. My entire life's dream is contained in some random warehouse inside your palace. And you want me to...to what exactly?"

Now it was all clicking into place. The thoughts were coming faster than I could vocalize and I hyperventilated as I came to the realization: none of these treasures were lost--*Gryphon stole them*. He had been traveling in time and collecting what he believed to be important items that would fit the bill to break his stupid curse. I personally knew archaeologists and historians who had been searching for decades for the Just Judges panel alone. One of my graduate professors at Harvard had traveled to eight different countries looking for it. And yet Gryphon had it hanging in his castle where no one could ever find it.

But why would he only pursue the treasure mentioned in the prophecy? What about the "mortal pairing" that he had to achieve, too?

Gryphon seemed to sense my growing hysteria and wisely said nothing, but gently rubbed my shoulders. As my breathing became more haggard, he guided me to lay on my back and ordered me to breathe deeply. I counted to ten as I exhaled. Then repeated the action five times to regain my bearings.

"Perhaps we should return to the library for the rest of this discussion," he suggested lightly as I returned to an upright position.

"Nope, I think you better tell me what in the world I am supposed to do about this! You have *centuries* worth of treasure in here, and you're telling me none of it means anything to you because it doesn't break your stupid curse!" I hissed.

He shrugged, an entirely human gesture. "It's just clutter," Gryphon offered.

His nonchalance made me thirst for violence. "IT IS ALL OF HUMAN HISTORY!" I bellowed. My echo carried into the void beyond. I scrambled to my feet, nearly knocking him over in my mania, and threw my arms wide to emphasize my point. "THIS IS WHAT I SPENT MY ENTIRE LIFE WORKING ON!"

This made Gryphon smile, a breathtaking smile that displayed gleaming white teeth and crinkled the skin around his eyes. It would have been jarring had I not been so hysterical. "And that is why I'm glad you're here."

I huffed in frustration. "You never met any other humans? How did you take all of this stuff if you never saw anybody else?"

My question gave him pause. He would not look at me as he answered, "I never said I had not encountered anyone else."

Blood was roaring in my ears. If I thought the shock from entering this room was too much, it was nothing compared to the outrage I felt now. There were other people. Other mortals, as he called them. That ice cell in the tower was there for a reason. He had more victims than just me, and it probably did include Mr. Cooper.

"You sick, son of a bitch!" I raged. I allowed my fury to take over, completely flying off the handle to hurtle myself at him. My fists swung blindly, connecting with any part of his body available. After the initial two strikes, Gryphon grunted in pain, then grabbed my wrists and locked them in cuffs that matched the ethereal green glow of his eyes. My knees shot together in the same instant, tied by more green power. The current of electricity that always ran between us nearly sparked an inferno as I festered in my rage. I crumpled to the ground, on my knees before him with my fists caged in my lap.

His breathing was labored, reminding me of a bull in the ring, and he drew himself to his full height, glaring down his nose at me. A faint golden glow outlined his entire frame, his eyes so bright they were practically translucent. I felt the impending sense of death and my only regret was not locating Mr. Cooper. I sent a sincere prayer to the Universe asking that his soul be located and laid to rest.

"You forget your place, mortal," spat Gryphon.

I glared at him defiantly, still too livid to speak.

"Let this be a lesson to you." And with a snap of his fingers, the black free fall of doom landed me flat on my face in my ice tower cell. My nose snapped on impact, but my hands and knees were still locked in place, preventing me from wiping the blood.

Groaning, I rolled onto my back and stared at the stones above. While I couldn't say I was surprised to find myself back here, I was still seething from Gryphon's revelation. How many humans had wound up here? Was Mr. Cooper one of them, like I suspected? It made my heart hurt to imagine my sweet old friend suffering and dying alone at the hands of a monster like Gryphon.

Once again, I succumbed to my sobs.

CHAPTER 12

Eating Crow

GRYPHON

I awoke in a cold sweat and sat bolt upright in my bed. Using my power to form chains around Mirielle had drained me, and I passed out cold shortly after I sent her to the tower. Darda must have brought me here to recover with her own magic. For some reason, the curse also gave her the ability to command objects within the castle to move, a power she had never retained when in her regular form. It did not seem to exhaust her the way using magic did to me, though perhaps that was my mother's act of gratitude for the centuries of Darda's service. It left me at a severe disadvantage, however, because the more I relied on my power, the more exhausted I became. It was yet another reminder that time was running out and I needed to break this curse.

My magic also had to continue operating the role I played in the human world, but that was an automatic bodily function for me, like breathing. Rather than hoard my magic for my own bene-fit, I maintained my assignment as the keeper of souls on Earth. Something I did not anticipate Mirielle handling well should she ever find out. Although she had not presented herself as particularly religious person, an instinct told me that she would not respond favorably if I were to explain my purpose. It was a subject I intended to hide from her for as long as possible.

My skin felt clammy and my stomach churned while the room swayed, but I shuffled into my bathing chamber anyway. The hot water in the basin was enough to scour my skin yet I did not register the temperature. My encounter with Mirielle had me reeling. I felt impotent and out of control, though rash anger had always been one of my biggest faults. Darda would call it "bull-headed." Mirielle had already lasted longer than any of the others and something told me she was the one, but if I continued to allow her under my skin, we would never succeed. I was desperate enough to try and curb my temper if it meant breaking free of this wretched curse.

Yet Mirielle's fiery spirit entranced me. It was like she had also cast a spell over me, a spell of attraction and awe, and I loathed it. Humans were not meant to know of Aeternitas, nor were any of its inhabitants permitted to mate with them, which made my feelings an abomination. My father's wrath would be swift and potent if he were to ever find out, but like a moth to a flame, I could not stop my thoughts from drifting to her delicious smell, her soft skin, or how arousing I found it when she challenged me. Everything about her fascinated me and fascination was dangerous.

It occurred to me that my desire for Mirielle stemmed from the final manifestations of the curse. Although I did not fully understand my mother's intentions when casting it, I suspected she sought to punish me by taking away my powers completely. Without my magic, Aeternitas could not survive, especially with my father's absence, and I would be doomed to life in the mortal world. I could not foresee her taking away my immortality—she was my mother, after all—but forcing me to abandon everything I held dear and reside in a foreign place without knowing how to survive sounded exactly like something she would cook up.

Have you ever held anything dear?

I frowned at the intrusive thought. It was true, though. If I was being honest with myself--and impending failure will instigate honesty--before the curse my life was not filled with joy. I had very few friends and wasted most of my days drinking or gambling. Pastimes grow tedious when you have an endless amount of time. My family was always in a constant state of turmoil and dysfunction. We fought like mongrels fight over scraps, clawing at one another over vanity and wounded pride...much the same way I had just fought Mirielle.

Ugh! Pushing the palms of my hands into my eyes, I groaned in frustration. Would I ever learn from the past?

With a snap of my fingers I manifested on the outside of Mirielle's cell, completely dry, with an apology on my lips. I grimaced as I realized my chains were still intact. They were supposed to disappear as soon as she left my sight.

Waving my hand, the cuffs disintegrated and she slowly turned her head in my direction. She remained lying on the floor, her feet firmly planted with her knees in the air. Her face was void of any emotion or expression and that gave me pause. It gave me a twisted feeling in my gut, making me feel sour and out of sorts. She had always been an inferno, her feelings dancing on the surface, revealing her thoughts and intent. This lifeless mortal was all but a stranger to me.

"My apologies for my impulsive behavior." I swallowed hard, trying to remember scenes from books where the hero made his amends. "It was wrong of me to hurt you."

To my surprise, she laughed, a bitter, hollow sound that made my skin grow cold. It was not the sort of sound I would have expected from a spirit like hers. It sounded like some of the war criminals Aeternitas captured during the last war with the Elementals, our sworn enemy.

"Everything about this has been wrong," she finally sputtered, the same venom saturating her tone. "Why should I care that you are cursed? Good riddance! You're a bully and an asshole!"

Her words rang true. She had no reason to help me since my mother's curse had not affected life in the mortal world. My parents had ensured Aeternitas operated in its own little bubble, the boundary between the two worlds impenetrable. Safeguards were in place to protect the humans from our squabbles, though I had reason to believe that was not always the case after some of the visits I had made to the mortal realm on my quests. Why else would hurricanes wipe out entire cities or generations of children die due to starvation? Those were all things under Aeternitas' control, and yet the humans suffered for it. I had no prediction for what would happen on Earth if my mother, father, and I no longer existed for the very nature of the human realm relied upon us. In all my selfish tantrums about the curse, I had never stopped to truly reflect on how the humans would be affected.

I decided that agreeing with her would be my best course of action. "Yes, you are right. I am a bully who is used to getting my way. But if you help me, I promise to provide you with safe passage home." Some of that queasy unease in my gut loosened slightly with my promise.

She rolled her eyes before pushing herself up to a sitting position. When her face caught the meager light of the torch bracketed to the wall behind me, I cringed. Her nose, mouth, and cheeks were caked in blood and her nose bent to the right. That had to have happened in this cell since I never struck her during our last skirmish.

"You should send me home anyway because that's where I belong! You *kidnapped* me, which is a serious felony where I come from! It's already the right thing to do, not some stupid incentive for me to care about your problems!" She huffed in annoyance.

I contemplated this for several moments. I had no idea what a "felony" was, probably some abhorrent mortal custom, but otherwise she was still right. She did not belong here and she deserved to return to her home at the end of this. For some reason that knowledge came with an ache in the pit of my stomach.

I pushed the feeling away for another time. "Fine," I hedged. "Then if you help me, I will help you search for your Cooper fellow and I will send you both to the mortal world." A triumphant smile broke across my face for surely that would be enough to entice her.

Instead, she hung her head and began to cry softly. The sound made something inside me shatter for it was the sound of heartbreak.

Her cries escalated into full on sobs and she pulled her knees up to her chest, circling her arms around her tiny frame. Clearly my offer was offensive in some manner, but I had no idea why or how to remedy the situation.

After several minutes, during which I stood awkwardly, uncertain how to proceed, her tears began to fade and she wiped her cheeks. She brushed the hair from her eyes and turned her head to the window before simply saying, "No."

Just "no." No explanation. No hesitation. Just a simple decline, but one that sent me into a blur of panic and rage. Savagely, I grabbed the bars and shoved my face closer to one of the openings, practically growling at her. "Then you have sentenced yourself to death!" I said maliciously.

She did not respond or react but continued to gaze out the

window. Even I could recognize the cloud of despair and resignation that hung over her.

With a final cry of fury, I teleported myself back to my private office chamber. As soon as my feet touched the ground, everything within reach became used as a projectile. Books, a hairbrush, a teacup and saucer, whatever I could get my hands on. When that was not enough, I kicked over the worktable and sent a wave of power strong enough to blast it to smithereens. I yanked the heavy brocade curtains from the windows, finding no satisfaction in the sound of the ancient fabric tearing at its seams.

By the time my rage ran out and my magic died, I sank to my knees amidst the chaos and held my head in my hands, whimpering like a child. That was how Darda found me.

"Master, you must pull yourself together," Darda admonished. Even though I knew she could not do it, in my mind's eye I pictured her pursing her lips the way she used to, what used to be a sure sign of her displeasure. "This will never right your wrongs."

I shook my head wearily. "It is too late, Darda. The human refuses to help me and I do not have time to find another. The treasure still remains a mystery and the rose is on its last few petals."

My cheek felt damp and I swiped at it in shock. There were tears running down my face. For the first time in my existence, I was crying. Not only that, but the uneasy feeling I experienced outside Mirielle's cell had increased tenfold. It was crushing me, and I wanted to shake off the burden it left.

Darda was moved by my misery. She inched closer, though the debris was piled so high it made that difficult for a desk. After a moment I felt her presence behind me and imagined myself as a young lad again, with her steadying hand on my shoulder to guide me. Thanks to me, she would never be able to do that again.

"I cannot handle all of these *human* emotions," I bit out in disgust. "It's like my body is no longer my own. I have this bothersome weight pressing on me."

"Sounds a lot like guilt," my nursemaid muttered drily.

"Your condescension is unnecessary! It does nothing to relieve all these feelings!"

This must have been the wrong thing to say for Darda immediately reappeared in the doorway. "Maybe a little emotion is what you need!" she argued. "Maybe then you wouldn't keep mucking it up with Mirielle! She's *scared*, Master, and you do nothing to prevent it!"

"That is not true!" I countered. "I just offered to help her locate her missing family member and send her home as long as she helped me!"

Darda snorted. "And what reason does she have to trust your word? The word of someone who sends her to a tower every time she speaks her mind? The word of a *beast*?!"

Her final exclamation hit me square in the chest like a sword to the heart. It was exactly what my mother had called me the day she cast her curse. My caretaker could not have chosen a better word to wound me, and she knew it.

My voice promised violence as I icily commanded, "Get. Out."

She teleported, slamming the door shut behind her.

Color Me Resigned

It was impossible to tell how much time had passed as the view from the meager window never changed. The fog remained, dense enough to hide most of the trees, and light and shadow ceased to have any meaning. Even with the foreboding weather outside, I fell into fits of sleep, panic, and resolve, which cycled without reprieve. There was no way out of my cell, Mr. Cooper was probably long gone, and I had never felt so alone in my life. All of the historical artifacts in the castle did not lure me into accepting Gryphon's offer. If anything, they served as a warning. This was a place where anything was possible with a creature who held extraordinary magical power.

Twice a day a meal would materialize in the corner of the cell accompanied by a steaming cup of tea. I grazed on enough food to keep my wits about me, but everything I put in my mouth tasted of ash. Idly, I wondered if I could starve here or if there was some sort of magical protection in place.

Gryphon did not return, for which I was grateful. Hearing more of his false promises was the last thing in the world I wanted and I saw no reason to interact with my jailer. His so called offer of helping me locate Mr. Cooper was a slap in the face seeing as Gryphon was the one who abducted him in the first place. There had not been any other signs of human life in this horrendous castle, leading me to the conclusion that Mr. Cooper was dead. Just as I would be soon, too.

A sharp crack reverberated through the air, waking me from where I dozed against the wall. My eyes burned from lack of good sleep and all of my muscles still ached from my last fight with Gryphon, making movement difficult. One eye peeked open to see the writing desk from my bed chamber on the outside of the cell. Darda.

This had me fully awake and wrenching myself upright.

"Now, dearie, this squabble has gone on long enough. I can't bear to watch you waste away before me eyes!" she said, her Irish accent thick.

I snorted. "Can you call it a 'squabble' when I fight back against captivity?"

She sighed heavily and I felt the weight of her burden in that sigh. "It is not as it appears to be, young miss. The Master has had a terrible life and he faces a terrible fate. He is desperate, and desperation makes people monsters."

For some reason her words make me think of my mother and her endless parade of pimps, dealers, and junkies on rotation in our apartment. Yes, desperation created monsters.

"We all have problems," I retorted. "Doesn't mean I have to be his punching bag as he learns to deal with his."

She surprised me by agreeing with me. "That's why I'm here to get you out of this tower, dearie. Let the Master sort himself out. You deserve a chance to do the same."

My frozen heart thawed a bit at her kindness. I imagined she was a maternal sort of woman before. "Why do you continue to serve him when he's done this to you?" I blurted out without thinking.

"Because I have cared for the Master since he was a babe and I have seen the destruction his parents have caused. I never wanted the same for him."

I rolled my eyes. "My mother was no peach, and I'm not out here kidnapping people and stealing history."

"Did your mother curse you to a fate worse than death?" Darda fired back.

Her response gave me pause. His *mother* had done this to him? Suddenly mine looked a whole lot better. And that made me feel some empathy for Gryphon, damn it. Ultimately, no one can choose who their parents are. It was not his fault he was raised the way he was. Reading between the lines of Darda's explanation, Gryphon never stood a chance. How could he treat me any differently when hostility was all he'd ever known?

I shook my head, angry with myself for my fucking bleeding heart. "It doesn't mean I want to help him," I hedged. "I want to find Mr. Cooper and get the hell out of this place!"

Darda's relief was palpable. "That's all I ask of you, dearie," she said. Before I could blink, we teleported into my bathroom, where the steam and bubbles were already rising from the tub. "Get washed up. I will send up a tray of food and then I expect you to get some rest. After you feel better, we will get to work."

"Oh yeah? When he decides to let me out of this cage? This room is just a fancier prison than the ice tower," I snapped. Deep down I felt guilty for taking all my frustration out on Darda, but I needed to get it out of my system before I had to see Gryphon again.

She chuckled. "I've fixed that." And she was gone.

Suddenly too tired to care, I sank into the scalding water and cleansed myself, washing my hair three times before I felt satisfied that it was clean. The bathroom provided me with fuzzy pajama pants and a simple shirt, and as silly as it felt, I thanked it. A steaming bowl of soup with a basket of bread sat at a small table before the fire in the bedchamber and I all but moaned as I ate. Wearily, I crawled under the covers of the bed, finding it to be just as soft and plush as I had imagined, and I sank into an exhausted sleep. My last thought before the world disappeared was that the door to the hallway looked different, but I was already too far gone to figure out why.

The next morning, my eyes snapped open as if a siren blasted in my ear. My body felt rested, almost relaxed, and I smiled despite myself. Stretching my arms over my head, I rolled my body to my side and faced the door. The door that now had an iron doorknob!

Bolting out of bed, I crossed the room in three strides and yanked it open. I could leave the room whenever I wanted! My happy dance had me twirling with giddy excitement and I discovered a small but heavy key on the table where I ate the night before. A note sat next to it from Darda, explaining the key was for my use with my bedchamber and Gryphon would no longer be able to enter without my consent if the door was locked. Darda rocked!

Happiness made me bold and the part of me who yearned to examine the artifacts from downstairs returned. I scrambled to get ready, requesting yoga pants and a shirt from the bathroom. It provided a bright blue crop top that matched the blue in my hazel eyes and yoga leggings that melded to my body. Too bad the magical bathroom couldn't return to New York with me because its style choices were on point.

My face beamed with triumph as I walked out of the room and down the hallway. I had only arrived at the first crossroads before Darda appeared. Thank whatever gods there were for that because I had no clue how to get anywhere. This place was a maze.

"Alright then, young miss?" she asked.

I smiled warmly at her. "I am great, Darda. Can you help me get to the warehouse?"

"Oh, you can't go in there just yet," she cautioned. "The Master is waiting for you in the library."

My face fell, but I tried to hide it with a small smile for her. I was not eager to see Gryphon again, regardless of my new privileges. Not trusting myself to speak, I nodded, and the familiar sensation of teleportation engulfed me. I landed squarely on my feet in the grand hallway that led to the library. Squaring my shoulders, I knocked before entering.

Gryphon sat at the desk in the center of the room with stacks of disheveled papers and open books spread across its surface. His golden hair was pulled back into a bun, though some strands fell loose around his face. The same golden paint covered his chest and torso, highlighting rippling abs and large biceps, but he donned hunter green trousers and black boots on his lower half. His skin appeared sallow, making his cheek bones more prominent. I would almost guess he was ill.

He did not look up as I approached and it was with great trepidation that I stood in front of him. Darda's history lesson taught me that I needed to set the example for him, but that was difficult to remember now that his handsome face was in front of me. Did he have something against wearing a shirt?

"Good morning, Gryphon," I finally settled on. I clasped my hands in front of me, hoping to demonstrate I was not confrontational at the moment.

He finally looked at me and dropped the quill he had been holding. I saw his eyes widen and something akin to lust cross his features, but he quickly schooled himself. I had to be mistaken. There was no way someone as beautiful as him would be attracted to a woman like me.

"Good morning, mortal," he replied slowly as he eyed me warily. My greeting clearly caught him off guard and I sensed that he was just as cautious of our exchange.

"Mirielle," I gently corrected him. "If we are going to work together, please call me Mirielle."

That made him smile and the beauty of it nearly bowled me over. He was radiant when he smiled, all golden light and rich emerald. I had to remind myself to breathe normally.

My reaction embarrassed me and I hastily tried to distract him from noticing. "What are you working on?"

He leaned back in his chair, scrubbing his hand over his face, and I noticed a thin layer of sweat across his brow. Definitely sick. I wondered if it had something to do with the curse.

"Nothing of value," he finally replied. He began to shuffle the parchment into a hasty stack, then shove them all into a leather messenger bag that he pulled from the desk drawer. Normally his movements were more decisive than this, a sure sign of how awkward he felt.

Perhaps it was my full belly and my night of solid sleep, or maybe I was just too influenced by Darda's explanation of his childhood, but I felt a surge of empathy for Gryphon that made me want to help him. I knew what it was like to have a shitty excuse for a mom, and although I had Mr. Cooper to guide me, Gryphon didn't have anyone like that. All the finery in the castle and his raging mood swings made me think he always viewed Darda more as a servant than as an example; she could not have held much sway over him if he ended up like this. I didn't exactly want to help him because he held me prisoner and stole Mr. Cooper from me, but I also didn't want to think the worst of him now that I knew what his mother did to him.

There was also still the warehouse full of historical artifacts to contend with. Every bone in my body was dying to examine them and restore them to their original glory. There were several pieces I saw before that were in desperate need of restoration, still covered in dirt and grime from wherever they were taken. I sincerely doubted the castle had any kind of cataloguing system to track what was here and where it came from, so much of it was simply tossed wherever it would fit. There was no rhyme or reason to anything stored in that room and the archivist in me itched to get my hands on it. None of it belonged here in Aeternitas. But how could I make him understand the importance of returning it?

I still hadn't fully decided how to proceed, but I spoke up anyway. "Gryphon, I am prepared to help you in some aspects of... all this." I gestured airily around the room. "Not because I believe you, but because I will feel better knowing all of that history is preserved properly."

His eyebrows rose quizzically. "You don't believe me?"

I rolled my eyes. "No, I don't believe you'll let me go home and I think you're lying about Mr. Cooper. I know you took him. This whole mess started because of some parchment he must have found that you wanted."

For once, a look of guilt and unease settled across his features. He would not make eye contact with me as he absentmindedly drummed his fingers on the desk.

"Look," I hedged, "I can't change what happened in the past. But if I'm going to change my future, I see no reason why I can't help you do the same." This statement sounded stupid now that it was spoken out loud, but I felt the sentiment behind it. I had always approached problems this way because while I loved history, it was meant to be a lesson, not a punishment. Actions always had consequences, so if they were bad, you made better choices the next time around and had better outcomes. It was a simple philosophy that Gryphon had never learned.

His intake of breath was sharp and he gazed at me incredulously. I could tell my silly speech moved him and that embarrassed me, so I began to walk about the shelves of the room rather than allow his breathtaking beauty to distract me. Randomly, I stopped at one and ran my fingers along the leather spines.

I sensed his presence behind me, his warmth seeping into my skin. He had moved behind me, all but caging me into the corner of the room. Slowly, I turned to face him and the intensity of his smolder locked me in place. A few stray locks of golden hair fell across his face that made me want to touch him so that I might tuck them behind his ear and feel the rough stubble lining his jaw. My body acted on its own as I all but closed the gap between us, looking up at him in wonder and confusion as my chest leaned into his. He smelled of roses, light and airy.

"I would have you believe me," he whispered. The musical cadence to his voice sent arousal straight to the apex of my thighs. "I would have your trust, for I have no desire to hurt you, Mirielle."

My name had never sounded so perfect as it did from his lips. Lips that were full and parted, begging to be kissed. His honesty shocked me, but it only added to his appeal in this moment as something in my gut told me he had never wished me harm. His moods were volatile and erratic, but unintentional.

Hardly believing my own bravery, I leaned up and briefly pressed my lips against his. Time froze as an electric current ran down the length of my body. When I tried to pull away, he cupped one hand around the back of my neck and the other around my waist to draw me back, crushing his lips to mine once more. My mouth welcomed him, our tongues clashing and greedy to explore, while my arms wound their way around his neck, molding my body to his. The passion in that kiss was enough to end wars and build empires. I felt him everywhere, all the way to my soul. It was the kind of kiss you got lost in and never returned to yourself the same.

It could have been lifetimes or mere seconds before he withdrew from our frenzy, his facial expression revealing shock and horror. Gryphon threw his hands up to cradle the back of his head as he slowly retreated from me. What startled me most were his eyes. They were now molten gold, prisms for the light in the room. The ethereal emerald color returned to them in the next second-- right before he teleported out of the room.

Are you freakin' kidding me?!

Gryphon had no sooner teleported than Darda appeared.

"He buggered it up, didn't he?" she asked. Had I not been so stunned and confused, I would have laughed. I settled for a weak smile, one that I'm sure looked more like a grimace than anything.

She huffed. "When I get ahold of him..." The desk lid slammed down hard in frustration. "I'll go sort him out while we get you to work, alright, dearie? I've brought you some help!"

I could sense her smile, even if the desk was not able to provide one. My heart broke all over again imagining how horrible it must have been for her to be cursed in such a manner for something she didn't do.

"This is Wade, and this is Ambrose," said Darda. A large quill made out of an eagle's wing appeared next to a thick blue journal. Both objects stood up on Darda's lid and shimmied as though they were waving to me.

"I'm Wade," the journal said. What startled me was his

youthful New York accent. It was like I had been transported back to the Bronx.

"Guess that makes me Ambrose," the quill huffed sarcastically. He was also American, although it was hard to pinpoint which part of the country. The tonality of his voice made me suspect he was a heavy smoker. Although, quills couldn't hold cigarettes, could they?

My mind was reeling. "Were you human?" I sputtered.

"Now, dearie," Darda replied gently. "Let's not start digging around and wind up back in that cell, shall we? The important thing is that they are here to help you."

She was right. If I started questioning and pushing things again, Gryphon was liable to fly off the handle and leave me up there permanently this time. I would have to find a way to talk to Wade and Ambrose without arousing suspicion.

"What are we going to work on now?" I asked instead.

I felt Darda's approval at my response. She probably assumed I would demand answers anyway.

"You know best, dearie. What do you think would be the most helpful?"

This shocked me because I had not anticipated them placing so much faith in me. It seemed like a wild leap to go from an icy prison cell to calling the shots on a mission to locate missing treasure, but then again, everything was off kilter here. My brain whirled with possibilities before finally deciding, "I'd like to start an inventory of what Gryphon already has. Perhaps if I can get everything dated and organized, we can determine a better time period to explore for this lost object."

"Then that's where you'll start," Darda replied simply.

With a jolt, I was transported in front of the warehouse door, along with Wade and Ambrose. They both hovered in midair next to me, but neither complained nor made noise, leading me to wonder if they had an on/off switch somewhere. In another one of my graceful landings, I stumbled and landed on all fours. It was timed perfectly with Gryphon's appearance...right in front of me.

Sheepishly, I peered up at him through my bangs and felt my face flush as red as my hair. His eyes were alight with lust and amusement, enjoying my position on the floor in front of him. It left me even more confused by his behavior before. Had he gotten over our kiss that fast? Did it even mean anything to him?

"As much as I enjoy your submission, perhaps now is not the time," Gryphon joked, an undercurrent of arousal to his musical voice.

This only made me flush harder.

Ambrose had the foresight to muster a fake cough and draw our attention away from one another, giving me time to stand up and avoid Gryphon's penetrating gaze. The same ornate key as before hung from a string around his neck, which he used to allow us entry.

All the flirtation went to the furthest corners of my mind when I took in the sight again. It was truly mesmerizing to see so many relics, artifacts, and artistic works before me. There was enough gold in this room to finance every country on Earth for the next 500 years.

"Where can we set up shop, boss?" Wade asked Gryphon. A roughhewn wooden table appeared just inside the doorway with a small table lamp in the righthand corner.

I shook my head. That would not work for me. "No, I need an air sealed room, nitrile gloves, a flat work top, some Absorene, a leather solvent...basically, I need my lab."

Gryphon fixed me with a cold stare. "That will not happen. All of the items are to remain in this room."

Rolling my eyes, I gestured to the table he provided. "Well, that's not a good surface to work on. Can't you at least give me something smooth? And some gloves to work with?"

Instantly the table was replaced with the polished desk from the library. White gloves were folded in the center.

"Satisfied?" Gryphon huffed. For some reason, he sounded annoyed again.

Ambrose moved over to the desktop and laid down. "Let me know when you need me," he barked. Wade followed, the journal opening to the first blank page.

Okay, I thought. *Let's do this!*

"As long as you have all you require, I must take my leave," Gryphon said. He turned on his heel before I could respond. I chased him out the door, my feet echoing loudly in the vacuous hallway.

His retreat confused me even further. "Wait!" I called out towards his back.

Abruptly he turned to face me, reaching for my waist to pull me close. His lips immediately sought mine, just as desperate as they had been in the library, and I melted into him with wanton abandon. My head tilted back, granting him better access, and I moaned as he moved his attention along my jawline. I felt like my whole body was on the brink of an explosion. Like kerosene to a flame, Gryphon's ministrations fueled a passion I did not know I possessed.

Our panting subsided as Gryphon rested his forehead against mine. He maintained a tight grip on my hips, allowing the moment to linger.

My brain was in overdrive and my heart couldn't keep up. I had to know what was happening because I couldn't make sense of it myself. This was emotional whiplash. "What are we doing here?" I whispered.

Gryphon's eyes remained closed as he gently shook his head against mine. "I am indulging in a pastime I had long forgotten. You are far too tempting for your own good," he murmured. "You have ignited the path to my deepest desires and darkest fantasies."

Jealousy and insecurity reared their ugly heads at his words. "I'm a pastime?" I repeated numbly. As gracefully as I could manage, I extracted myself from his arms, relieved at the space between us. I gave him my back; I was too much of a coward to face the rejection I could feel coming.

"Mortals are not permitted to mate with residents of Aeternitas," he explained. "Long ago, humans were deemed unworthy." But his rationalization only made the sting grow worse.

"So I'm some piece of garbage you're using to get your rocks off?" I countered. My fists were clenched so hard that my knuckles were ghostly white. "And what residents? You're the ruler of nothing!"

I was not prepared for the yank on my shoulder and tumbled against his chest. He smoothly caught my wrists to stop my fall, then pinned them against his chest to keep me close. "Please," he begged. "Please do not ruin this for me." Glowing green eyes pleaded with me.

It was the worst thing for him to say. "You already did." Swiping my hands from his clutches, the tears blurred my vision as I ran away. Pain seemed to be the only constant in this castle.

CHAPTER 15

Laying Claim

GRYPHON

I didn't need Darda to tell me I had royally screwed up this time. The intensity of my feelings led me to blurt out the first thing that came to mind because insulting her was easier than anything else. It shamed me, and I had little doubt that I would be berated for my actions once my caretaker found out, but for now I needed to escape.

Summoning my magic, I deposited myself inside my private office and sealed the door to bar any interruptions. While most days I felt like a weak imitation of my former glory, right now the power coursing through my veins would be enough to resurrect mountains. I was invincible, on a high that had no fallout, and it made me bolder than any potion or tonic ever could. If I had been practical in any sense, I would have concluded Mirielle had something to do with the sudden buzz of life coursing through my veins, but blissful ignorance suited me just fine.

Originally, I planned to bring Mirielle with me on my next quest, but invigorated with this feeling of strength and force, I would dare the journey on my own. It would also serve as an apology because I regretted the way I acted. She managed to bring out the worst in me no matter how hard I wanted to be better for her.

I paused by the door to ensure no eager ears were listening before crossing to the torch mounted on the opposite wall. With a swift tug, the bracket lowered, causing the stones to shift and reveal a Baroque style mirror, gilded and ancient. The top and bottom featured the original fleur de lis symbol, from before the French stole it and used it to propagate their royal line. Each symbol was embossed with my mother and father's motto, *temporis et naturae*. "Of time and natural order." It served as a reminder of the significant role Aeternitas played in the universe. As if anyone here could forget.

If Darda knew I still possessed my mother's mirror, she would have me chained in the castle dungeon. This mirror had been the cause of years' worth of strife and discord between my parents. My father sought to use it for its powers, while my mother did everything she could to conceal it from him for this was no ordinary mirror. This was a portal between all worlds, regardless of time and space, and it allowed the seer to transport themselves anywhere they desired. Unlike my powers, which only continued to dissipate as time ran out, the mirror remained fully functional. It was how I had been accessing different locations for missing treasure, for the most part, with Mirielle's extraction being the most recent exception. Before the curse, I had the ability to manipulate myself in and out of time due to my lineage. It was my birthright as the Crown Prince of Aeternitas. However, as I fell more and more into despair and my magic came in shorter supply, I had begun to rely on the mirror.

Although I felt stronger now than I had in years, I did not want to push myself to the brink of exhaustion. Especially when I had no way of knowing what awaited me on the other side. While time moved far differently here than in the human realm, some time would have still passed, and Mirielle's lab could be in complete disarray, swarming with other humans searching for her.

It was time to retrieve that parchment.

Thankfully, the lab was not occupied when I entered, and there were no signs that anything had been disturbed. The entire room was still in utter disarray as though it had been ransacked; my powers had been out of control so far away from home. I felt the painful transformation into my beast-like form as I stepped through the portal, my wings growing from my back and fanning out behind me. My fingers morphed into sharp talons in a burning sensation that traveled all the way up my arm, mimicking the agony of my face forming a beak. It was difficult to breathe in this form, an intentional part of the curse my mother set to make it harder to find mortal help. Approaching someone as this monster only terrified them. Most humans believed themselves to be insane when they saw me, and a gibbering human could not comprehend my questions enough to answer.

I found the parchment on the floor beside the table where Mirielle had left it. All of the equipment she had planned to use was still there, so I waved my hand over it and sent it to the castle library. I was positive she would find a use for it.

The parchment was significant because it had been torn from my personal journal, something much like a diary. It was how I had been able to track my progress as the curse had worn on, and it held sentimental value to me, a rarity in my existence. On one of my acquisitions, the journal had fallen out of my pocket and landed on a battlefield, where a human had picked it up and turned it in to a shop more than a hundred years ago. I had been trying to locate a trace of its magic when it brought me to New

York City recently after a human man bought it. He was looking through the pages when I arrived and this piece was torn in the scuffle. Now I could reunite it with my original journal once more.

A squeak several feet away had me peering cautiously over my shoulder. Several tense seconds passed, but no one appeared and the sound was not repeated. Inwardly I groaned at my own trepidation. Some warrior I turned out to be...Mirielle had me questioning my own instincts now.

"Put your hands up where I can see them, freak!" a man shouted from the doorway behind me.

I whipped my head around and realized the human had a gun pointed at me. My blood curdled in rage. Guns were brutal weapons made for savages. A creature should not be allowed to wield a weapon if they had no regard for life, and if all of my history lessons with the humans had taught me anything, it was how little they respected the laws of natural order.

This arrogant mortal was of average height with a slightly muscular build—nothing that would indicate he was a fighter. However, I caught the gleam of plated gold on the right hip of his belt and all but sneered in disgust. He was a police officer, one of the mortal peacekeepers who did little to keep the peace unless it was for someone just like them. I had no tolerance for their so-called justice.

"I said to put your hands up!" the man barked again.

I made no move to raise my hands and instead closed the distance between us until the barrel of his firearm was inches from my chest.

His facial expression told me how petrifying my beast form was and how uncertain he felt. This was not a man who was confident in his actions. When faced with death, humans always showed their true nature.

"Where's Mirielle?" he demanded, only he used the Americanized version of her name, something akin to *Muriel* rather than the harmonious *My-rye-elle* the French intended. Americans really were the worst of the humans.

"Mirielle," I enunciated her name clearly so the fool had the opportunity to learn, "is not your concern. Leave. Now." Any other mortal would have been cowering from the venom laced in my voice.

This one only seemed to grow more resolved. His jaw tightened and his eyes narrowed as he called my bluff. "Where is she? Did you hurt her?!" There was an edge of hysteria to his voice, indicative of just how desperate he was for answers to Mirielle's whereabouts. As if he had any right to that information!

I raised one eyebrow at the man's audacity. My movements and reflexes were much faster than a human's, and before he had the wherewithal to stop me, I removed the gun from his hand and crunched it into a metal paperweight.

His eyes grew as wide as saucers. I couldn't stop myself from smirking at his incredulity.

This exchange was already tedious. Since I had everything I needed, it was time to go. To return home to Mirielle and the emotions I couldn't escape but did not know how to feel.

A piercing cry of anger met my back when I was just outside the mirror's portal, a shimmery wave in the spectrum where space met time. I glanced over my shoulder to see the man's blue eyes filled with hate, his body leaning towards me and preparing to fight.

"You better not hurt her, you fucking freak!" he roared. "I'll find you!"

The proclamation only made my smirk grow into a wicked smile. "And who, pray tell, is braving to the fair lady's rescue?"

He swallowed hard and dared a few steps closer, his fists clenched at his sides. "I'm Detective Barrett Collins and I'm a *good* friend of hers. Touch a hair on her head and you'll regret it! If I find out you have her locked up somewhere, you can bet that you'll be seeing me again real soon."

His words sent a sliver of ice down my spine. They were too familiar, too possessive...I didn't like it. The implication hung in the air that this was someone Mirielle knew intimately, and I faced the stunning realization that I had no idea what kind of relationships she had here in the mortal realm.

I would sooner see his head on a spike than allow Mirielle to belong to him. She was *mine*.

The urge to claim her roared through my body and sent a wave of power so strong, it knocked the detective back several feet. His body skidded along the laminate floor before slamming into a cabinet at the opposite side of the room. Without a backward glance, I exited through the portal, simmering with wrath and lust.

Make no mistake about it. If Mirielle confirmed a relationship with that pretty boy human, she was signing his death warrant. That mortal woman belonged to me—she just didn't know it yet.

CHAPTER 16

Boundaries are Important

I hovered outside the door to compose myself before entering the warehouse. Gryphon's words played on repeat in my head, making me flush with shame and embarrassment. Romantic relationships were a completely foreign concept to me. I had never really had a boyfriend, although there was a guy friend I fooled around with in college. It never amounted to much of anything since we both agreed we were better off as friends, which meant my V-card was still *technically* intact.

Maybe it was growing up with a revolving door of gross men coming in and out, but abstinence had never been difficult for me. I was so repulsed by the sounds, smells, and occasional visuals coming out of my mom's room that I never considered experiencing it myself. My own company had always been enough for me, and even Paul, the friend from college, was really more due to peer pressure than anything else.

That made Gryphon's rebuttal so much more painful. It was my first time ever experiencing this sort of vulnerability and I loathed how weak it made me feel. Yes, I was the one who kissed him first, but he led me on by kissing me back! He didn't need to awaken this blazing passion I never knew existed! It was a mistake that would never be repeated. We would keep our distance unless absolutely necessary. Besides, I had already sworn he was my mortal enemy. A few tawdry kisses would never be enough to right the wrong he committed by stealing Mr. Cooper away from me.

Satisfied with my decision, I wiped the tears from the corners of my eyes and joined Wade and Ambrose inside. The monumental task before me was almost repellent—almost. A much bigger part of me was thrilled at the prospect of examining rare artifacts that had been lost in time. It was every historian's dream.

Wade exuded enthusiasm when I walked through the door. He rose eagerly to meet me. "Can we get started? What should I call you? What are we gonna look at first?"

I laughed at his questions and wondered again about his age. He sounded so young!

"Will you quiet down?" Ambrose huffed. Definitely curmudgeon-y Grandpa vibes. I pictured him as the old man from *Up* and laughed again.

"Alright, gents, let's get to work!" I clapped my hands gleefully.

Hours passed quickly, but I barely made it through one shelf of scrolls. Without a computer and my lab equipment, the work was extremely time consuming. I longed for technology to streamline the process because after I started, I realized just how daunting it truly was. There was so *much*.

In order to create an easier visual for myself I removed the stolen Rembrandt from the wall and hung up several pages from the journal (which Wade assured me did not hurt and were magically replaced within an instant) to draw a rough timeline of human history. My plan was to notate the dates and locations of each of the items so we could determine if there were any important eras or places that Gryphon missed in his search. And if I could get away with it, I might preserve and restore a few things along the way.

Based on my initial examinations I determined the scrolls to be from the lost library of Alexandria, making the documents almost 2,000 years old. All of them needed some serious restoration. Not only was there sand and sun damage, but it looked to have saltwater damage as well. That could be tricky to restore because of the porous material of the paper, which wasn't really paper, but actually thin strips of the stem from the papyrus plant. I would need a wheat starch paste to go line by line on each scroll, then go over it again with a cellulose solution several times. Papyri typically required repeated cleanings to fully restore them to their original glory. It was time consuming, but given the significance of these scrolls, it was a job I was willing to sign up for.

I made a mental note to request better equipment from Gryphon.

Wade and Ambrose were excellent company, with Wade's snickers filling the air every time I picked him up. Ambrose was quieter, more reserved, but posed periodic questions if he sensed my frustration or puzzlement, which always served to redirect my feelings until I resumed productivity. Neither of them could tell me about their life before, so I did not have confirmation that they were human, but both dropped hints unconsciously. Wade repeatedly referenced a park that I knew was located in Harlem while Ambrose made an offhand comment about the Ohio River. It was like their memories were repressed, but certain topics or information filtered through the cracks.

As the hours waned, my eyelids began to droop. There were no windows or clocks of any kind, so it was impossible to determine how much time had passed. I never stopped to eat anything and my stomach growling jerked me awake. I hastily brushed the bangs from my eyes and returned to my notes.

"Uh, maybe it's time to call for the Master, My-my," said Wade. We had shared a good laugh earlier as he tried to pronounce my name and mutually agreed that "My-my" was an acceptable alternative.

My head felt heavy as I shook it in disagreement. "I just need a power nap," I mumbled. I laid my arm across the desk as a pillow, intending to rest for a few minutes. Darkness enveloped me as sleep took over.

I woke up in my own bed after rolling into a hard wall beside me. Wearily, I peeked out through one eye to find the wall was actually Gryphon's firm chest. He lay on his side, head propped up on one elbow, and his emerald eyes danced with amusement as he took in my sleepy state.

"I did not know mortal women to be capable of such sounds in their sleep," he teased.

His throaty chuckle shouldn't stir something in my chest. He was meant to be my enemy, I reminded myself. I rolled onto my stomach and breathed as best I could with my hair surrounding my face, shielding me from further mocking. The dragon breath I was sporting would *not* be his next target!

As I slithered out from under the downy blanket, I realized someone had removed my clothes and I only wore a sports bra and panties. They were boy shorts that weren't really boy shorts given the round backside my mother gave me—let's just say, J. Lo and I would have something in common. I snatched the blanket from the bed, but it would not yield to me with Gryphon's bodyweight on top of it.

Smiling cheekily at my predicament, Gryphon's mirth only

grew. "I am enjoying the view, but I will not complain if you return to the bed with me."

Embarrassment burned white hot through my body coupled with my rising desire. *No, bad Mirielle!* Refusing to let him win, I dropped the blanket and held my head high as I stalked into the bathroom. I immediately began turning on the many faucets to fill the bathtub. It should have been a signal that I wanted him to leave, but when I turned to the vanity to retrieve a hair tie, I found Gryphon sitting cross-legged on the counter.

"Jesus!" I sputtered, clutching my chest. "Do I not have a right to privacy?"

He grinned. "Do you wish for privacy?"

"Yeah...a little bit!" I snapped.

Gryphon rolled his eyes and unfurled himself before exiting through the tapestry.

Despite the basin only being half full, I stripped down and stepped in the hot water. The aroma of roses permeated the air as I sighed with relief. I wanted to soak for a little while before actually scrubbing myself, but not even 30 seconds later I heard Gryphon call through the tapestry.

"Are you going to be much longer?"

"Why are you waiting on me?" I countered.

Even without seeing him, I could sense his irritation growing. He needed to get a grip on his anger issues.

Another minute or so passed before he tried again. "Are you finished?"

"If you wanted this process to go faster, you should have installed a shower in your magical bathroom!" I snapped in exasperation.

Gryphon's head poked through the tapestry, causing me to sputter and sink further into the bubbles. "All you ever need is to ask," he said simply. With a snap of his fingers, a glass encased shower was positioned next to the door to the water closet. It had three shower heads on the ceiling, with another nine on the three walls of the interior, and looked big enough to house a soccer team.

My eyes wanted to pop out of my head. "Do you ever do anything half-assed?"

He smirked. "Do you ever stop the mortal vulgarities?"

"Go away so I can shower in peace!" I chided him. His aversion to swearing was actually amusing when it didn't make him fly off the handle. He wouldn't last two seconds in New York City, though.

For once he did as I asked and the tapestry swung back in his retreat. I tried not to squeal in delight as I turned on the shower and tried all the different settings. When I finished, I asked the bathroom for skinny jeans and my black thigh high boots back. It provided a simple black shirt, but it was skintight-- not my usual style. Probably something Gryphon wanted. I rolled my eyes at the thought, but still had to stifle my smile. My hair was too thick and heavy to keep down, being that it almost reached my waist, so I piled it on top of my head and used a straightener to fix my bangs. I felt confident enough to wear makeup, so I drew on winged black eyeliner and thick black mascara. Overall, I was pleased with my appearance. Other than the shirt being a size too small, it was how I normally dressed, which gave me the confidence boost I needed after my insecurity yesterday.

I found Gryphon pacing before the fireplace. The small table from the other morning was back with a covered platter on top. Two deep green silk chairs framed the table, although there was only a place setting for one. He stopped abruptly as I entered and I could tell from the way his eyes surveyed my frame that he approved of the outfit. My cheeks burned at his attention and I crossed my arms across my chest.

"Perhaps the view *has* improved," he commented lightly.

Deciding to ignore him, I sat at the place setting and pulled the cover off the platter. It contained a tray of pancakes and a small pitcher of syrup on delicate China plates accented in gold. The same hourglass insignia was etched into the center as I had observed on all the banners in the main hallway. It had to be the royal crest. I tried not to pucker my nose at the food selection— breakfast wasn't really my thing.

Gryphon must have noticed my grimace because he snorted derisively. "What's wrong now, mortal?"

"I'm just not really a fan of pancakes. Is there any chance I could get some chicken fried rice and an iced coffee?"

His expression turned puzzled. "Fried rice and iced coffee? Do humans normally combine those for a meal?"

I laughed. "I've never really done what other people do. I like what I like, I guess."

Gryphon nodded once before snapping his fingers. A steaming plate of chicken fried rice appeared in place of the pancakes, with a tumbler full of iced coffee next to it. Another small pitcher of creamer arrived a moment later.

"How did you know I liked creamer?" I asked in surprise.

He raised an eyebrow but did not answer my question. "Poor Cook must be beside himself with worry over satisfying you."

This was a revelation to me. "You have a cook?!"

"Of course I have a cook. The castle is equipped with a full staff."

"How come I've never seen any of them?"

Gryphon's eyes darkened. "Because I did not wish for you to see them. Servants are not meant to associate with my guests."

On the one hand, his consideration of me as a guest was unexpected. I certainly hoped he didn't routinely send his other guests to an icy tower whenever the whim suited. However, the disdain with which he spoke of his staff sent off alarm bells in my head. You'd have to be incredibly arrogant to have that kind of perspective.

"I am not your guest, I am your prisoner," I corrected him, knowing this would set off his temper.

I was not disappointed. He slammed a closed fist down on the table and when he spoke, his words were like venom.

"If you would like me to demonstrate how I treat my prisoners, I would be happy to do so."

He was far too easy to rile up, but I mutely shook my head. No good would come from me berating Gryphon for his reaction. It was several more tense minutes before I resumed eating. I was never returning to that cell, or any other cell for that matter.

Gryphon pondered me as I ate, his body leaning back on the elbow of the chair as he cuffed his chin with his hand. I tried not to be distracted by his look, or the way his pinkie finger traced along his bottom lip. His hair was down today, in all its golden glory, falling in slight waves past his shoulders. Although he had on a white linen shirt, the top was untied, exposing the hard planes of his chest. I could see the faint outline of the key to the warehouse falling below his right nipple. In my mind, I pictured myself running my hands along the muscles of his abdomen, tracing lightly upward to feel the thrumming beat of his heart, then using my lips to follow their ascent.

"Is fried rice a typical food for humans to break their fast? Is it not customary to eat eggs or meat from a swine?" Gryphon suddenly asked.

The disconnect between his thoughts and my own could not

have been farther, and I burst into a peal of giggles at his question. "Food is food, in my opinion. Doesn't really matter what time of day you eat it."

His face lit up. "The sound of your laughter is enchanting."

The echo of my last laugh froze on my face. No one had ever given me such a beautiful compliment before. It unnerved me because I did not know how to respond.

"Does that trouble you?" he inquired.

"Your opinion of me does, yes," I whispered. The room felt too hot, too crowded, his gorgeous face too close. The walls were slowly closing in on me.

Gryphon growled, a sound meant for a beast. "And I suppose your human companion's opinion pleases you."

My mind drew a blank. Was he talking about Mr. Cooper?

"Um, Mr. Cooper is old enough to be my grandfather, and he would never discuss something like that."

"No, your suitor. Barrett, I believe his name was." The tone of his voice implied how vile he found the name to be.

I leapt from my chair, furious. If I stood close enough to deck him, this encounter would end badly. I needed distance *now*.

"I don't have a 'suitor!'" I hurled the word at him. "And if you are referring to Barrett Collins, the bully of my adolescence who has now turned into a bully of a detective, I suggest you have your head examined. Clearly your brain is missing and we should be looking for that instead!"

For once his anger did not rise to meet mine, but I could tell my words affected him. His features softened and his body visibly relaxed. I expected something more explosive and found myself willing him to challenge me.

"Wait—how in the hell do you know anything about Barrett?" I asked.

Gryphon shrugged. "As the Crown Prince of Aeternitas, I know many things, human."

His condescension would be my undoing. The only sound in the room was my own harsh breathing as I tried to calm myself. It felt like hours before he rose from his chair and slowly stalked towards me. His eyes never left my face, the heat of his gaze making my knees quake and my thighs clench. My daydream from before returned in full force, and I leaned towards him, beckoning him forward. Now he had my feelings all over the place as well as his own.

Gryphon did not blink as he towered over me. I was average in height, but I might as well have been a dwarf for the difference between us. His shoulders were massive, reminding me of the impressive wingspan of his other form. He was an indomitable figure, imposing, and I had studied combatives enough to recognize a predator when I saw one.

"What are you doing to me, mortal?" Gryphon whispered. His gruff hand was surprisingly gentle as he cupped it around my cheek.

I blinked, too entranced with the moment to maintain my mantra of him being my enemy. His eyes were glowing again, on the verge of the molten gold I saw once before.

"It's Mirielle," I replied weakly.

A ghost of a smile crossed his lips. "Mirielle," he breathed. It sounded angelic in his musical voice, the accent rich and alluring. "My miracle."

Mr. Cooper had translated my name for me once before and his wrinkly face burst into my mind at Gryphon's words. This was all wrong. Gryphon was keeping me prisoner. I could not allow this flirtation to grow.

Taking a giant step to the side, I turned my back to him and took a few steadying breaths. The spell of the moment was broken and I heard Gryphon's harsh exhale behind me. "I am nobody's anything. Not Barrett Collins' and certainly not yours. I am here to find Mr. Cooper and then I'm going home."

The temperature in the room dropped by several degrees until I was almost shivering.

"Then while you are here you will maintain yourself properly. Meals at least twice per day and rest as your body requires," Gryphon ordered. I could hear the effort he was using to maintain his composure. His anger wanted to explode.

I nodded. "I don't need your help to do any of it, so it's probably best that we keep our distance."

A tense pause followed my statement as I waited for Gryphon to erupt. I turned back around after several moments and found him to look stricken, almost hurt. It was his turn to nod.

"As you wish, mortal. You need only say Darda's name and she will come to you. She can provide whatever you need going forward." And with that, he was gone.

CHAPTER 17

The Ultimate Surprise

Time began to pass in the same routine. My days followed one after the other like clockwork, waking up in the morning, showering, eating, working in the warehouse with Wade and Ambrose, eating a final meal, and then bed. It was much the same schedule I had back in New York, so I found it easy to slip into the simple practice. Wade and Ambrose remained excellent company, helpful and inquisitive, and for once I found enjoyment in sharing my workspace with someone. It made the time pass quickly and kept my spirits up as the task grew seemingly endless.

Despair was all I felt as I explored further into the warehouse and discovered more artifacts, for there was too much to be done. It would take years to comb through the document archive Gryphon had created as there were scrolls, books, treatises, and more from not only the lost library of Alexandria, but other lost libraries, such as the Nalanda library from India, the Mayan Codices, which had originally been believed to be burned in the 16th century, and the Imperial Library of Constantinople. These works barely scratched the surface of Gryphon's collection as the rows went on for well over a mile and were just as deep. All of the works I had examined needed to be cleaned, restored, and properly preserved, let alone catalogued and accurately dated. While my knowledge of ancient languages was more extensive than most, even I would seek the help of a colleague to identify most of what this library contained.

Gryphon provided more equipment, which I strongly suspected came from my lab back home, but I did not have the courage to ask. We were avoiding each other. He even tasked Darda with the key so she was responsible for unlocking the door to the warehouse each morning, and although Gryphon was the one who always arrived at the end of the day to signify work was over, he would merely examine the progress I made on the timeline and then hold open the door for Ambrose, Wade, and me to leave. The coldness we had developed was just as jarring as the attraction, and it made me wonder if my life was incapable of happy mediums. Perhaps I would only ever experience emotions in extremes. I was too embarrassed to try and repair the damage between us, and Gryphon was far too stubborn, so we both simply avoided eye contact and maintained our distance.

Ambrose, Wade, and I were growing far closer. The more we talked, the more their memories seemed to surface. I was certain now that both of them had been human. Gryphon had plucked them from their homes, but why? Why were they now cursed here in Aeternitas like Darda when they did not belong here?

These questions swirled around and around in my head until I thought I might go crazy. Even as I added more and more to the timeline, I grew despondent. There were still more questions than answers, and it was hard to find motivation when all the work was leading me nowhere.

One morning I asked Darda if it would be possible to have the morning off from the warehouse, surprising both of us.

"Are you feeling ill, dearie?" she asked kindly.

I shrugged. "I'm a little homesick and just feeling kind of down. I just need a day to myself."

I could feel Darda's empathy surrounding me, bright and warm. It was all she could do when she was unable to hug me.

"Why don't we take a little tour of the castle instead?" she suggested.

I brightened at her offer. That would be an excellent change of pace!

By now I was accustomed to free fall into nothing, so when Darda transported us, I landed easily on my feet. The amazement came from the garden I found myself in. It was a courtyard of the castle I had never seen before, with all four walls made of the same steely gray stone. Large archways opened on opposite ends, with a winding path through the garden connecting the two. A small pond with lily pads was to my left and a large willow tree towered to my right, extending up beyond the castle walls as it searched for light. One branch hung lower than the rest, and a wooden swing hung from it, large enough for an adult.

Everywhere else were bursts of color; roses in scarlet, yellow, white, and the palest pink were the predominant choice, growing up the corner farthest from me. Peonies, fuchsia and hot pink, were the size of my fist. Tall dahlias in reds and yellows circled around the outer edge of the pond, and heavy purple wisteria grew up around the wall behind the willow tree. It formed a canopy of sorts in the corner opposite the climbing roses. There were more flowers I did not recognize, equally resplendent in purples and bright blues, and the air was so rich and fragrant it made me dizzy. It was paradise.

"But how do the flowers grow? There's no sunlight," I inquired curiously. The thick fog had never lifted the entire time I had been here. Even now, overhead, the sky was impenetrable.

Darda chuckled. "We have our ways, dearie," was all she said.

"I help a bit, don't I, Darda?" came a voice. A small gardening shovel emerged from an azalea bush near our path.

Darda agreed, "Yes, you certainly do. Anastasia, may I introduce you to Mirielle?"

The shovel leaned the handle part towards me as though it were bowing. "It's a pleasure to make your acquaintance," Anastasia said. Her accent gave me pause for it was distinct, yet uncommon. Dare I say eastern European?

"Do you take care of this garden?" I asked her. "It's so beautiful here."

"I do what I can," she replied quietly. Her voice was laced with sadness, and it made my heart break for her. I could feel her pain and wondered if it came from her life before Aeternitas or after.

"Would you like to join us on our tour?" I offered. "I would love to make another friend here."

Even though she could not give me a facial expression, I had the sense that Darda approved of my invitation. It was uncanny how sensitive I seemed to be to the feelings of these objects, although it was probably more magic at work. I would never disregard the improbable again after my time here.

Anastasia giggled in delight. "I would love that! I could use a new friend, too!"

Over the next few hours, Darda showed me several rooms in the castle. I learned that it had been modified as the human world changed, so different areas reflected different styles that were popular at specific points of time. We saw an art gallery that was filled with landscape paintings, which she swore up and down were of landscape in Aeternitas, but I doubted mostly due to the inability to see anything outside of the unnatural fog. We toured a trophy room that displayed cups and medals for tournaments I had never heard of as well as games that did not exist in the human world.

Next, Darda took me to a ballroom that had glittery glass chandeliers reflecting prisms of light onto a mirrored ceiling. It was a room large enough to accommodate three hundred people and a mosaic of the same hourglass insignia I saw everywhere else was built into the main dancing floor. A raised stage in the far corner contained several musical instruments, like a black grand piano and a gold harp.

Everything in the room was dusty, with cobwebs hanging amongst the chandeliers, and Darda whispered quietly that the Master had not had cause for celebration in quite some time. She described the lively parties they used to throw in the ballroom, then opened a set of double doors made of mirrors into an adjoining dining room with two dark wood tables running the length of the room. Each table had golden chairs lining both sides, and by estimate, could have sat more than two hundred people for a meal. The hourglass crest was etched in gold every six feet along the table. A gold chandelier as big as a Buick dropped down from the center of the room, and I could not help but gasp at the grandeur of it all.

Anastasia was excellent company on the tour. She was witty and managed to crack a joke any time I found myself awestruck. Based on the way she spoke of certain things, I had the impression that she was used to living in a palace, and therefore did not find the lavishness all that imposing. The only Anastasia I knew of was the Russian princess who had supposedly disappeared after the revolution, but that myth had been debunked years ago in 2007. This could not be her, could it?

As the tour wound down, mostly because I was starting to get tired and had no sense of direction, we walked through a hallway that remained true to the medieval style of a castle. Here the walls and floor were stone, making the temperature colder. Our footsteps were muffled by a red carpet runner and torches were bracketed every few feet along the walls. Despite the disparity between the opulence I had already seen, I found that I liked this atmosphere better. It felt more like an actual castle and less like a palace.

We rounded the corner and I could hear the splash of water and some indistinct shouting. Darda paused, which made me wonder if we were allowed to be here. We had all been so caught up in conversation about the castle that I didn't think she meant to turn down this way.

"What's back there?" I asked, trying and failing to keep the curiosity from my voice.

"Never you mind, dearie," Darda said stiffly. The desk turned abruptly and began gliding back in the direction we came from.

It was Anastasia who answered. "That's the kitchen."

I remembered Gryphon mentioning a cook, so my interest was piqued. Before Darda could stop me, I raced down the hall and burst into a room that would have been confusing had I not already seen so many unusual things in Aeternitas. It was a kitchen that was as modern as it was medieval. A colossal black cauldron sat over an open fire right next to a gleaming stainless steel oven with eight stove top burners. Long fluorescent lights hung from the ceiling, but more bracketed torches dotted in between cabinets that hung on the walls. There were several butcher block islands throughout the room, each looking as if they were workstations designated for a specific type of cooking. There were stone counters along one wall, but each contained a small appliance like a coffee maker or an air fryer.

The hodge podge of new and historic was not even the most jarring part. What stopped me in my tracks was that there were no humans working in any of the various stations through the kitchen, but more objects. Scrub brushes moved on their own over bubbly water in a circular fountain. Pots and pans were simmering on a second stove top, this one dating to the 1950's. Knives chopped vegetables at a butcher's block station closer to the cauldron. A restaurant-sized refrigerator was barking out orders in an Irish accent similar to Darda's. All activity stopped as I stepped farther into the room, glimpsing an open storeroom to my left that served as a pantry. All of my favorite foods were inside.

"You can't be in here, young miss!" Darda gasped from the doorway behind me.

"Is everything here *alive?*" I whispered. The implication of my statement made me queasy.

At the same time that Darda ordered me to leave the room, Anastasia answered in the affirmative.

"Everything is fine here, miss," a soup ladle hanging from a hook on the wall next to me said. I heard several other voices confirm the statement, with some objects moving up and down as though they were nodding.

I ventured farther into the room to judge the scope of the activity. Anastasia followed me, hovering next to me as I finally sank down onto a small stool near the wash fountain.

"Don't fret, Mirielle," she said. Her words were meant to be soothing, but they rankled me to my core. This was exactly the kind of thing I should "fret" over!

"Mirielle," one of the scrub brushes said mildly. "That's a pretty name."

Ice crusted over the blood in my veins and my heart stopped beating. Everything in the room began to swim as I slowly turned towards the brush and desperately tried to breathe in enough air to prevent myself from passing out. I would recognize that voice if I lived to be a thousand years old, the voice that had haunted my dreams for weeks.

"Mr. Cooper...?" I murmured.

CHAPTER 18

Curse of Consequences

MIRIELLE

The brush stopped scrubbing the cutting board it was working on and turned so that the bristles faced me. "What did you call me?" he asked.

Tears streaked down my face as I choked back a sob. "That's your name," I replied softly. "That's what I've always called you."

"No," the brush said, "my name is Emil...do I know you?"

It was like a sucker punch to the gut. Mr. Cooper was alive, in a manner of speaking, but he didn't remember me or who he was. How had he come to be afflicted by this curse?

"DARDA!" I roared. "TAKE ME TO HIM NOW!"

She did not need to ask. She knew exactly who I meant.

I snatched Mr. Cooper by the handle as the black void swallowed me. Darda and I emerged in the library, Gryphon already standing before the fire with quiet fury rolling off him in waves. The tension in his jaw and shoulders should have terrified me, but I was too blinded by my own rage to notice.

"CHANGE HIM BACK!" I bellowed at Gryphon, holding Mr. Cooper out in front of his face. "Right now or so help me, I'll destroy that entire room full of treasure!" It was an empty threat, something he should have called me out on right away, but he remained uncharacteristically quiet. He did not so much as flinch as I thrust the brush closer.

Instead, Gryphon turned his head to Darda and the look on his face promised violence. "You will return to my quarters immediately while I sort out the consequences of your idiotic actions." Now he turned back to me, his tone cold and deadly.

"You were never to see that room or any of my servants," Gryphon hissed.

It was the worst thing to say and set off my temper like a firework. "YOU KEPT HIM FROM ME! THIS WHOLE TIME HE WAS HERE IN THE CASTLE AND YOU COVERED IT UP!" My anger only escalated as I began to call Gryphon every name I had ever learned in the Bronx projects. I had only gotten through my second "mother fucker" when a glowing green gag caught in my mouth and the same shimmering ropes as before bound my wrists and knees together. They forced me to the ground in a kneeling position as the cuffs fastened to my knee constraints.

More infuriated tears ran down my cheeks, and I glared up at Gryphon with what I hoped served as a warning. Mr. Cooper, meanwhile, floated near Gryphon and began backing away as though he wanted to distance himself from my outburst.

"Master," he said, "I had nothing to do with this! Please let me return to the kitchens!"

Gryphon nodded once, his eyes never leaving mine. "Yes, I think that would be wise, Emil." With a snap of Gryphon's fingers, Mr. Cooper disappeared.

My simmering rage did not. I screamed into my gag, trying desperately to fight against my bonds so that I could launch myself at the atrocious creature before me. Gryphon had let me believe Mr. Cooper was dead! All of the anguish I had felt for months had been for nothing, and while I was so relieved I did not need to plan a funeral, I was incensed that Mr. Cooper had been right under my nose all this time. I should have been helping him escape, not charting history for a monster!

"Mirielle," Gryphon began, making my name sound like loving caress, "I did not know that 'Mr. Cooper' was who I knew to be 'Emil.' Last names are not used here like they are in the mortal world."

I only screamed harder into my gag. Adrenaline was coursing through my veins, demanding vengeance. His excuse was weak, at best.

"If I let you out of these bindings, you are not permitted to fight me, for I cannot be held responsible for the aftermath." It was a direct warning, one that matched the look in his eyes, but I could not heed the threat. I was too lost in my own suffering.

The moment Gryphon snapped his fingers to remove the ropes, I aimed for his jugular. I attacked with vigor, all of the pain and rage channeling into my attack. My right fist connected with his cheekbone while my left pummeled an upper cut into his abdomen. The sound of the bone breaking did little to satisfy me— I was out for blood. As I reared back to throw another punch, Gryphon held up a hand to stop me. It was exactly like the fight when I first arrived; I was frozen in place, my muscles straining to break free and continue the assault. Unlike the previous time, however, his hold over me only lasted a few seconds before he visibly wilted and stumbled backward.

I was not one to miss an opportunity and ran the few steps towards him, using my body's own momentum to crash into him. He fell backwards, breaking a couple bookshelves, and sending the books crashing to the ground. Groaning loudly, he tried to sit up, but almost immediately slumped back against the broken shelves.

"Change him back NOW!" I screamed.

Gryphon shook his head. "I cannot," he sputtered. "I did not put him in this state. The curse did."

It was a revelation that did not make sense, but it brought me up short. My body tensed, prepared to deliver a high kick to his face if his next response did not satisfy me.

"Explain," I commanded.

Gryphon extracted himself from the shelves and promptly stumbled forward, reaching out for an armchair. Sweat ran down his face, which had returned to the sallow white color I had seen only once before. I had thought he might have been sick then, but in this moment, he looked like a corpse. The gold in his hair lost its luster and his face was gaunt.

I reacted instinctually and dove for him. My legs strained to lift him upright into a sitting position, but after a moment, he was settled. I pulled the other armchair directly across from him and sat down, refusing to even blink lest he use that as a chance to escape or overpower me.

"You were right before," Gryphon whispered. "There have been other humans, people I extracted in hopes they were the ones from the prophecy. But whenever they could not help me success-fully retrieve an item, we would return to Aeternitas and they would morph into something else. I could not stop it and I had no control over it. I can only assume it is part of the curse."

"The curse your *mother* inflicted," I snapped, the word tinged with disgust. His mommy issues didn't need to be Mr. Cooper's problem. Or mine, for that matter.

His eyes jumped to my face and I realized belatedly I had probably just gotten Darda into more trouble. No one else could have told me that truth. However, rather than question it, he simply nodded gruffly. His breathing was becoming more and more labored the longer he sat there.

"That's why it is so important that we break the curse," he continued. "It will save all of them."

I fervently shook my head and began pacing the room. I felt hysterical now, my desperation leading me on the road to insanity. "No, no. You have to change him back! You must know a way to do it—look at all the other magic you do! There has to be another way! CHANGE HIM BACK!"

Gryphon truly looked pained. "I cannot, Mirielle. If I could spare you from this agony, I would. Channel this energy into finding the missing treasure."

His pleas fell on deaf ears. "I will never help you again! This is *your* problem, not mine. What even makes you think I can find it? I haven't accomplished anything so far and it's been weeks!"

"Because you are the only one who has lasted this long!" Gryphon barked suddenly.

This declaration made me stop short. He pushed himself up a little straighter in the chair, his damp hair now plastered to his face in sweat. If I had to guess, he was on the brink of collapse.

"No one else has lasted more than a day or two at most," he continued. "You are the only one. You, Mirielle Townsend, are who is meant to save us all."

With that, his eyes rolled back into his head and his body slumped to the floor, limp and covered in a sheen of sweat. I rushed to the ground beside him, cradling his head in my lap as I frantically called for Darda.

CHAPTER 19

Borrowed Time

GRYPHON

Random images appeared in my dreams after I passed out in the library, images that had already begun to haunt my waking hours. Aeternitas was not under threat just from the curse. The Elementals, a warrior group from where my mother originated, were always looking for a way to breech the gate. As I grew weaker, it became more and more likely that they would attack. Their soldiers were fierce and swift, a mixture of the four elements found in the human realm—fire, air, water, and earth. The king of the Elementals, my uncle Vulcan, could manipulate all four, which made him incredibly deadly. Now that Aeternitas' army was lost to the dense fog, another product of my mother's curse, the only defense we would have would be my powers. Powers that were disappearing rapidly. It was only a matter of time before they came to test me.

Even before I rose from my bed after my library episode, I could already tell the equivalent of several days had gone by. My throat was parched and my skin was clammy. I needed to bathe, and I was desperate to get some food in my belly. I sent the order to Cook for a Philly cheesesteak, a mortal sandwich of which I had grown preferential, and slid out from under the silk sheets. I was completely naked, not in itself unusual as Darda had undressed me before, but I stopped abruptly when I made eye contact with Mirielle.

She was sitting a few feet away on a makeshift cot piled high with fluffy pillows and blankets. A tumbler of her favorite iced coffee sat next to her on the table, along with a tray of half-eaten food. At my movement, her eyes widened, and I could tell she was trying hard not to glance down at my cock, which was only growing harder with arousal as I observed her there in my bedroom.

No one had ever been inside this room beyond Darda and myself, not even my parents. Bedchambers were sacred places of privacy in Aeternitas, which was how I reminded everyone in the castle that Mirielle was, in fact, my prisoner—I frequented hers and denied her that privacy. Sharing this space with her felt intimate and erotic, and I was suddenly very aware of the enormous bed behind me.

"What are you doing here?" I rasped. It sounded like I was a human smoker.

Her cheeks flushed a deep shade of pink. "After you blacked out, I called for Darda. I begged her to let me take care of you," Mirielle explained. "You have been out of it for a few days now. We had to change your sheets twice. Darda said you don't have medicine here?"

"No, that is a mortal custom that would not have any effect on me," I murmured.

It was actually touching to see her concern. No one had ever cared about me or for me like this. After the first time I raged at Darda as a lad during a sickness, she would do nothing more than deposit me in this room whenever I felt ill, not that I could blame her. I was an absolute menace when that happened.

I offered Mirielle a small smile, one that she returned. Several heated moments passed with bated breath. I felt happy, but awkward. How did I proceed forward now?

"Thank you for your care," I said.

My words must have broken her out of a daze because she dropped her eyes and shrugged. "If something were to happen to you, then I'd never break the curse and Mr. Cooper would be stuck as a brush."

It was like a knife to the chest. Of course she didn't actually care about me. This was all about the stupid curse, a millennia's punishment that my mother bestowed upon me. There was no way someone as kind and compassionate as Mirielle could ever care for someone as volatile and violent as me. For whom could ever learn to love a beast?

The change in my mood brought an icy chill to the air and I swept from the room into my bathing chamber. After her request in her own bath, I had modified mine to include a shower, although mine was far grander than Mirielle's. Now it irritated me to have the jarring reminder of how much she influenced me. She was determined for her stay here to be temporary, so why was I permitting such drastic changes in my habits and activities for her?

Why would I want her to stay longer anyway? She was a human. My father would never accept her.

Out of spite more than need, I filled my bathing pool, which was large enough to accommodate me in my beastly form. Glowing embers ran underneath the tub to keep the water warm for as long as I cared to bathe and today, I felt like stewing in the water until my dark mood passed. Three tall windows lined the wall beside the tub so that I had a clear view of the tree line and fog just beyond my chambers, trees half-filled with crimson, gold, and ginger leaves. The colors were muted through the mist, but the familiar sight still brought me some comfort.

I was so lost in my own thoughts that I did not hear Mirielle approach. Her statement startled me and I jumped up in a defensive stance.

"Those trees are beautiful!" she cried. She stared out the windows in awe, her mouth forming a perfect O. What I longed to do to that mouth...

But she did not want that, did she? Huffing, I returned to the pool, giving her my back as I hung on to the edge closest to the window and allowed the rest of my body to simply float. I did not trust myself to speak to her when I was in such poor spirits.

"Why is it that the landscapes are always so different here?" she inquired.

It was vanity that urged me to answer and I could not keep the pride from my voice as I explained. "Aeternitas represents the stages of human time. We are the reason your world experiences the four seasons of summer, autumn, winter, and spring, and so it is reflected here."

I could sense her incredulity without looking at her. It probably was impressive to a mortal.

"Is there anything else you need?" she finally offered.

Without meaning to, I snorted derisively. "Nothing you can provide."

"What's that supposed to mean?"

Angrily, I turned in the water to glare at her. She had stepped closer to the tub, close enough that if I stood up, I could grab her biceps and yank her in with me.

"Leave. Now. I no longer require your pitiful assistance."

She flushed, eyes bright with animosity. "Most people are grateful when someone takes care of them," she reproached me.

"I already thanked you. We are done here, and soon you will be done altogether. You should return to the treasure room and resume your research. You must return to your precious home," I sneered before giving her my back once more.

I half expected her to challenge me further, so I was momentarily caught off guard to hear the echo of a door slamming from my bedchamber. Sullen and now emotionally drained, I lingered in the water for far longer than normal.

Darda's presence filled the room after some time, a signal that she was outside waiting for me, and I reluctantly exited the bath. I found a clean pair of breeches waiting for me on the counter, which I was still tying as I entered the bedroom.

"Master, what have you done?" she chided me gently. There was empathy in her voice, and I was infuriated with how weak it made me feel.

"I have done nothing! Mirielle wishes to leave Aeternitas as soon as possible, and I have done nothing to delay that. Thanks to your meddling, she now has an extra incentive to break the curse. Then she will be out of my life forever." The words tasted bitter leaving my mouth.

She chose her next words with care. "And...and is that what *you* want?"

Vulnerability felt hollow and empty, a fitting prison for a monster like me. "It no longer matters what I want, Darda. I shall see her dream to fruition."

With a snap of my fingers, I sent Darda from the room.

CHAPTER 20

Rejection Breeds Planning

MIRIELLE

s I stormed from Gryphon's bedroom, a torrent of emotions battled for my attention. On the one hand, it hurt how dismissive he had been, especially after the vigil I kept at his bedside for the past three days. I had been terrified when he collapsed in the library, then utterly repulsed when I summoned Darda and she seemed unperturbed. She simply whisked him away to his room and was aghast that I wanted to nurse him. No matter what kind of magical powers Gryphon possessed, it was *not* normal for someone to black out like that and I needed to make sure he was okay.

That's all it was, I had constantly reminded myself as I wiped the sweat from his brow and kept watch over his fitful sleep. I was only worried because it was traumatic to see someone I normally saw so strong and composed reduced to a sick weakling. I refused to entertain the nagging in the back of my mind that my concern stemmed out of an attraction to Gryphon himself. That I actually wanted Gryphon-the-man to be well, not just Gryphon-who-passed-out-in-front-of-me.

He had made it clear on more than one occasion that nothing was ever possible between us. While it was obvious he was physically attracted to me, I had no idea what—if any—feelings went beyond that. And let's not forget, he was still my jailer. I would not fall prey to some convoluted Stockholm's Syndrome as he kept me here in a beautiful palace, making real friends for the first time in my life, and allowed me unimpeded access to the world's most valuable historical artifacts. No, it was definitely a prison and I didn't want to be here...did I?

There was still a huge sense of relief and anger surrounding how I found Mr. Cooper, but it reignited the fire in me to locate the missing object and return him to his natural form. Now it wasn't just he who needed my help, it was everyone in the castle. And rather than crush under the weight of responsibility, I found myself embracing the challenge with open arms. Up the ante and my determination would increase tenfold. That had been true in all of my academic pursuits since high school. New motivation invigorated me and I was eager to return to the warehouse. It would also serve a good distraction so I did not ruminate on how badly Gryphon's rejection continued to sting.

By the time I reached the end of the hallway I had enough sense to recognize I was lost and called for Darda. She appeared instantly and voiced concern right away.

"What happened, dearie?"

I both hated and loved that she had come to recognize my feelings so quickly. She only needed one look at me and Darda would read me like a book.

I shrugged. "I don't know why I keep getting hurt when Gryphon rejects me. He's right, I don't belong here, and I have to return home."

Darda hesitated before responding. "Surely going home is what's best for you..."

Shrugging again, I turned my attention to the floor. My cheeks flushed as I finally admitted, "I don't really have anything to go back to. All I wanted was Mr. Cooper and I've found him."

It was several awkward seconds before Darda finally responded. "Well, let's get you back to work, and I'll have Mr. Cooper come join you."

My smile was so wide that my jaw hurt. "And Anastasia, too! She seemed like she needed to talk."

Darda's approval rippled over me. "I'll send them both, dearie."

The next week passed in a blur. Mr. Cooper, who insisted I call him Emil now (I never would), and Anastasia joined Wade, Ambrose, and I in the warehouse. It was actually far more helpful than I anticipated because Ambrose could write more rapidly on his own than I could, so I allowed him to take over the actual writing while Mr. Cooper and Anastasia assisted me with dates and locations. Both of them retained a sense of geography and were able to piece together approximate cities of origin. The best part about their presence was simply the laughter that ensued. The five of us were constantly cracking up, usually due to Wade's hysterical commentary, although Anastasia gave him a run for his money.

One day Mr. Cooper commented that the others in the kitchen were envious of the fun we were having, so without thinking, I invited him to bring some of his friends to join us. The next morning when I arrived at the warehouse door, Mr. Cooper hovered with three more scrub brushes, two spoons, three knives, a colander, and a cheese grater. He introduced them to me and then assigned them tasks to help make the job go by faster.

By now, organization was the name of the game. Most of the magical objects could read and several of them spoke languages other than English, so I set them into translations. Wade ripped more pages out of the journal and Mr. Cooper dictated the translations to Ambrose to write down. I was attempting to locate an end to the warehouse because my catalog currently stood at over 1,000 items. There was treasure, ships, a small airplane that looked like the Electra lost aviator Amelia Earhart was last seen flying, different sarcophagi from ancient cultures, primitive paintings chiseled out of stone walls, and enough dazzling jewels to blind someone. It was seemingly endless, involving every culture and people I had ever known, and many which were unfamiliar to me.

I began to mull over the possibility that there was another clue hidden in the prophecy and requested an audience with Gryphon one afternoon so that we might discuss it. After I called his name, I was transported to the intimacy of the library rather than summoning his presence directly to me. I found him seated in an armchair before the fire, a glass of amber colored liquid on a small table beside him.

We had hardly spoken a word to one another since I had left his bedchamber, and I avoided eye contact at all costs. It felt uncomfortable being near him, mostly because my feelings were still at war with each other, and now that I faced him, I was overcome with shyness. He was still too breathtaking to look at. His golden hair was pulled back from his face once more in a bun at the back of his head. He was shirtless, his ab muscles rigid as though he were flexing. Dark gray pants prevented me from seeing the outline of his powerful thigh muscles, but some twisted part of me longed to kneel between them and see if Gryphon responded the same as any other human man.

"Why didn't you come to me in the warehouse?" I asked instead, cheeks flushing at the turn of my thoughts.

Sadness filled his eyes and he turned his attention back to the fire to avoid my gaze. "Laughter tends to die when I enter a room," he commented offhandedly.

My heart fractured a tiny bit at this confession. He felt unworthy to be around all of the humans he cursed. I suddenly realized how much of a burden Gryphon must carry to hold onto that kind of guilt. He was just as helpless as I was in these circumstances.

I needed to do something to show him how important he actually was to our cause and how welcomed he would be, but that would have to wait for another time. We needed to discuss the prophecy now.

"Did your mother say anything else when she cast the curse?" I asked.

My question must have caught him off guard for he drew back to glare at me before downing the glass next to him in one gulp. He pondered for a moment before shaking his head. "No, what I showed you is all that the prophecy said."

I tried not to let his answer defeat me. "What were you doing when she did this? Why would she curse you?"

Gryphon gave me a wry smile and indicated I should sit in the chair next to him. "To understand that would be to understand my family's dynamics. My parents are both very powerful beings in their own right, but with power comes ambition. They both sought to rule Aeternitas outright, excluding the other, and I was left in the midst of their dysfunction. Each used me against the other in their squabbles." He shrugged, feigning nonchalance, but I could tell how much it bothered him to admit this out loud. "The day she cast her curse was the first day in months that I had seen my mother. She claimed I had taken too much after my father and she couldn't stand the sight of me. An argument had broken out, like it always did, and suddenly, she cast her curse. It impacted everyone I ever cared about."

His bravery summoned my own. "I don't even know who my father is," I offered. "At least you've met yours."

Gryphon's eyes softened and he moved to take my hand before stopping himself. "And your mother?" he prompted.

It was my turn to shrug. "She sold herself for drugs, so she wasn't around much. Whenever her customers came around, I would escape. I would go to Mr. Cooper's."

Understanding dawned on his face. "That is why he means so much to you."

I nodded. "Mr. Cooper was...there," I awkwardly tried to explain. "He let me stay at his apartment as much as I wanted, he fed me, he helped me with homework. He's the reason I amounted to anything and didn't wind up another strung out addict like her." I hated how bitter my voice sounded, but the years' worth of resentment came pouring out. It was almost cathartic to finally give these feelings life outside my head.

This time Gryphon did grab my hand, giving me a gentle squeeze of comfort. "Then I am forever indebted to Mr. Cooper as well for your life is a gift to me, and to my people."

A single tear rolled down my cheek. His words stirred something inside me, and it made me shy and awkward once more. My face warmed under his gaze, making me snatch my hand away. I could not allow this to mean something. Gryphon's attention was misplaced.

He seemed to sense the turn of my thoughts and walked over to the globe on the other side of the room. "Was that all you came to discuss?" he asked without looking at me.

I cleared my throat before answering, inwardly cringing at how raspy I sounded. "Yes, I guess that's all. Can you send me back to the warehouse?"

Gryphon's shoulders slumped for a moment before he turned to face me. "As you wish," he said quietly. With a wave of his hand, I fell into the black void and reappeared at my desk.

Mr. Cooper was there, muttering a dictation to Ambrose about a rough Armenian translation from a manuscript that likely came from a Russian museum around 1916. It was calming to hear his heavy accent, grounding me in a way that nothing else could. Still, I could not shake the sense of loss from leaving Gryphon's presence, nor could I stop my mind from lingering on the look of defeat on his face. Had it been the reminder of his childhood? Or was it the fact that I left so quickly? Did I really hold that kind of sway over his mood?

When Darda came to collect us at the end of the day instead of him, I knew Gryphon continued to dwell on his negative thoughts. Inspiration set in, and I enlisted Darda's help for a surprise. Hopefully I wasn't getting in over my head.

Darda begrudgingly agreed. She seemed anxious about Gryphon's reaction, so I informed all of my castle friends before she could change her mind. They were jubilant and promised to bring more help tomorrow.

I woke with the sun the next day, eager to put my plan into motion. Darda retrieved me as soon as I called and teleported us to the ballroom. Within minutes, Ambrose, Wade, and Mr. Cooper arrived along with about 25 other household objects, ranging from hand mirrors to mops to coat racks. Some of them knew more about the castle than others and I suspected they were servants like Darda rather than humans who had been swept up in the curse. They were the ones I placed in charge of the day's require-ments—cleaning and prepping the ballroom for a party.

We spent the entire day cleaning the chandeliers and mirrors. It was exhausting work, but by the end, the floors were polished until I could gaze at my reflection and there wasn't a cobweb in sight. The instruments were cleaned, which awoke them, and a music stand named Glenn came forward with an offer to lead the band. He said he had an inkling that music was important to him. We set them to tuning and rehearsing for the rest of the afternoon.

A collection of animated sewing needles and pin cushions had been working in another room on a gown for me that Darda commissioned. She refused to let me see it until tomorrow evening when the party would be held, but I was frequently stopped in the ballroom by a very agitated measuring tape who barked out demands for various measurements. Darda's excitement was palpable over the dress and she promised me that there would be a team to help me get ready.

By the time the dinner hour came, I sank gratefully into the chair in my bedroom and could barely lift my arms to hold the fork. My poor friends had all been enlisted in the kitchens for the night as Darda wanted to plan a special meal for the party. For not being so keen on the idea in the first place, she sure had come around after she saw how many of the castle's inhabitants wanted to attend. Darda was used to being in charge of the castle opera-tions and I was grateful to hand the reins over to her. Especially now when I felt sleep overcoming me.

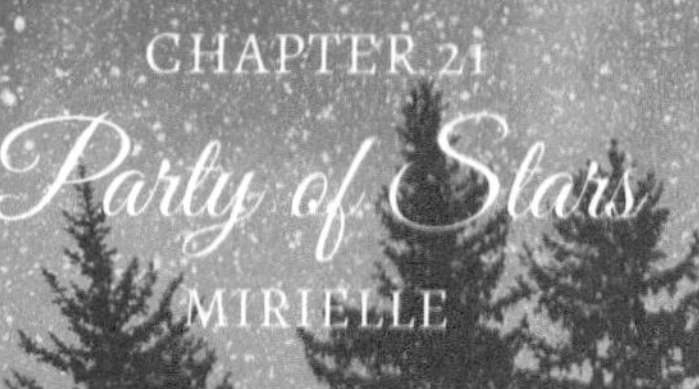

Sitting upright in bed, I slowly blinked as I took in my surroundings. Everything looked the same, but it all somehow felt different. Perhaps that was what happened after a good night's sleep? It had never happened often enough for me to know.

I sensed Gryphon's presence before I noticed him, hovering near the bedroom door that had been left open. He hesitated on the threshold and offered me a small smile when I made eye contact. Waving him in, I recognized the same awkward ticks as myself whenever I was about to ask an uncomfortable question. Although he came all the way into the opposite side of the bed, he stared steadfastly at the floor, his hands clasped behind his back.

"Good morning," I finally said to break the uneasy silence.

He snorted, eyes still on the floor. "You must mean 'good afternoon' because it's after lunch time."

That baffled me. I had slept for almost an entire day, which I had never done before in my life. "I must've been really tired after all the work yesterday," I commented.

"Yes, I am told there's to be a ball this evening," Gryphon replied quietly. "It is kind of you to delight the staff like that. We have not hosted a bit of revelry in quite some time."

I giggled. "The ball is for you, silly. We are throwing it in your honor."

Gryphon's eyes shot up with a look that I recognized. Hope.

"Am I to attend?" he asked.

This time I outright laughed and threw the covers off. Someone had once again changed me into a bright pink sports bra and black boy shorts that left little to the imagination, but I found myself past the point of caring with Gryphon. Now that I had seen him sick and suffering, it felt only fair to let him see my vulnerable points, too. I felt his eyes on my backside as I walked into the bathroom to brush my teeth.

He abruptly followed after me, standing behind me to lock eyes with my reflection. He was close enough that if I allowed my body to relax my ass would touch his crotch. "Is that a yes?"

I rinsed my mouth with water before answering him. "Of course that's a yes, Gryphon! You're the guest of honor!"

At my words, his face darkened and he backed away to sit on the stone wall of the bathtub. "They should not honor me," he replied quietly.

His self-hatred stirred something in me and I found myself squatting down between his knees, forcing him to look me in the eye as I made my next statement. "You *deserve* to be honored, Gryphon. You are their prince, and you are doing everything you can to break this curse. Maybe you didn't always go about things the right way, but it's not like you have a guidebook to follow." I rested both of my hands on his knees in what I hoped to be a soothing gesture that demonstrated my sincerity.

Gryphon watched me in amazement. "You really believe that, don't you?" he murmured.

"Of course I do. Everyone deserves to be appreciated for who they are," I shrugged. It was certainly all I had ever wanted.

The movement made Gryphon's attention drop down to my chest. The slinky straps of the bra were not enough to provide decent support if I were actually exercising, and the low cut of the garment only made my cleavage that much more pronounced. My nipples began to pebble at the heat in Gryphon's gaze.

Ever so slowly he inched his fingers forward to graze along the outline of my right nipple, pinching it slightly to make the peak more pronounced in the thin spandex. He kept his eyes on mine the entire time, judging my response, but I was far too mesmerized with how good and sinful it felt, and how his eyes were morphing into the same molten gold color I had seen before. It must have been a sign of his arousal. I stole a glance between his legs, the thick bulge in his black pants confirming my suspicion.

He noticed where my attention had gone and gave me one of his sexy smirks. It emboldened him to reach inside the bra and continue his gentle ministrations. My heart quickened and my knees began to quiver from how good it felt. A pool of warmth was collecting in the apex of my thighs.

"Has anyone ever touched you here before?" Gryphon looked pained, like he worried over my answer.

Not trusting myself to speak, I merely shook my head. He continued his slow assault on my nipple and withdrew my breast completely.

"Not even Barrett Collins?" he prompted.

By now his entire hand was caressing my exposed breast while the other had begun to tease the nipple peak on the other side. It felt like a direct line to my clit, which throbbed with the need for release. Even the mention of an asshole like Barrett couldn't dissuade my attention now.

"Nope. Nobody." My voice was breathy, the air in the room suddenly disappearing as my body reacted to his touch. "I fooled around a bit with a friend in college, but he never touched me below my clothes."

It sounded stupid to my own ears to admit something like that out loud. Gryphon probably thought I was childish.

His eyes, however, warmed at my confession and he slid both of the spaghetti straps down my shoulders, gently tugging so that my other breast came free. The intensity of his gaze led me to sink to my knees, drawing me closer to him, and he surprised me by then pushing my chest towards him as his mouth descended on my right nipple.

I whimpered in shock, but wound my fingers through his silky gold hair as his tongue swirled around a peak that was now rock hard. His other hand continued to play with my left breast, alternating between kneading the flesh and pinching. The little flashes of pain felt incredible and made my arousal increase tenfold. I was sopping in the boy shorts and before I realized what I was doing, my hand slipped beneath the seam as I began to rub my clit.

Gryphon groaned against my breast, then snapped his fingers. We were instantly transported to my bed, me on my back with my legs spread open for Gryphon lying between them. With another snap of his fingers, the door slammed shut and the loud click of the lock echoed throughout the room. My lips parted in a breathy pant as I tried to make sense of the inferno in my core, my desperation for Gryphon clogging my senses. His eyes were swirling now, a mirror to my intense passion, and I grew wetter knowing my body yielded the same response in him. He scrutinized my face for a reaction as he dipped his hand beneath the seam of my panties. At this point, he could have convinced me to train unicorns if it meant he would finally touch me there.

"This is something you do not have to share with me if you do not wish it," he murmured. His hand stopped just above my lower lips, softly tracing his fingers along the downy hair there. I sent a silent prayer of thanks to whatever had prompted me to trim up my nether regions while showering yesterday.

One heated exchange with his glowing golden eyes told me how desperate he was for me to say yes. To finally let whatever connection that burned between us turn to flames and consume us. He wanted this—wanted *me*.

I smiled and reached up to trace my fingers along his jaw, his skin smooth to the touch. "Yes, please," I breathed before pulling his lips to mine.

Gryphon sank into the kiss, parting my lips wider, and letting his tongue sweep across mine. His fingers slid across the seam of my pussy and he groaned at the wetness he found there. He used his thumb and forefinger to swirl around my clit, starting at a slower pace that quickly began to build. Immediately my body responded, relaxing and spreading my legs wider. Suddenly he thrust one callused finger inside me. It was both jarring and decadent, like finding a forbidden sweet was actually better than all the other desserts you had ever tried.

His thrusts grew faster as I became wetter, my own arousal dripping down between my thighs. A moan tore its way out of my mouth and I felt my will power disintegrate as my muscles clenched around his intrusion. My body began to writhe beneath him, and Gryphon pinned my arms above my head in response.

"Just let go, Miracle," he whispered, his voice catching in his own passion.

Gryphon added an additional finger, then a third before I

cried out in both pain and jubilation. It felt as though my body was stretched to the limit. A tingling sensation was building in my core, and one look into the liquid gold of Gryphon's eyes made me detonate. The orgasm that racked my body barreled me over until I was a pool of jelly beneath him, barely registering my surroundings.

As the high began to fade away several minutes later, I blinked rapidly to bring myself down to reality. Gryphon propped his head up by leaning on his elbow, a small smile of triumph lighting up his whole face, his body stretched across one of my thighs to pin me down and prevent my escape. He had waited until my soul returned to my body so that I could watch in a mix of fascination and horror as he sucked my juices from his fingers. A satisfied groan escaped him and all but primed my pussy for another round.

Now that my orgasm was gone, however, my behavior shocked me. I let Gryphon, the most spectacular male specimen I had ever seen, finger me like some horny teenager!

My anxiety began to rise and I fidgeted with the straps of my bra to regain some sense of modesty. Gryphon seemed to sense my growing unease and began softly rubbing his hand along my exposed stomach.

"You are the loveliest woman I have ever seen," he said. His eyes were starting to transition back to their normal emerald, though I vaguely still sensed his erection pressed against my thigh.

Flattery worked, however, and eased some of my anxiety. "I can't believe you would think so," I said.

He pushed himself up farther on his elbow so that his face hovered over mine. "Mirielle, know that I have seen mortals across every dimension of time and civilization, yet my heart has never beat for another the way it beats for you."

I could feel myself glowing from his words. Suddenly shy, I shimmied out from under him and dashed towards the bathroom to clean up. Turning on the water in the shower, I vaguely wondered if I should invite him to join me before Gryphon followed me into the bathroom, setting a rectangular black velvet box on the counter.

"Wear this with your dress this evening, please," he instructed. He winked at me before leaving the room.

I showered in a daze, lingering far longer than should have. The water calmed the tension in my muscles as I replayed the events over in my head. Gryphon made me feel beautiful, like a real woman, something I had shut myself out from feeling before. Yet I craved to have that same sense of desire, of power, radiating from within based on the knowledge that this god of a man wanted me. He was hard for *me*, Mirielle Townsend, the nerdy, rejected child of a drug addict.

I frowned as I tried to picture him in my apartment back home, or even just New York City itself. I had never asked him why he turned into an animal when he was outside the gates of Aeternitas, but even in his regular form, he would look out of place and draw far too much attention. It would be impossible to maintain the sense of peace and invisibility I had enveloped myself in.

These were not the sort of thoughts a woman should have after her first real sexual encounter and it soured my mood as I left the shower. Wrapping myself in a large bathing sheet again, my long hair soaking down my back, I stepped into the bedroom and found Darda already waiting for me along with several hair and makeup brushes.

"Dearie, say hello to Rita and Pamela, and their team. They are here to help you get ready for tonight," Darda explained. It was then that I noticed a long white box on the bed behind her. I craned my neck in an attempt to see its contents, certain I would find my dress inside, but they all ushered me back to the vanity inside the bathroom.

Rita and Pamela barked out orders to the others while asking me questions about my life back home as hair dryers, curling wands, eye shadow pallets, and more hovered around me. Each waited their turn, dabbing make up in various places or spraying hair products, but never saying a word. I could never tell Rita and Pamela apart, and I suspected even they could not tell the difference since they both tended to answer my questions, no matter to whom it was directed. My hair alone took hours, though Darda complimented me on how long and lush it was, and everyone agreed. The curling wands created a large braid that swooped around the crown of my head before cinching into a ponytail of large curls wound over my shoulder. A faint sparkle of silver shimmer was sprinkled into the red, highlighting the rich color.

I gasped, awestruck, when the velvet box Gryphon left behind was opened to reveal a long string of diamond stars, each slightly bigger than a thumb nail, that was then woven into the braid and tail. They twinkled in the bright light of the vanity, and I knew they would dazzle around the many mirrors of the ballroom.

Finally, Rita and Pamela pronounced my makeup to be complete, and when all their assistants drew back to let me see my reflection in the mirror, my jaw dropped audibly. I had always been under the impression that my complexion was too pale to contour properly, but the brushes had somehow managed to evoke a naturally rosy glow from my skin that did not make me look over-heated. My eyebrows were plucked and shaped in a way that better suited my face, drawing attention to the dramatic sliver eyeshadow and thick eyeliner around my eyes. The color made the blue of my irises pop, which matched the faint sparkle of the silver star at the outside corner of each eye. My lips had been painted a luscious pink color and the sheen of gloss over the top made me look kissable. Pale blue diamonds that resembled falling stars hung from my ears. I looked like a radiant fairy made of starlight, beautiful and otherworldly.

"Come, dearie. Now you can finally see what the seamstress whipped up for you!" called Darda. You could hear the excitement in her voice and my own exhilaration nearly pounded in my throat.

A navy blue mannequin had been brought in to showcase a dress that stopped me in my tracks. This was truly a gown, with a wide A-frame skirt of silver silk and shimmery white tulle. It featured more diamond stars woven into the bodice, smaller than those in my hair, and along the edge of the sweetheart neckline that gave way to more silver silk in an off the shoulder capped sleeve. It was a gown of starlight, just as ethereal as the man who would escort me tonight.

My cheeks flushed at the thought of Gryphon seeing me in this gown and what he would say. Since he had given me the stars for my hair, did that mean he had already seen the dress?

As if sensing my thoughts, Darda scooted closer and whispered, "The Master designed this dress for you himself, dearie."

I wonder why he designed a gown for me if he didn't think he was invited tonight, I thought. Maybe Gryphon just wanted me to feel special?

I eagerly stepped forward before I could overanalyze her revelation and simply held out my arms. The dress acted of its own accord, floating up above the mannequin before gently sliding down my body. The ties of the corset pulled tight, forcing my breasts up and making a rather blatant display of my cleavage, in my opinion. Silk silver heels with the same pale blue stars as my earrings completed the look and raised me several inches taller.

These pumps must have been bestowed with magic, for despite how high and thin the heel stood, I was able to walk with ease and comfort.

"Oh!" Darda cried, her voice thick with unshed tears. "You look every bit a princess, dearie! Just wait til the Master sees you!"

She teleported us to the top of the grand staircase and tittered. I never thought I'd hear the day where a desk giggling like a school-girl would make me smile, but I couldn't help being infected by her joy. Darda's excitement was contagious.

"I'll see you there, miss!" she said before disappearing at my elbow.

Inhaling deeply to calm my nerves, I gathered my skirts and stepped to the stair landing. My eyes immediately connected with Gryphon's like we were magnets drawn to one another. All sense of sound and place faded away in that moment as I watched his eyes widen and his lips part. He leaned towards me as though the distance was too great to bear.

I could not contain my smile and it widened to the point where I feared my cheeks would break. Gryphon looked divine in a charcoal gray topcoat and breeches, with a silver silk waistcoat that matched my dress. His entire ensemble looked to be out of the Regency era, including the palest of blue neckerchief and white stockings. Gryphon's hair had been styled so that it half hung in golden waves about his shoulders while the rest was pulled back from his face into a small bun at the back of his head. He could not have looked sexier to me.

Gryphon stepped forward to take my hand once I reached the bottom of the stairs and just his touch alone sent quakes of desire through me. His eyes were pooling back into gold, and while I had suspected earlier that was a sign of lust, now I wondered if it was something more because I did not recognize the look in his eyes. I wanted the ability to read his emotions the way I read my own, which caused me to blush at the brazen nature of my thoughts. Intimacy like this was such a foreign concept.

Thankfully he did not question why my cheeks were suddenly flushed and my breathing erratic. He pulled me closer, one arm wrapped around my waist, and kissed me full on the lips. "You are exquisite," he murmured against them. His words had my pussy clenching.

"We'll never make it to the party if you keep talking like that," I warned him.

He grinned. "Maybe I'd rather a party with just the two of us in your bedchamber."

I swatted playfully at his chest and extracted myself from his arms. "Not after all the work we've put into this! Come on!" I tugged his hand down the hallway that led to the ballroom. It was surprising how familiar I was starting to be with the castle and how much it had begun to feel like home.

Gryphon pulled me back into his arms and smirked as he snapped his fingers. We instantly arrived at the doorway to the ballroom, still holding one another, and I rolled my eyes at his "subtle" show of power. "What are you going to do with the extra 15 seconds you just saved?" I muttered sarcastically.

Music was already playing from the grandstand in the corner, though I noted there were far more musical instruments than yesterday. A song that sounded reminiscent of Fall Out Boy made me grin because that could have only been a selection for my bene-fit. The rest of the ballroom was filled with chatter from the objects of the castle. I spotted Wade first, who came over and greeted me with his signature exuberance. A feeling of warmth, like Wade's essence, enveloped me in what felt like a hug.

"Yo, catch you later, My-my!" he cried, taking off after one of the makeup brushes who had helped me get ready.

I had not realized Gryphon came to stand beside me until he leaned down in my ear to whisper, "My-my?"

Giggling, I elbowed him. "It's a nickname!"

One golden blonde eyebrow arched and a smirk played at his lips. "And what do I have to do to be on a nickname basis with you?"

"Dance with me," I breathed.

His smirk grew into an actual smile and he pulled me tightly against him by the waist, the other hand holding mine near shoulder level. The music transitioned at that moment to a more classical piece, and Gryphon whisked me off in an elaborate twirl.

Everyone else faded away as I gazed into Gryphon's eyes. They were smoldering, surely looking straight into my soul, as we whirled around the center of the ball room. He was an excellent dancer, his large body somehow graceful and refined enough to move rhythmically to the beat. I had never danced in this manner before, but it felt comfortable letting him lead. The lights began to dim and I glanced up to notice the night sky overhead.

"Gryphon!" I exclaimed. "Look!"

He did not break his eyes from my face. "I know," he said, "I brought the stars to you."

My eyes fell back to his in wonder. He used magic to create a sky for me? "It's miraculous!" I murmured, looking back up to examine his work.

Gryphon gave me a soft smile. "That's because you are my miracle."

My smile could not be contained. I pulled him in for a kiss, my arms snaking around his neck. His hands moved to the small of my back to grip me tighter and I thought my heart might actually burst. This felt so right, so perfect, and that overwhelmed me.

Cheers rose up around us from the occupants of the castle and I broke away from Gryphon in a fit of laughter. I had laughed and smiled more here in the past few weeks than I had in the rest of my life combined. Gryphon finally huffed out a laugh, too, and smiled wide as he turned to wave at everyone in the room. He turned back to me and took both my hands in his. "I think my realm approves," he joked.

I rolled my eyes. "It's not exactly like there are a whole lot of options!"

Darda called out the announcement for food, but not before I saw sadness cross Gryphon's features. He had carefully schooled his expression by the time I looked back, but I could sense the wall being built between us. What happened?

Whatever, I refused to let Gryphon's ridiculous mood swings ruin my night. Spotting Mr. Cooper, I let go of Gryphon's hand and joined him across the room as everyone made their way into the dining hall.

"How do you all eat?" I asked in surprise. The entire table was set and objects were sliding up to place settings as though they were prepared to sit and eat.

"We just...eat," Mr. Cooper said. Had he been in his regular form, I knew he would have shrugged and thrown up his hands to demonstrate how stupid he found my question. I stifled a laugh and watched in wonderment as the plates in front of the castle subjects began to fill with food, then disappeared bite by bite as though it was being eaten. Was this part of the curse as well? They were still human enough to need to eat, but it was conducted through magic now?

I filed these questions away for later because I had been toying with an idea for weeks about investigating Gryphon's family in his library. I needed to keep that idea on the down low, however, because I already knew Darda and Gryphon would both shoot it down. There was something missing from the puzzle, though, and I firmly believed his family held the answers.

Mr. Cooper began to move towards the food, so I followed along before glancing around to look for Gryphon. I was certain he had been next to me just seconds ago, but his domineering presence left a noticeable absence in the ballroom. Still, I scanned the entire ballroom for him a second time before sighing in acceptance. He was gone.

The party continued well into the night, but Gryphon never returned. I danced with everyone—Mr. Cooper, Wade, Anastasia, even Ambrose—yet it all felt forced. This was *his* party! How could he just leave like that?! After all the work everyone put in to show him how much he was appreciated, Gryphon couldn't be bothered to stay. It rankled me, yet something in my mind kept dragging me back to that moment where I saw his face change. I replayed our conversation over and over in my head and could not figure out what would make him so upset.

It must have been close to daybreak by the time I finally excused myself to go upstairs. Exhaustion was about to claim me, and I longed to slide in between my sheets and succumb. My gown returned itself to the navy mannequin as soon as I closed the bedroom door behind me and I took the world's fastest shower to scrub off the makeup and hair spray. I did not even bother to put on underwear before climbing into bed fully naked and passing out as soon as my head hit the pillow.

My dreams circled around Gryphon, some so real and life-like that I almost felt I could touch him. I saw him lying in his bed, sweating and clammy again like his illness before, and Darda stood next to him. They were arguing, and even in my dream I could sense Darda's disapproval.

"My lord, you are misreading this!" Darda said. "I saw how she looked at you!"

Gryphon shook his head. The action took too much effort and his eyes closed wearily. "She does not care for me, Darda. I must send her home."

Are they talking about me? I wondered. It was unnerving, like a dream that wasn't quite a dream, with everything tinted in a sepia filter. Deja vu with twist.

Darda sounded incredulous. "*Send her home?!* After all the work she has done? After the hope she has inspired in the staff? She is the only one who can help us!"

Gryphon raised an arm and laid it over his eyes. "Then I shall return to my quests so that we do not cross paths. It must be so, Darda." Even in my dreamlike state I recognized a Gryphon order when I heard it.

Darkness began to swirl around me and the image of Gryphon's room disappeared in black smoke. A figure stood before me that I recognized but could not place. I assumed it to be female based on the dirty blonde curls that fell from beneath her dark green hood, but her face was hidden in shadow. Her cloak fell all the way to the floor and shielded her body. She stood before me under the same sort of hazy filter from Gryphon's room and although I sensed immense power, I did not detect any danger. Something told me this woman would not hurt me even though she was capable of doing so.

"Mirielle," she said, "find the journal. All will be revealed in the journal."

The smoke swirled thicker than ever and the cloaked woman disappeared into the haze. I drifted back into the lull of a deep sleep, my conscious self hoping I remembered this when I woke up.

I awoke later to the heavy scent of roses. Gryphon stood at the foot of my bed, shoulders braced as though ready for a fight. I was beginning to think that was just his normal posture.

Sitting up and stretching, it was too late to remember that I had fallen asleep naked. Gryphon got an eyeful before I pulled the sheet up to cover myself. He smirked, but did not move towards me as I might have expected. The wall from last night was still firmly in place and barbed wire was about to be added to the top.

"I will be leaving Aeternitas until further notice," Gryphon stated flatly. The musical cadence of his voice was gone and only a cold, detached echo remained.

I was immediately suspicious. "Why? Where are you going?" It took me a moment to realize I was actually upset; I didn't want him to leave.

My questions irritated him. I could tell by the clench in his jaw and the way his nostrils flared as he sought to control his temper. "If you needed to know, I would tell you, mortal," he ground out through his teeth. Hearing his use of that infernal word again hurt. Gryphon only called me that whenever he wanted to push me away. He turned and strode toward the door, but I scrambled out of bed and was hot on his heels.

He was just flinging open the door as I grabbed his elbow to spin him towards me. One glance at my naked body and he growled in rage, slamming the door shut behind him. "The entire castle is not permitted to see you like this, Mirielle!"

"Oh, so it's Mirielle again? A second ago we were back to 'mortal!'" I snapped back. It infuriated me that we were having the same arguments due to Gryphon's unstable mood. "What happened last night?"

Gryphon ran his hands through his hair in frustration and moved towards the bathroom.

"Where are you going?" I demanded. "I'm talking to you!"

"I can't talk to you when you are standing before me as seductive temptation!" he barked out over his shoulder. He returned a moment later with a pink sherpa bath robe that he threw at me.

Rolling my eyes, I slipped it on without tying it and threw my hands in the air. "You are insane! What are you running from, Gryphon?"

He paced in front of the fireplace and refused to look at me. He was like a caged lion, ready to attack.

I put myself in his path and grabbed his face to make him look me in the eye. "What are you running from?!"

At this, the fight in him seemed to deflate. He visibly wilted beneath my touch and fell into my embrace, leaving his head resting on my shoulder. I cradled him, winding my arms around his neck, and pressing my entire body into his.

"I cannot escape these feelings, Mirielle!" he whimpered. Fresh, hot tears coated my neck and I gasped. Gryphon was *crying*. And I had never been more confused.

"What feelings? What is going on?" I shouted. "You have to talk to me!"

Gryphon pulled on the sides of the robe, covering my stomach, and hastily tied the belt. "I can't talk to you like this, vixen," he muttered. He righted himself and wiped the tears from his face before backing up from me a few paces.

I tried to wait patiently because if my time in Aeternitas had taught me anything, it was that patience was a virtue I actually possessed. I pulled the robe tighter around my body and adjusted the belt, keeping my eyes downcast to allow Gryphon some semblance of privacy to collect himself.

"I have all these feelings, Mirielle! Emotions that I have never felt before," Gryphon sighed. "It is overwhelming to feel so much at once, and there's never any reprieve!"

Okay, so Gryphon was tapping into new territory. While I could respect that, I had no clue what it had to do with me or why he resorted to all the distance between us. Especially not after what had transpired in my room only yesterday. Did he mean feelings related to me?

"So...what can I do?" I asked. If he was overwhelmed from emotions, I was probably not the right person to help. I barely addressed my own.

He sighed again. "Do you not feel this thing between us? Is it all in my head?" He motioned between us as though a thread would suddenly appear and explain.

I stalled by opening and closing my mouth several times. This topic was as foreign to me as it was to him, and it made me far more uncomfortable to articulate any of it. I could not deny that there was some sort of electric current that sparked between us any time we were in close proximity, but beyond acknowledging it, I had not given it a second thought. I didn't *want* to give it a second thought because I did not want to feel anything anymore than he did.

"It's not for me to say," I finally sputtered out. Even my conscious groaned in frustration. *Coward!*

How could I admit to him that I didn't know how to address it either? That it was impossible to understand the way I felt about him when I felt trapped? As intelligent as Gryphon could be, I sincerely doubted he had any idea what Stockholm Syndrome was, and I wasn't ready to accept that I might have possibly fallen victim to it. Whatever was growing between us was convoluted and writhing with obstacles, and I already faced too many of those at the moment.

Gryphon's eyes dulled at my response and he visibly wilted for the second time.

I opened my mouth to speak again when a loud clang from a bell rattled through the room. The reverberations rattled the floor and my bed shook as it moved an inch or two to the right. Crying out, I stumbled to the mantel above the fireplace and held on for dear life.

The sound served as an alarm for Gryphon, who immediately transformed into the battle body paint I had originally seen on him, the golden scales trailing up his muscular torso and down his powerful thighs. His hair was pulled back into another bun, with a golden sword hilt protruding just above his right shoulder. Most startling of all was the return of his iridescent wings. They ruffled behind him before spreading out to their full width. Emerald fire blazed in his eyes as he turned towards the sound.

"Mirielle," he said slowly. "Get dressed immediately and call for Darda. She will take you to the warehouse where it is safe. Do not come outside until I retrieve you, no matter what. Do you understand?" The bell sounded again, louder this time, and I clapped my hands over my ears like a child to block out the noise.

Before I could say another word, he vanished.

Like hell was I going to stay inside. Something was wrong; I sensed danger looming. Dashing into the bathroom, I called for leggings and a shirt. My bathroom always knew how to deliver and provided black leggings made of a thicker, heavier material than spandex, but with far more stretch. A black, long-sleeve shirt of the same material appeared along with black combat boots. I haphazardly threw my hair into a pile on top of my head and ran out to the hallway. Chaos met me.

CHAPTER 23

Strength in Catastrophe

No matter how many times I blinked the logical side of my brain could not reconcile the sight before me. Several of the knights' armor from the castle entryway were fighting with swords and axes against creatures made of water. Their limbs moved like the crest of ocean waves, and wet spots appeared on the carpet beneath their feet, yet they stood and moved like a normal human. But bigger. Much, much bigger. The ceilings in the hallway were approximately twelve feet and each of the water creatures could have easily jumped to have their limbs touch the ceilings. They wielded weapons made of ocean shells and seaweed. And from my estimation, there were far more of them than there were knights of Aeternitas.

I ran back inside my room and locked the door, then barred it with the chair and table at which I normally ate my meals. It probably wouldn't do much to stop the creatures, but it gave me a small sense of security at the moment. I began to pace, unsure of what to do, and yelled out in frustration. "I need a weapon!"

A loud clank echoed from the bathroom. Inside I found a thin sword made of a silver so light it was almost translucent. It was not metal and it glowed as I moved it. There was a slight heat radiating from the blade and when I tried to bring my hand closer for inspection, a force field of some kind pushed my hand away. There was just one problem—I had never fought with a sword before.

The sounds of the battle outside grew louder and something pounded on my door. "Guess it's time to learn," I mumbled to myself. Thanking the bathroom, I returned the sword to its hilt and tied it through a sash I wound around my waist. Going out the bedroom door wasn't an option, which only left the balcony. A balcony I still hadn't approached because I was so fearful of heights.

Emerging outside, I saw the area of the castle to my left was on fire. Strong gusts of wind were yanking trees from their roots on the snowy mountain side, and the ground rumbled as an earthquake shook the foundations of stone. There weren't any stairs and with the thin layer of ice on the stone, I did not think it wise to try and jump one balcony over. For that matter, I did not even know what rooms that balcony would lead to since I had not explored the castle on my own floor.

The only escape I could see was the banner hanging off the edge of the balcony bearing the Aeternitas crest, the familiar hourglass ensconced in roses and stars. The idea made my stomach churn in dread. A loud cry from behind me alerted me to the fact that the fight had now burst into my room. Without pausing to reconsider, I quickly laid my body chest side down on the railing, using my left arm and leg to grasp onto the banner. It hung three stories down, level with a window that had a wide ledge. I would have to figure something else out once I got to that point.

It was now or never. Bracing myself in case the banner would not hold my weight, I swung the rest of my body over the railing to grip the heavy velvet material. For once I was so grateful for all the upper body strength my trainer at the MMA gym made me build. Although I was out of shape compared to my normal standards, I had enough muscle to slowly lower myself down the banner, like descending the rope climb in junior high gym class. It took several seconds for me to breathe through my nerves at the high altitude, clenching my eyes shut and counting to 50 in my head. I could hear shouting from above as well as from the open windows below, so there had to be more of the water warriors. Where was Gryphon?!

My descent was slow moving, primarily because I kept stopping to breathe through my anxiety so that I did not vomit. It felt like hours passed before I reached the window ledge. Now came the hard part. I had to use my body weight to build up enough momentum so that the banner would swing closer to the window. I was already winded from the climb down, but adrenaline was coursing through my system, making me grit my teeth and ignore the fatigue. My hips swung to the right while my upper torso went left, pushing each side a little more with every swing. It was exhausting, and I could feel my muscles straining to continue. Inch by inch I swung closer until it was just enough to catch the end of the ledge.

Thankfully my hands did not slip on the rough stone, though they might bleed from how tightly I gripped the ledge to pull myself closer. I was able to grab onto the ledge on the inside wall and hoist myself in. My landing was less than graceful as I tumbled headfirst into a hallway. The faint sounds of swords came from my left, so I sprinted that way in search of Gryphon.

I raced to the end of the hall and finally recognized enough of the décor to know that if I turned right I could follow it to the landing on the grand staircase. Heart hammering in my chest, the clinking of swords grew louder and the smell of smoke began to permeate my nostrils. It was getting brighter and I stopped abruptly as I emerged on the landing, too stunned to move.

More of the water warriors were battling coats of armor with their seashell swords, but they were not the only fighters in the fray. Tall flames of bright orange and red used hand to hand combat against the knights, setting fire to anything in their path. There were large holes in the walls of the castle and giant creatures made of boulders with dark eyes could be seen through the openings. They were banging their fists against the outer walls of the castle, causing the ceiling to crack and crumble. The wind howled outside furiously like we were caught inside a giant tornado.

I spotted Gryphon right away in the thick of the action at the landing. He moved faster than should be possible, his lethal blade swinging everywhere at once, taking down multiple monsters with one fell swoop. Seeing him like this, a warrior in every sense of the word, was frightening. My attempts to fight him before seemed trivial compared to this skill.

Still, I needed to help him. The other fighters outnumbered Aeternitas by four to one. Using the sword from the bathroom would probably be pointless since the only instruction I had on sword fighting were Antonio Banderas' lessons in *The Mask of Zorro*, but seeing Gryphon so hopelessly outstripped spurred me on. There were so many of them!

Drawing the weapon, I raced down the stairs two at a time before leaping down the final four. A water creature rushed toward me, shell axe drawn, and instinct told me to swipe from left to right at his waist. The sizzle of heat and water could be heard above the din of the fight, and the water warrior collapsed into a puddle at my feet. My starlight sword glowed brighter, making me laugh incredulously at what I had done.

I closed the distance to Gryphon quickly, shoving the point of my sword into the back of a fire demon attempting to attack him from behind. The fire roared in rage before disintegrating into a cloud of smoke. Gryphon turned towards the sound and his eyes nearly bulged out of their sockets when he saw me.

Before he could take a step in my direction, a large portion of the ceiling fell between us, causing me to tumble out of the way. Some of the bigger fragments still managed to catch my left tricep as I went down. Blood oozed from the wound, running over my elbow, but I did not have time to assess the damage before another water creature came in for the kill. I managed to roll on the ground to dodge the blow, and when I sat up, I grabbed my sword's hilt with both hands to swing it upwards and block the creature's next attack. The force in his swing rattled my sword, and therefore my arms, which was the main reason I did not notice the creature's equivalent of a hand slamming against my cheek. The water shot up my nose and down my throat, choking me. I could not break my head free from the watery bubble the creature created around my face, and I began to panic as the lack of oxygen burned its way through my lungs.

Suddenly the water bubble burst, along with the creature, and I coughed up salty liquid.

"Mirielle!" Gryphon cried, kneeling before me. "Mirielle, look in my eyes!" He was frantic, rubbing his hands on both my cheeks, his weapon lying forgotten on the ground beside him.

I shook my head and sputtered. "I'm okay! We need to stop them!"

He ground his teeth in frustration. "I told you to barricade yourself in the warehouse!"

"I had to know what was going on! That you were safe!" I argued.

His entire demeanor changed with my confession. Despite the fire and battle around us, he pulled my face to his for the most passionate kiss I had ever imagined. His lips were fierce and dominant against mine, making me pant with desire. It contained the promise of a future, hope, and stirred something deep inside me. It did not last nearly long enough before Gryphon pulled away, his eyes once again a swirling, molten gold. "I cannot protect you here," he yelled above the noise. "You must return to the warehouse! Darda will let you inside!"

Several more water creatures descended on us in that moment. No doubt to draw them away from me, Gryphon flapped his wings and flew over their heads, using his sword to slice as many of them open as he could along the way. More water washed over me as the bodies collapsed on me like the others and I jumped up in a defensive stance. My sword lay forgotten on the floor. Two more water warriors and a fire demon circled me, their eyes cold and menacing. They were out for blood.

All three rushed me at the same time, preventing me from blocking their strikes. The hilt of a seashell sword struck the side of my head and I cried out in agony as my right leg caught fire. I kicked into a water warrior just to douse the flames, though the salt in the water made the burn all the more painful. It brought me to my knees. Another blow to my face drew blood, thought I could not say from who, and I spit the tangy taste on the ground at their feet. My vision was beginning to blur.

"MIRIELLE!" Gryphon bellowed. It echoed in the chamber louder than the clashing of swords or the crunch of more stones falling.

A force rippled out through all the fighting, causing all the water warriors to wash away into long puddles and the fire demons to curl into more puffs of smoke. The boulder men outside shuddered and fell lifeless to the ground, and I could vaguely register that the wind had stopped. A preternatural silence descended upon the castle as all of the enemy fighters collapsed at once. I was slipping away too quickly to process what was happening, and the last words I heard before blacking out from the pain were Gryphon's panicked cries for Darda.

CHAPTER 24

Mother Hen

GRYPHON

Watching Mirielle fall would forever be engrained in my nightmares. It was pure torment to see her beaten and bleeding, utterly helpless to stop it. The power that surged from me at that moment was stronger than I had ever created before, and for once it did not drive me to bed in exhaustion for several days afterwards. I pulverized every enemy in Aeternitas with that one spell, which definitely sent a message to Vulcan, my villainous uncle, who should have known better than to test me. They would not attack my realm again any time soon.

I was far too distracted with Mirielle's care to concern myself with why they had attacked in the first place. Once Darda had appeared we whisked Mirielle away to my bed chamber and I personally attended to her over the next several days. I channeled as much of my power into her as I could to heal her injuries like I did my own, but mortals are built differently, so her body did not respond the same. It forced her into a deep sleep where nothing could wake her.

Darda assured me it was probably for the best because Mirielle would be in a lot of pain without it. Aeternitas was not equipped for human injuries beyond that of a standard first aid kit I plucked from a caravan in the Congo around 1983. I was too scared to return to the human realm for one of their healers; I could never forgive myself if something were to happen to Mirielle in my absence.

I had taken to crawling into bed next to her simply to hold her, hoping my presence alone would make her wake up. I longed to hear her laugh again and imagined the way her cheeks would flush in embarrassment if she awoke in my arms after days of not brushing her teeth. The daydreams led me to such distraction that I did not even think about the curse. The lost treasure could rot in the mortal realm forever as far as I was concerned. Mirielle was the only thing that mattered.

After a few days of restless pacing at her bedside, sleep overtook me as well, no matter how hard I tried to force my eyes open. I jerked upright as an arm clamped around my waist.

"Hey," Mirielle offered weakly. Her voice was gravelly after five days without water, but just to see her round hazel eyes look up at me made my heart flutter.

I sprang into action instantly, barking an order for Cook to send up a large pitcher of ice water and something to eat. Then I summoned Darda, asking the bathing chamber for fresh clothes as I was sure Mirielle would want a proper bath. I had gone through eight sponges while cleaning the burn on her leg and the cuts on her face and arm, but a bedside sponge bath would not be enough to make her feel clean. She had better grooming practices than most humans I had encountered.

Mirielle rubbed her hand across her forehead and frowned in concentration. "What happened?" she croaked.

A small smile was all I trusted myself to give as I fought back tears of joy. *Tears of joy.* That's who I had become, a warrior who literally cried in delight when the woman he cared for healed. Those thoughts and feelings terrified me, and I shut them back in the dark corners of my mind with a key, determined to ignore them for eternity.

Darda appeared with a tray of food and a buttery soft night-dress for Mirielle to put on after her bath. She gently instructed Mirielle to sit up, with me gripping her shoulders to help guide her upright. I pulled the table directly in front of Mirielle at her bedside rather than risk her tumbling while trying to walk to a chair. Darda's smug satisfaction at watching me play nursemaid barely infiltrated my thoughts, and I could feel her smile as I rolled my eyes at her.

The covers toppled down, exposing Mirielle's bare chest. I had to cut her clothing off with a knife after we brought her here because it was so caked with blood. The leggings had singed to her skin and required laser-like focus to peel off thread by thread. Now, it hurt to see how her once round breasts sagged on her thin frame, her ribs poking through from the weight loss of the past several days.

She glanced at my face before pulling the blanket up to cover herself. "And why am I naked?"

Fire blazed within me to say the words out loud. "You were hurt in my realm. Something that will never happen again, I assure you. I had to cut your clothing from your body in order to clean your wounds."

"I see," she whispered. She greedily drank a full glass of ice water, allowing some of it to dribble down her chin.

I gestured towards the meal of simple broth with a crust of bread in front of her and stood up to pace the room. "You should not have been in the fighting, Mirielle," I scolded her. "You are lucky to be among the living."

From the corner of my eye, I saw her shrug and then wince at the pain. "I have had lots of hand to hand combat training," she replied.

Stopping short, I turned to glare at her. "That is not the same thing, nor is it useful against an Elemental!" I snapped. Her indifference was infuriating.

"What's an Elemental?" she asked curiously.

"The warrior race you fought. They belong to a neighboring realm, the place where my mother grew up. Her brother, my uncle Vulcan, rules there now," I explained. It was the simplest explanation I could give to her at this point, but I longed for her to better understand. The gag order my mother had placed on me was too great a risk for Mirielle, though. I would not hazard turning her into another household object like the other mortals.

Mirielle merely nodded and did not press any further. She slurped a few spoonful's of broth and began to sway. Clearly it was too much exertion for her at this stage.

I rushed forward to catch her before she fell, then gently guided her onto her back on the mattress. Drawing up her legs, I tucked the covers around her and fluffed her pillows.

Her eyes instantly closed, but when I moved to retreat, her hand darted out and grabbed my wrist.

"Please stay with me," whispered Mirielle. Her eyes were open again, round and hopeful. I would have done anything she asked at that moment if only to see happiness return to them.

Trying not to jostle her, I pulled back the blankets and crawled in, angling my body to face hers. She turned her head towards me and offered a small smile in thanks before closing her eyes again.

Her hand sought mine and wove our fingers together, pulling them against her chest.

"Gryphon," she sighed before succumbing once more to sleep.

My name on her lips was the most beautiful sound in the world, maybe only second to the sound of her laughter. It promised more, but more was terrifying. It was the unknown, and if time had taught me anything, it was that the unknown was the worst state of being for any creature to dwell. Mirielle gave me hope and I didn't want hope. I didn't want to see my dreams shatter again like they had when my mother cast her wretched curse.

As Mirielle's gentle snores filled the room, I allowed my mind to wander back to my life before the curse. It was bleak, even then, long days of endless training or council meetings before a night spent drinking and gambling, culminating in whatever female's bed I sought out. As the crown prince of Aeternitas, women of all realms and manner of creature were throwing themselves at me constantly, more eager to bed my title than me. It was a lonely existence, only made worse by the fact that I was always caught up in my parents' squabbles. No one wanted to be on the wrong side of their fights, so the residents of Aeternitas kept their distance whenever any of the royals were around. Until the liquor came out and the chance to warm my bed presented itself, of course.

I shuddered involuntarily when I pictured Mirielle as a part of that world. She would loathe my realm in its true form; it held nothing but vices and sin. While she had not presented any religious affiliation like most other human mortals I had met, the purity of her soul shone like a beacon in the darkness from a mile away. She represented the goodness that still existed in the world. Had her actions not already demonstrated such?

Throwing herself into the heat of battle without any training made my blood boil. It was foolish and reckless, and I still had not yet determined how she had managed to escape her bedchamber. Darda had informed me afterwards of the wreckage inside the castle and Mirielle's quarters had been one of the hardest hit. She put herself in mortal danger...for me.

And therein laid the problem. I could not identify anyone else who had ever laid their life on the line for me like that. Yet Mirielle always referred to me as her "jailer." She said at the ball that anything between us was merely a lack of options, not an indication of real attraction on either side. Did that mean she didn't care for me as I had grown to care for her?

She had to have acted based on her knowledge of the curse. There was no way to know what would happen to Mirielle or the residents of my castle were I to perish before the rose's final petal fell, which was a possibility at the hand of an Elemental. They were one of the few races of creature with the necessary weapons. Perhaps my mother put in a safeguard of some kind, perhaps not. I certainly could not predict what she might have done because it still confounded me that she had done it in the first place. While she and I were never as close as I was to my father, I never doubted her regard for me. Not until that fateful day.

It was enough to make my head spin. Sighing heavily, I leaned over to gently place a kiss on Mirielle's temple and joined her in sleep.

Lust and Confusion

Over the course of the next week, I slowly built back my strength and stamina. Gryphon was very attentive, always within a hand's reach of wherever I sat, walking next to me in case I fell, and eating meals with me in his private chambers. He would help me into the bathroom when I needed it, but did not linger or join me in the bath like I expected. While he was polite and kept up the modicum of conversation, it felt forced and awkward.

I had finally had enough after the ten day mark. Broaching the subject cautiously, I said, "Darda told me I could pick another bedroom in the castle. She's going to show me my options this afternoon."

Gryphon was sitting at a small table closest to the hearth and writing in a ledger. At my words, he slowly placed the quill down and faced me completely. "No," he replied with a tight smile before returning to his task.

"I wasn't asking for permission," I huffed. Leave it to Gryphon to try and call the shots on this.

He shook his head without looking up. "You will remain here in my rooms until I determine otherwise."

I jumped out of bed and rushed towards him. "Like hell I will!" I cried, barring my teeth at him. "This isn't working for either of us."

Gryphon's eyebrows cocked in response. "It's working just fine for me," he shrugged nonchalantly. "You stay, Mirielle."

"So you're back to treating me like a prisoner?" I fired back.

His eyes darkened ominously as he turned to glare at me. "When did I ever stop?"

Roaring in frustration, I stomped towards the bathroom and closed myself inside. Perhaps a hot shower would relieve some of the tension building up in my muscles. It would at least serve as a distraction so I didn't choke the life out of him in anger.

Steam quickly filled the room as I let the scalding water run over my body. I kept my back towards the door and did not notice Gryphon's presence until I felt his chest meet my back. His erect cock was enormous as it pressed into the small of my back. His arms caged me in as he braced himself against the wall to loom over me, all while inhaling deeply into my hair.

Glancing back over my shoulder, Gryphon's eyes met mine, alight with more swirling gold. Ever so gently, he pushed away from the wall and ran his fingers down the sides of my arms, keeping his gaze only on my face. His lips were parted, close enough that I could feel his cool breath on my face, and suddenly the temperature in the shower went up another hundred degrees. He was so achingly beautiful, especially now with his long hair wet and his muscles on full display.

"Do you not find me to be a hospitable host?" he whispered. Gryphon leaned slightly forward and began nibbling at my ear lobe. He traced light kisses along my neck as he waited for my response. I turned to face him, my nipples pebbling as the hard plains of his chest grazed them.

"It's not about hospitality," I managed to pant. My breathing was so erratic that my heart was likely about to stop beating. Evidence of my arousal was already beginning to seep down my thigh. How could he make my body ignite with such a simple touch?

Gryphon redirected his attention along my jaw line, pulling my face closer to him. "Then what is it?" he murmured before searing his lips to mine. It was so passionate that my knees began to tremble and I had to brace my arms against the wall to hold myself steady.

I twisted my face up to his, wrapping my arms around his waist to eliminate all space between us. It was like I could not get close enough to satisfy the current that always connected me to him. His hands moved to my hair and he pushed me back roughly against the shower wall. Our kiss grew deeper, his tongue moving quickly in my mouth, his cock a rigid line of steel up my abdomen. Even though the movement was foreign to me, the heat of the moment spurred me to wrap my hand around his shaft, stroking up and down his hard length. I had no comparison other than awkward glances at some of my mother's clientele as they sauntered out of her bedroom, but Gryphon's cock felt gigantic. My thumb could not reach any of my other fingers as I grasped him, and I had been teased more than once for having long fingers.

He groaned in my mouth as I continued light strokes, pausing only long enough to grit between his teeth, "Harder!" I squeezed tighter and felt an exhilarant thrill as he began to pant from my movements. He broke away from my mouth to lean down and suckle at my nipples, his left hand expertly sliding between my thighs. As soon as his fingers found my clit, I matched the pace of my strokes to his. Within minutes we were both screaming as we came together, his cum a thick, white stream on my hand.

I looked down at the evidence of his orgasm in awe, completely transfixed at the idea that I had done that to him. Gryphon noticed my reaction and smirked.

"It's a flattering decoration on you, Mirielle," he murmured. Raising my chin with his fingers, he drew my attention back to his face. Gold lava swirled in his eyes, so bright they were almost blinding.

I finally gathered the courage to ask. "Why do your eyes change like that?"

Gryphon frowned. "Like what?"

"They're gold, almost metallic right now. I've noticed they change like that whenever we're..." I trailed off, too uncomfortable to finish the statement.

"Whenever we're physically intimate?" he offered with a crooked smile. I think my embarrassment amused him.

I shook my head. "It happened at the ball, too. You looked at me in my gown and they changed. It was like they were glowing."

A faint trace of suspicion and uncertainty crossed his features, but he tried to hide it with his usual mask. It was only there for a moment, but I knew him well enough by then to realize it meant he was hiding something from me. "What is it?" I asked again.

He shrugged. "Just something that happens in Aeternitas," he said simply. He abruptly turned and exited the shower, however, making sure to place a fluffy bathing sheet and my pink sherpa robe on the small stool outside the shower door.

Sighing, I turned off the water that had now run cold. Much like whatever this was between Gryphon and me. As much as it pained me to admit to myself, I missed his warmth and smiles. It had been pleasant having someone taking care of me. Gryphon had reminded me of Mr. Cooper in how he doted on me for the past several days. And yet I knew it needed to come to an end. All I had heard was his disdain for my humanity; there could be no future between us. Having our own separate living quarters would be the logical way to start creating a boundary. While he might fuss at first, eventually Gryphon would come to see I was right.

Nodding to myself, I slipped on the bathrobe left for me on the counter.

CHAPTER 26

Learning New Tricks

When I emerged from the bathroom, Gryphon was nowhere to be found. Darda stood in the center of the room, however, and her comforting presence surrounded me like a hug.

"Get dressed, dearie," she instructed. "The Master has made all the arrangements. You're to start lessons today!"

"Lessons?" I repeated. "What kind of lessons?"

"You'll see," she replied.

I returned to the bathroom and found clothing already waiting for me, dove gray leggings with a bright purple sports bra and a see-through mesh gray tank top. A pair of purple ombre sneakers rested on the floor. Apparently, Gryphon's bathroom had the same excellent style as mine.

"Hey, Darda!" I called over my shoulder.

"Yes, dearie?" she replied.

"How does the bathroom know to pick out my favorite colors and styles?"

She chuckled. "A good designer never reveals her secrets, love!"

I snorted and thanked the bathroom before changing quickly. As soon as I arrived at Darda's side, she teleported us into a room I had never seen before. We were standing inside a gymnasium that reminded me of Madison Square Garden without as many seats. The wood floors were polished to a shine and the Aeternitas hourglass crest was inlaid at center court. Gryphon had told me only recently that the insignia was meant to represent the union of his mother's and father's realms, but would not elaborate further when I asked.

A set of double doors opened to the left, revealing a modern gym to rival Dwayne Johnson's Iron Paradise. There were free weights lining an entire wall of mirrors, with machines, a treadmill, an elliptical, a Stairmaster, and more filling the rest of the room. A rock climbing wall hung in the mirror's reflection, and giant fans circulated cool air.

Additional doors were closed on all sides of the gym where I stood and I could not help but marvel at the magic of the castle. It never ceased to astound me.

"Young miss?" Darda prompted. "Meet your instructor, Jimmy."

A tapered medieval sword approximately three feet long hovered in the air before me, the hilt bobbing slightly at Darda's introduction. It was made of silver steel and looked to have been recently polished. It had a simple black grip, but the cross guard had an unfamiliar insignia etched into the metal. When I tried to take a step closer to examine it, the blade pointed at me.

"Let's keep our distance here, okay, doll?" Jimmy said. His accent was definitely Midwest American, although it was his word choice that startled me more than anything. Men didn't tend to use terms like "doll" very often anymore.

I turned to Darda. "What exactly is the lesson? A reminder of what feminism has accomplished?"

Jimmy snorted indignantly.

Darda tried to cover her chuckle with a harsh (but very fake) laugh. "Jimmy is going to teach you how to fight."

I rolled my eyes. "I know how to fight!"

"Not with a weapon, you don't!" Jimmy sneered.

"Jimmy is our head of security," Darda offered instead.

It was my turn to snort. "Looks like you need some lessons yourself there, Jimmy."

"Why I oughta—" Jimmy snarled, closing the gap between us, grip side forward.

"Now that's enough!" Darda barked, her voice rippling with authority. "The Master has ordered these lessons, so both of you will see it through!"

Sighing, I took a few steps back, recognizing there was no sense in arguing. If Gryphon had made up his mind about me learning how to fight with weapons, there was nothing I could do to change it. And honestly, if we were going to face any more Elemental attacks, learning how to wield the heavy sword my bathroom had provided probably couldn't hurt.

"Where is my sword?" I asked.

A gust of cold wind blew through the room as the sword appeared. It was still glowing faintly, heat radiating off the blade like before. A sense of calm sank over me as I grasped the grip. That feature was new. Or maybe I just hadn't noticed in the middle of battle before.

"Whoa!" Jimmy breathed. "That's Stellarum...the sword of starlight."

"Okay, so?" I huffed out.

"That's the sword of Aeternitas. No one's seen it since the queen went missing. Where did you get that?"

I stood up straighter and examined the sword more closely. The hilt was made of a silver metal that rivaled titanium. It was polished enough that I could see my own reflection. The hourglass crest of Aeternitas was engraved on the stop of the hilt, with a swirling fleur-de-lis style design along the grip. Heat radiated from the blade like before, but I only now noticed it resembled a bright white light more than any recognizable metal.

"It just appeared in my bathroom after I said I needed it," I whispered in awe. The glow emanating from the blade flashed a rainbow of colors before returning to its original white.

"What about the lost treasure?" I cried. "Shouldn't I be focusing on that instead?"

"Let the Master worry about breaking his curse," Darda said. "We all need to know you're safe, dearie."

It didn't escape my notice that she said "we all" needed to know. My friends had attempted to visit me the entire time I was recuperating in Gryphon's bedroom, but none were permitted inside. Gryphon valued his privacy too much.

Accepting I was not going to leave the room until Gryphon was satisfied, I turned back to Jimmy. "Where do we start?"

By the end of the day, I was a sweaty pile of mush. I did not think my legs would cooperate to do more than stand, and even that would be difficult. Forget about touring other bedrooms with Darda. Jimmy had led me through exercise after exercise of how to properly stand to distribute my body weight in my feet while holding the sword, the proper way to grip in both hands, the angle of my body in relation to an attacker, and more. It was exhausting and probably derailed half of what I had learned in my karate and MMA training. We did not really get into the mechanics of actual sword fighting, but Jimmy said we would not be limiting our lessons to Stellarum. He was meant to show me other weaponry and survival skills. Master's orders.

Jimmy snickered as he hovered near the door. "Might wanna step inside that gym there, doll. You need to build up some serious muscle."

I groaned rather than say something snarky in return. He was right, but I did not have the energy to admit it. Instead I called out for Darda, who appeared instantly, and transported me back to Gryphon's bedroom. She told me there was already a bath drawn for me. Who knew someday I would want to kiss a desk in relief?

Large bubbles floated around me as I sank into the hot water with a contented sigh. Gryphon's tub might as well have been a swimming pool. There were spots along two sides meant for soaking, but I could have swum laps in it had I the urge. It felt decadent to soak my tired muscles. Maybe Darda could give me a magic potion to ease away the pain. Anything seemed possible in Aeternitas.

The thought made me giggle, which was how Gryphon found me minutes later. He leaned against the door frame, arms crossed over his chest, and eyed me with amusement. His hair was down in long waves past his shoulders despite having on what I knew to be his fighting attire. It wasn't quite body paint as I had first thought, but rather a shield provided by his magic, according to him. He said it was easier to fight without clothing restricting his movements.

As he stood there in all his muscular glory, I didn't really care what we called it. I just wanted to stop my jaw from dropping.

"Is something funny?" he asked lightly.

I giggled again. "Nothing important. I am incredibly sore."

He nodded once. "Jimmy informed me you have potential."

Rolling my eyes, I grabbed a sponge and lathered it with soap. "How generous of him," I muttered dryly.

Gryphon stepped forward and tugged the sponge from my hand. "Allow me," he murmured. He began gently exfoliating along my shoulders and neck, the bubbles stopping at my collarbones. Although the room felt like it was now engulfed in flames and my skin was flushed with a new kind of heat, Gryphon pretended to be immune to my physical reaction to him and kept his attention on the task at hand. He washed both arms and motioned for me to turn so he could wash my back.

"Why don't you join me?" I offered. My own boldness surprised even me, and I kept my eyes downturned so I would not have to see his rejection if Gryphon said no. Somehow, I still managed to catch his sexy smirk.

With a wave of his hand, he stood before me naked, pure strength and power. His erect cock jutted out almost at eye level and I felt my cheeks flood with both lust and embarrassment. Climbing into the tub, Gryphon immediately circled behind me and used his hands to wash along my back, taking them lower with each rub.

"You're tense," he admonished. His voice was barely above a whisper, but perhaps that was the ringing in my ears at having his hands on me once more. Raw desire wound its way down to my core, and I had to clench my thighs together to stop myself from reaching for my clit.

He began to massage the knots in my back, tutting incoherently whenever he found another. Never once did he make a move that made me believe he found the act to be erotic or sexual, yet his length was a steel shaft against my lower back. I let out a grateful moan as strong hands worked out the kinks along my shoulder blades and let my head fall back against his neck. His jaw shifted as he smirked, and he placed a soft kiss on my temple.

"Is that better?" Gryphon asked.

"It's heavenly," I sighed.

Wrapping his arms around my waist, he pulled me back so that I was flush with his chest. He leaned into my ear to murmur, "Because you are my miracle."

My heart could burst from happiness. No one had ever cared for me the way Gryphon had, and I knew without a doubt that the lines between captor and captive were being blurred. Maybe Stockholm's Syndrome wasn't so bad if it made my pussy wet and my self-esteem soar? I had certainly been through far worse.

"Come," he finally said, hands still firmly locked around my waist. "Let's to bed." He had not made a single move to escalate the intimacy, yet his words flooded me with want.

Still, I needed to establish some boundaries with him. "I need to find a room."

I felt him stiffen for a moment before he relaxed again. "This is your room now. You will remain here with me."

Shaking my head, I pulled away and turned to face him, swimming backwards by a few feet. Distance helped clear my head.

"Gryphon, I need my own room," I demanded.

His nostrils flared at my defiance. "No."

"I can't share a room with you!" I argued. "You live in a palace--it's not like you don't have the space!"

My words might as well have been snowflakes melting into stone. He did not respond, and instead swam over to the edge of the tub to pull himself out. Even the sight of his back muscles flexing did nothing to distract me.

"Gryphon!" I cried in frustration.

"Mirielle, you are safer here than in any other room in the castle," he explained, drying himself off with a large gray bathing sheet that appeared beside the bathtub. "Do not challenge me further."

Okay, so he had a point. If those Elemental things attacked again, it would be safer for me to be with Gryphon. I didn't exactly want to have my head in a floating ocean again. However, it seemed like a dangerous precedence to let him believe he could continually have my submission. I practically tasted blood from how hard I bit down on the inside of my cheek to stop myself from arguing further.

I stood up to follow him, climbing out of the tub far less gracefully. At least the fatigue in my muscles no longer bothered me. Seeing my naked body seemed to anger him, however. He quickly snatched my sherpa robe from the hook by the bathroom door and threw it over my shoulders.

"Really?" I snapped. "You can massage me in a bathtub, but seeing me naked is going too far?"

I barely heard the word "vixen" again as he stalked from the room, but it did help ease my mood somewhat. Gryphon must be a visual kind of guy. I would store that tidbit away for a later time.

Letting out a heavy sigh, I asked the bathroom to send me something to sleep in. It immediately provided a lacy babydoll teddy in an emerald green that would perfectly match Gryphon's eyes. I snorted. "Yeah, he's not gonna get that lucky," I advised the bathroom. The lingerie disappeared and a pair of cotton shorts and a sports bra arrived, both in a royal blue color. It wasn't ideal, but it must have been the typical form of pajamas in this place since I was never provided with any other option.

I wanted to stall the fight with Gryphon so rather than entering the bedroom, I pulled a brush through my hair, lost in thought. My gut told me that he meant well, although I had nothing to really base that on. Maybe he was just trying to protect me. He couldn't know how much the thought of sharing such a personal space made me feel like there were pinpricks of sharp needles all over my body. How desperate I was to have a private place where I could be alone and think. An introvert like me needed to have their own space where they could simply *be*.

I needed to approach Gryphon differently, I reminded myself. Mind-reading was not one of his powers (to my knowledge) and he did not really know much about humans based on all our previous interactions. If I explained it in a way he understood, he had to reconsider.

Nodding to my reflection, I placed the brush back in the drawer and returned to the bedroom. Gryphon was sitting at his same small worktable, the worn brown leather journal open in front of him. He glanced up briefly when I stopped in front of him, then did a double take. His eyebrows rose as he took in my sleeping clothes.

"Remind me to instruct Vogue on appropriate clothing for you," Gryphon said.

I grinned at him and dropped into the chair across the table. "Is that someone I know?"

"She is the castle seamstress. She provides all of your clothing when you ask," he explained.

My eyebrows rose in shock. "Those were coming from an actual person?"

He paused before glancing away. "Not exactly," he muttered.

Belatedly I realized Vogue was probably under an enchantment, too, and therefore no longer human. Gryphon hated reminders of the curse, and as I spent more time with him, I concluded that it was primarily due to guilt. It was eating away at him piece by piece and he did not know how to handle it other than breaking the spell to free everyone. We had not discussed what would happen to everyone if that day came.

He gestured towards the bed without looking up from his journal. "I will only be a moment. Go lay down."

"Yeah...about that. I have never had to share my space with a man before and I don't know that I'm ready to start." I kept my eyes on my knees as I spoke rather than let the embarrassment flood me again. I had no idea why it mattered so much what Gryphon thought of me; no one else's opinion had ever occurred to me, but everything with him just felt different. More significant.

Gryphon set the quill down and closed his journal. "Nor have I ever shared accommodations with someone. In fact, you and Darda are the only people who have ever been permitted inside these rooms. Not even my parents have entered."

His admission surprised me, and my eyes shot up to meet his, hopeful that he was finally beginning to understand.

Instead he smirked at me. "I suppose it will be a learning curve for both of us."

Before I had time to whip out a scathing comeback, he held up a hand to stop me. "You will remain in my rooms so that I can protect you and so that I can learn from you."

"Learn from me?" I echoed.

He nodded. "Yes, Mirielle," he whispered. "There is much you can teach me."

His green eyes began to transition to the same molten gold, but I was too infuriated with his answer to care. I shot up out of my chair faster than you could blink, then darted over to the bed and crawled under the covers, bunching the blankets and pillows around me like a cocoon, leaving only my nose and eyes exposed. This was not a fight I was ever going to win, no matter how much I argued and his pretty gold eyes weren't going to distract me. Nor were lovely sentiments. I certainly didn't have anything worthwhile to teach him, unless he had a sudden interest in human history.

"Well I'm not having sex with you," I countered through the covers instead.

He chuckled from across the room. "*Yet.*"

A Happy Place

MIRIELLE

The next several weeks flew by in a blur. I had never had such a packed schedule before, and although I did not have long to rest at night, I slept soundly in Gryphon's bed, normally waking up with his strong arms around me. At Jimmy's request, I began to use the gym each morning, running through strength training exercises meant to build more muscle. It made it easier to wield a sword, though we had not yet graduated back to Stellarum. Jimmy seemed to revere the sword and expressed repeatedly that I had to be "worthy" of it.

Most mornings Gryphon joined me, and if someone ever discovered a sexier sight than a shirtless, sweaty Gryphon running through this training exercises, all the women of the world were in trouble. It drove me to lose count of my reps or drop my kettlebell on more than one occasion. I swear, he always flexed a little more whenever I did that.

After the morning workout, I would shower—always fighting Gryphon to stay out and let me bathe without his help—and then he would transport me to the warehouse. Our team consisted of more household members now, people Mr. Cooper had recruited. Greco was a small rubber mallet with a thick Italian accent who proved to have invaluable strength. He was able to move many of the large items about in the warehouse for me without other help. Pranee was a lock pick who more than earned her keep with her ability to open various drawers and cabinets presumed to be locked. One turn from her head and the items in question always opened. Conversations were limited because she did not know much English or French, the only other language I could speak fluently, but she was learning quickly.

Mr. Cooper said he thought she might be speaking a dialect from Thailand, but he could not remember why he would know that. I had to choke back a sob at that point because I knew it was from one of his old bridge club friends who had passed away a few years ago. He had emigrated from Thailand around the same time as Mr. Cooper arrived from Armenia.

Ambrose and Wade were stretched so thin between all of us that after two days I requested another pen and journal from Gryphon. The next morning a binder full of loose leaf paper arrived, introducing herself as Nenetl, along with two quills who identified themselves as Temujin and Batzorig. Wade immediately took them all under his wing and began to serve in a supervisory role, assigning translations and helping to build a timeline on the wall.

By mid-afternoon Jimmy would arrive to escort me back to the training gym where we would work through various weaponry. He tried to keep it varied enough that I did not lose interest, but detailed enough that I could easily defend myself. We practiced the basics of swordsmanship and knives before progressing to firearms. Jimmy said that since it was possible I would go on a field mission with Gryphon at any point in history, I had to know how to use different kinds of weapons because I never knew what I would have at hand.

I felt more comfortable with knives, especially after Jimmy taught me how it was actually more lethal to hold the blade against my forearm and not out above my fist. I retained more control over the blade, and therefore my movements. My speed was picking up a lot, too, because I found myself idly playing with the cold steel I now kept on my belt at all times. We would be standing in the warehouse, discussing the timeline or notes on an artifact, and I would suddenly notice the blade in hand as I unconsciously twirled the handle through my fingers. I wanted to practice Bucky's move from all the Captain America movies where I dropped a knife from one hand to the other and kept fighting, but Gryphon told me we couldn't use cinema as a model for training. Rude way to crush a girl's dreams, but maybe someday I would get through to him.

Muskets, rifles, bayonets, all the way to modern pistols—I had to demonstrate proper use of them all. A gun range was hidden in the depths of the castle, and we spent hours inside while I learned how to line up my sights properly and aim for center mass on paper targets in the shape of a person. Jimmy had me practice at various distances and in various lighting because he said I needed to be able to defend myself in the dark, too. The gun range provided me protection in a pair of fluffy purple ear covers that I adored, while Jimmy told me I looked like a Muppet.

He said eventually we would progress onto moving targets after he got permission from Gryphon to set up an obstacle course of sorts where I would have to run around various blockades and clear buildings while shooting at whatever "bad guys" popped up. Trepidation filled my gut whenever he talked about it, but I tried not to push it for the time being. Guns were definitely *not* my thing.

One of the doors off the gymnasium led to an archery range where we practiced using a standard bow as well as a few variations of a crossbow. They were often heavy and extremely problematic to aim, but for once Jimmy assured me that I was doing well. I preferred the barebow style and found that more of my shots reached center mass in my targets when practicing with those, but I practiced for hours with them all. It was a hobby I actually wouldn't mind continuing if I ever got to return to New York.

By late evening I would always be a sweaty mess, my muscles aching, but my spirits high. It felt good to challenge myself again, to learn a new skill that might wind up saving my life. Gryphon would meet me in the gymnasium and then join me in another room built for Ninja Warrior style training. He called it "life training" and thought it was odd that I had never learned to rock climb or sprint across short planks or any of the other ridiculous activities he conjured. I always pointed out that he hardly needed to learn any of it when giant wings sprouted from his back whenever he needed. He artfully changed the subject after that.

We would practice some hand to hand combat skills every few days, but as he tactfully reminded me when I asked about it, I had already demonstrated I could best him in that arena. It was hard to ignore the hint of pride and awe in his voice when he said it, and I couldn't help the smug grin from crossing my face. I didn't want to grow lax with my training, however, so I requested a punching bag to be installed in a corner of the gym. Even if it was just a quick, 20 minute routine, it always felt comforting to go through the familiar motions.

Gryphon and I would then return to his chambers and enjoy a

meal together, just the two of us. Those meals were always the highlight of my day because I grew to enjoy his company so much. We talked about many different things like books, philosophy, history, and art. I even dared to open more about my childhood, confiding some of my most shameful moments at the hands of my mother's many "boyfriends." When I revealed how Mr. Cooper made me stay in his apartment after one particular boyfriend ripped my shirt open to glower at my budding chest when I was only twelve, Gryphon snapped the arm of his chair clean off in a fit of anger.

After a few weeks, I could tell it pained Gryphon to ask about Barrett. He confirmed that the equipment in the warehouse had in fact come from my lab and briefly described the run in he had with the detective at that time. Gryphon sneered as he said, "That human spoke very possessively in regard to you."

I snorted in derision. "Barrett Collins bullied me from the first day of junior high until the day I graduated high school. I hadn't seen him in almost ten years."

Gryphon's beautiful features pulled downward into a scowl. "I still don't much like him."

Nodding, I agreed. "I don't much like him either." That answer seemed to pacify him because he abruptly changed the subject and never brought up Barrett again.

On the nights when we opened a bottle of Aeternitas wine, our conversations often turned far more intimate. Wine, much stronger and sweeter than anything I had tasted back home, made Gryphon's defenses drop instantly. He confessed one night that he used to have such a strong tolerance for the stuff from drinking it all the time that he could have polished off the entire bottle by himself and still fought in battle without stumbling. I shuddered to think of it.

"Why were you drinking so heavily?" I asked.

He sighed and stared into the fire for a moment before responding. "Everyone was always around me," Gryphon began, "and yet I was always alone. I never had a true friend in all my existence. My parents were too swept up in their responsibilities to our realm, and then in their quarrels with each other. It made me invisible. The wine helped me feel numb in addition to invisible."

My eyes filled with tears that he snorted away. "I don't want your pity, Mirielle!"

I shook my head, blinking them back. "It's not pity," I whispered. "It's grief for the life you should have had. You didn't deserve that, Gryphon. You're worth more than that."

It was Gryphon's turn to have his eyes glaze over with unshed tears. We both fell into silence and went to bed quickly that night.

Although we had reached a new level of intimacy, things did not progress sexually. While it was very apparent how desirable Gryphon found me (he could often be seen adjusting a large erection in his trousers while watching me), he did not breech that boundary. Small traces like a lingering hand on my waist in the gym or a tender kiss on my forehead when he left the warehouse in the morning were the most that occurred between us, but it was enough. Just having his eyes on me, sensual and darkened with lust, made my confidence skyrocket. I had never felt so beautiful and comfortable in my own skin. Gryphon often gave me seemingly random compliments, such as how much he loved the way my hair curled down my back or how he found green to be a flattering color on me, but I lived on that flattery like a starving child finding scraps. They were not intentional or insincere, more so just Gryphon's own habit of saying whatever he thought was important. And praising me was always important to him.

He had long since ceased referring to me as "mortal" and

instead often called Miracle. Wade's nickname for me of "My-my" brought out an eye roll, but it was followed by a look of affection that pulled directly at my heart strings whenever Gryphon said it. I was feeling something I had never experienced before and instead of being terrified, peeking behind Gryphon's bristly exterior made me want to open up more and allow him behind my walls. Vulnerability did not seem so bad when someone made you feel wholly accepted. Although I was hesitant to put a label on it, my hesitation lay in his reaction more so than my fear.

I noticed Gryphon was smiling more and made more of an effort to interact with the staff. Mornings when I could convince him to join us in the warehouse were the best because Anastasia had a way of teasing him that brought out loud peals of laughter, although we rarely accomplished anything productive on those days. His megawatt smile could melt a glacier, and it drew me in like Icarus to the sun. I was transfixed and only a fool would ignore love when it finally knocked on your door. For the first time ever, I understood what Mr. Cooper believed me to be missing out on, though the fact that he was right shouldn't have shocked me. Mr. Cooper was right about most things. Happiness felt good. Happiness felt right. And falling in love with Gryphon was the happiest I had ever been.

CHAPTER 28

Tick Tock

Spending all of my free time with Mirielle was like living in a dream. She was constantly laughing, lighting up whatever room she was in. Although she claimed to be socially awkward and ill at ease in a room full of people, my experiences with her were just the opposite. Members of my household were drawn to her planets in orbit—ever circulating and basking in her radiance. She could incite conversation with the shyest servants and welcomed everyone no matter their station. Several of the people effected by the curse did not speak English, yet she tried everything to communicate with them and include them in her plans. The lunch hour had become a group affair, everyone eating in the grand dining hall cafeteria-stye now. I even caught her reading a book from the library on introductory Mandarin after she discovered a floor cushion with whom no one had been able to converse.

I could not deny that I was just as enchanted with her. She consumed my every thought, and I found myself rushing through my tasks in order to return to her sooner. Working in the warehouse with her was too distracting, she often said, so I had relegated myself to overseeing the repairs on the castle. My masonry staff had morphed into shovels, London trowels, jointers, and the like, and were happy to leave "retirement" as they called it to reassemble the parts of the castle that had been destroyed during the Elementals' siege. Some of the damage was too extensive to attempt without magic, but I was not above rolling up my sleeves and pitching in. Together we replaced walls on the interior, painting, and laying down new wood floors. It was grueling, but for the first time in my life, it felt rewarding to see the results of my labors take shape before my eyes. I think it may have helped gain some of their respect, too, which was something I had taken for granted until then. It would be more of a priority in the future, I promised myself.

Most afternoons were spent practicing combat drills with my forces. The knights of Aeternitas had been cursed into coats of armor, but their dedication and loyalty to my realm remained as steadfast as ever. We had become too complacent since then, which was why the Elementals were able to darken my doorstep in the first place. Now that I had someone as precious as Mirielle to protect, my need for security increased tenfold. I could not bear the thought of any more harm coming to her.

The best part of my day was always returning to my private quarters in the evenings with Mirielle on my arm. It wasn't even being physically intimate with her, something I practiced great restraint against, it was enough simply to bask in her presence. The way she listened raptly to the stories I shared or remembered seemingly small details about me, such as my preference to write in my journal each night by the light of the fireplace made me accepted—understood, even—each night as I returned to my writing desk to a fresh quill and full ink pot. She didn't make me feel special for being the crowned prince of Aeternitas, she made me feel special for being myself. Lying in bed next to her each night, longing for the inevitable moment when her body would naturally gravitate towards me in her sleep and I could finally hold her close, was the most delicious kind of torture.

Something held me back from pursuing something more physically intimate with her. While her innocence was the biggest aphrodisiac and an innate instinct in my core wanted to mark her as mine by claiming all of her first sexual experiences, a voice in the back of my head that I could not identify cautioned me against doing so. *Mirielle is special*, the voice warned me. *If you hurt her in that way, she will never recover.* The last thing I wanted to do was be the cause of more anguish in her life, so I succumbed to the voice's caution and resigned myself to long showers with only my hand for company.

Days were long, but fulfilling, and it had been many centuries since I had known such peace. I felt content, and were it not for the many souls who deserved to return to their natural state, I would have preferred for things to stay exactly the way they were. Our little bubble felt blissful, which was far more than I ever hoped.

Hope, however, was corrosive. As the days wore on, no matter how joyfully they were spent, the clock continued to count down towards a conclusion of my mother's spell. My magic grew weaker as I tried to maintain my role in the human realm, leaving me feeling vulnerable and ashamed. These feelings were easier to hide beneath a cloud of anger and it made me lash out on innocent soldiers or masons just to quell my simmering rage. Never did I feel better afterwards, but day after day, my frazzled nerves gave way to wrath. Mirielle called them my mood swings, which she said was a common human thing, and advised everyone to avoid direct contact with me when they struck.

It was Darda's passive aggressive remarks that finally burst the cocoon of joy I had created. She repeatedly made tick tock noises whenever I summoned her and had taken to leaving notes in my room indicating how many days it had been since I last searched for the missing treasure. After over a month of ignoring that truth, I was forced to agree. One day I could not summon the magic I needed to bring out my wings and the panic I felt at being permanently grounded was enough to have me run into the warehouse demanding an update.

Mirielle just so happened to be conferring with Wade on the status of the timeline when I entered. He floated next to her, happily jabbering away about dates and locations, while she pensively stared at the figures on the wall. It stretched nearly eight feet now, with miniscule writing to mark the origins of my collection.

Her smile when she caught sight of me was so dazzling that I stopped in my tracks just to soak her in. She wore her long hair straight down her back today, the bright red bangs falling just above her eye line, with a soft lavender sweater and black leggings that molded to her body. Her ass looked luscious in those pants, stirring unholy thoughts across my mind that involved her not leaving my bedchamber for several days.

Instead of acting on them, I returned her smile and felt a tremor of excitement when she jumped into my open arms to clamp her own firmly around my waist. I engulfed her in my embrace, her head nearly a foot lower than mine. It did not prevent me from leaning down and pressing a kiss into her hair and inhaling the strong scent of roses and vanilla she now embodied. They would never smell the same to me after this.

"Good afternoon, Miracle," I whispered into her hair as I clutched her closer to me. "We must discuss our next step."

She peered up at me in surprise. "Did Darda tip you off?" she asked.

I cocked my head at her odd turn of phrase. "I beg your pardon?"

"We were just telling Darda that I have a rough idea in mind of what the missing treasure might be," she explained.

I grinned. "Where do we start?"

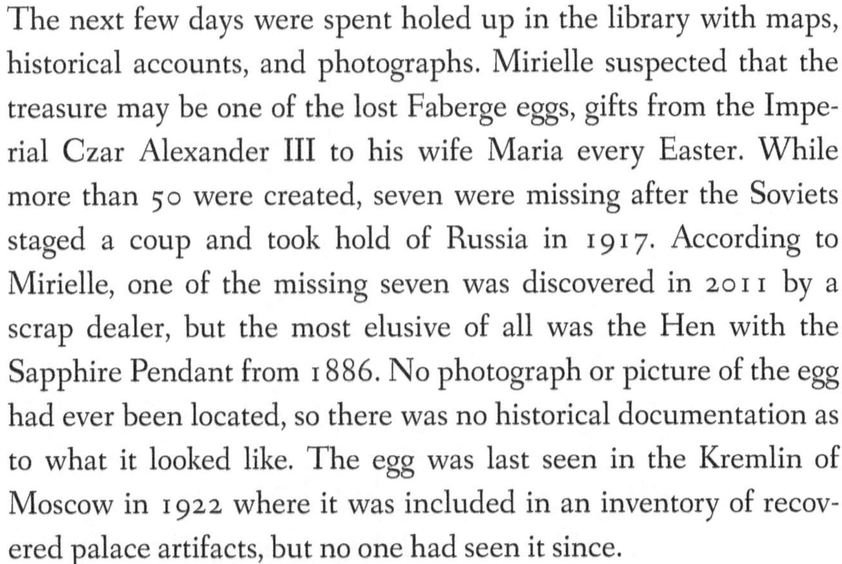

The next few days were spent holed up in the library with maps, historical accounts, and photographs. Mirielle suspected that the treasure may be one of the lost Faberge eggs, gifts from the Imperial Czar Alexander III to his wife Maria every Easter. While more than 50 were created, seven were missing after the Soviets staged a coup and took hold of Russia in 1917. According to Mirielle, one of the missing seven was discovered in 2011 by a scrap dealer, but the most elusive of all was the Hen with the Sapphire Pendant from 1886. No photograph or picture of the egg had ever been located, so there was no historical documentation as to what it looked like. The egg was last seen in the Kremlin of Moscow in 1922 where it was included in an inventory of recovered palace artifacts, but no one had seen it since.

"It's a mystery!" Mirielle stage whispered with a twinkle in her eye.

She subtly explained that since it sounded like my parents often quarreled (she knew they did) and these were a gift from a loving husband to a wife, perhaps my mother chose one of them to symbolize the love she wanted from my father. It didn't exactly sound like the kind of sentimental choice dear old Mum would make, but then again, neither did cursing our entire realm. I had never before considered how hurt my mother may have felt from my father's actions or that there may be a deeper reasoning behind her curse, and the more I thought about it now, the more I wondered whether she did, in fact, want me to see beyond the idea of a jealous monarch. It was something to consider at a later time.

"So we can go to the Czarina's jewel room and simply take the eggs," Mirielle explained with a flourish.

I shook my head and felt a slither of guilt when her face fell. It gave me no pleasure to dash her hopes.

"Why not? It's the safest way to get them!" Mirielle argued.

"If we take the eggs from the royal family before they were last reported missing, it will disrupt the fabric of time," I explained.

Her jaw dropped with an audible click as her eyebrows receded into her bangs.

I rolled my eyes at her dramatics. "Think of it—you know of these things as treasured objects partly because of their notoriety after being identified as 'lost,' yes?"

She nodded.

"If we do anything that changes that from happening, it alters what history is to become, meaning the world would not have made Faberge's eggs famous, you would not have learned about it in any of your history classes, and they could therefore never be considered a valuable treasure to my mother." My frustration grew as I tried to verbalize the mechanics surrounding the philosophy. "We can only go to their last known point."

Her eyes were darting rapidly from side to side as she considered the implications of everything I said. It would not have surprised me if steam came out of her ears, for I could see how quickly her mind was trying to process this information.

"So you're saying that unless the object has already been labeled with infamy, taking it would change the trajectory of how history plays out?" she finally asked. Although I should know better than to doubt her at this point, I still hid my incredulity at how quickly she connected the dots.

Sighing, I corrected her. "I'm saying that if your historical accounts say the eggs were never seen after a certain date, it's because it has already been determined I would take the eggs from that time period. That's why all of the objects are in the warehouse, remember? Fate willed it so."

She rolled her eyes. "Oh, are you and Fate on close terms?"

"We have always been cordial, but she typically prefers to isolate herself on her island," I commented offhandedly with a shrug.

I could tell Mirielle was fighting the desire to scoff at me, but wisely chose against it. After a few moments with more rapid eye twitches and far off gazes she leveled her eyes to mine.

"Then I guess Bolshevik Russia, it is!" she said weakly.

Despite the dangers of our plans, Mirielle's enthusiasm was palpable. She was thrilled with the prospect of going back in time to locate a long lost artifact while I was so anxious that I struggled to sleep at night. So many things could happen to her in 1922's Russia, and that was with the best laid plans in a country that wasn't in turmoil. With my magic so weak and sporadic, who knew if I would be able to protect her? Or worse—what if I could not bring her home? My mother's mirror was the only way we could safely travel there, but that was not without risks of its own. While I did not think the Elementals would attack again any time soon, should anything happen in Aeternitas at the time we tried to travel through the portal, it would automatically seal itself. The same way it would not deposit us in the middle of an active battle in the human realm. A stop gap, my mother had called it, meant to protect her on either end from walking into a blood bath.

Mirielle was able to navigate the books in the castle library far better than I ever could and had soon discovered that all of the books were blank until you specifically asked for whatever it was you wanted to read. She was very specific in her requests for building schematics, aerial maps, and weather patterns for the area around the Kremlin where we would be going. We both agreed that it was the best place to start looking since it was the last known location for someone to have eyes on the Hen with the Sapphire Pendant. While she wanted to obtain all of the missing eggs, that was the one she felt might be the key since it was so elusive and existed under the veil of such secrecy.

The structure of our days changed as we ensconced ourselves in the library, permitting only Darda to enter with food that neither of us touched without my housekeeper's scolding. Mirielle's focus was as intense and laser-like as my own; she wanted everything meticulously planned down to the minute. I discovered she hated surprises and being caught off guard, so in order to assuage her anxiety, we needed to discuss hypothetical, what-if scenarios and have plans in case they came to fruition. My method had always been more get-in-grab-get-out, which Mirielle reminded me was due to my immortality. An unbidden image of her corpse began to haunt my dreams after that conversation.

The Kremlin was an odd title for a fortified wall around a hill that originally served as the city center in what humans knew to be Moscow. There were various buildings inside, mostly churches and smaller storage buildings, however it also contained the Ivan the Great Bell Tower (which she assured me was quite famous, but immobile) and the Patriarch Palace. It was the palace we were most interested in because that was where she believed the jewels were held after they were seized from the Winter Palace in former Petrograd, what was now known as St. Petersburg. That was where she said we needed to go.

After weeks of planning, she finally announced she felt ready. Mirielle spent all day at the vanity with a team of castle hair stylists who temporarily dyed her hair a sooty brown color and helped pile it into a loose bun at the nape of her neck so that a black felt hat could rest atop her head. The seamstress had created a black shift-like dress, baggy and worn, that stopped at mid-calf for Mirielle to wear over heavy gray stockings and black leather boots. The makeup team tried to downplay Mirielle's natural beauty, marking her face with blemishes and ruddier complexion than normal, but there wasn't enough makeup in existence for me to see her as anything other than the most stunning creature of all time. We needed her to blend in as a young communist, though, if we were going to gain access to the eggs, and a woman with bright red hair and perfect skin would only draw attention.

As she emerged from my bathroom, bundled in the misshapen clothes and frumpy hat, I felt a surge of something so strong that I wanted to fall to my knees. It was beyond gratitude, though I had that in spades for what she was willing to do for my people. Mirielle was literally risking her life to set us all free. But there was something more, an intense feeling hovering just above the surface, that I could not name. It made me that much more determined to protect her and make myself worthy of the kindness she continued to bestow upon me.

Hairbrushes, cosmetics, and the like all filed out of the room, followed by Darda who closed the door with a snap. Having so many servants in and out of my private chambers would have felt like a huge invasion of privacy months ago, but right now, with all they were doing to protect my Miracle, it barely even registered in the back of my mind. Our little world here in the castle had grown closer—like family—and as I was coming to learn, one didn't need to shut out one's family. I heard the lock twist and sent a prayer to the Universe that they would all be safe while we were gone. Although I had knights posted all along the perimeter, everyone knew the true threat in Aeternitas was me.

Mirielle approached me, gazing up at me with her wide hazel eyes. Her bangs had been brushed back as they would not have been considered normal in the time period to which we were traveling, but I loved the way it opened up more of her face. Even the fake dirt on her nose and forehead could not sway me.

She was gorgeous. And she was *mine*.

I clasped both of her hands in my own and noted a faint tremble. "Everything is going to be fine," I assured her with a confidence I did not entirely feel. "If it is too dangerous, I shall bring you back and return on my own."

"No!" She shook her head and pulled my hands to her heart. "I want to do this! For Mr. Cooper and all my friends...and for you," she finished in whisper.

Sincerity rang from her words. Without giving it a second thought, I crushed my lips to hers, twining my arms around her torso to bring her body flush against mine. This was a kiss to convey a promise, but what that promise was, I did not entirely know. That I placed her life above my own wellbeing? A kiss meant to reveal every thought and feeling I could not put into words? Tightness spread across my chest as my euphoria rose, for she was matching my passion breath for breath, and I swore I felt her heartbeat in time with my own. We were as one in that moment, and it was the greatest moment of my being, no matter what came to pass.

Panting and breathless, Mirielle pulled away, resting her forehead on my chest as she regulated her breathing. My arms wove tighter around her back as I let happiness wash over me like a wave.

"I trust you," she finally whispered.

Just when I thought it impossible for my heart to swell any more, she had to prove me wrong. Mirielle was not someone who trusted others. Her guard had been up since the moment I encountered her at her lab all those months ago. Her confession solidified my resolve and sent an ache through my chest.

"I will protect you. Forever," I swore firmly. No matter what happened, Mirielle would make it out of this day unharmed.

CHAPTER 29

A Dangerous Rendezvous

MIRIELLE

Gryphon led me over to a flaming torch bracketed in a small alcove of the room. It was seemingly innocuous, a space created to provide some light between a long side table and brocade curtains framing the entrance to Gryphon's massive balcony. Yet he stopped abruptly in front of it and turned to face me, his eyes grave.

"What I am about to show you cannot leave this room," he explained. "Nobody can know of its presence here...even Darda," Gryphon added with a sigh.

I could not fathom anything in the castle that Darda did not know of, but still I nodded. "I'll take it to my grave."

He frowned at my words, but did not comment. Turning to pull down the bracket, the stone wall slid away to reveal an antique mirror, curling with the ostentatious swirls of the Baroque period. I barely held back a gasp when I noticed the mirror was not reflecting Gryphon, rather rippling like water after someone dropped a stone in its clear surface.

"This was my mother's mirror," he explained, glancing at me

out of the corner of his eye. "It is enchanted to take us anywhere in time and space I wish to go."

I gulped audibly, but merely nodded. I didn't trust myself to speak at the moment because my stomach wanted to spew the contents of my breakfast.

Without looking back, Gryphon reached his left hand out behind him for me. He had warned me from the beginning that the portal we would use would automatically transport us to the safest location closest to the Faberge eggs. It was a safety mechanism, he had explained, to ensure that we were not walking into an ambush or a trap. But it also meant we had no idea how close we would actually be to our destination.

Gryphon, of course, never had to worry about such things. Even if he didn't have immortality, he was a lethal warrior, built to annihilate in a single blow. When needed, he could sprout wings and fly wherever he needed to go. He had nothing to fear. A fact that I was blatantly reminded of as I side-eyed him now with his sword strapped across his rippling back muscles and magic painting a protective shield over his body.

I shook my head at my misgivings and took his hand, following him through the mirror's portal.

It felt like walking under a cold waterfall without getting wet. One moment I was in Aeternitas, the next I was back in the real world. The portal deposited us in a muddy alley in the dark of night. Stars blinked wearily overhead as if they, too, were cautious of what the night held for us, but it was so refreshing to finally see them again that I couldn't bring myself to care. I didn't realize I had stopped to stare at them, still clutching Gryphon's hand, until his hot breath tickled my ear.

"We can go star gazing another night, Miracle," he murmured.

I turned abruptly away from the sky, noting the tall buildings flanking our sides. There was a small flicker of light at one end of the alley while the other was cloaked in shadow. I didn't see anyone, but that didn't mean there weren't eyes on us like sitting ducks.

"We are alone," Gryphon whispered, reading my thoughts.

It took me a moment to register his beast-like form had returned, wings furled in tight against his back given the tiny space, long claws rippling and posed to strike. His beak was prominent, longer than I remembered, and had I not known his true form, I would have been terrified. He had only explained that it was part of the curse when he entered the human world, but as I observed him in the weak light I wondered if it caused him pain. It certainly looked like it would hurt to undergo such a transformation.

Nodding, I followed the alley towards the light, sticking to the side of the building in the shadows as much as possible. The light shone from a lone streetlamp across the way, making the boarded up shops and restaurants appear much more ominous in the mustard yellow light. The streets were muddy, filled with potholes and puddles of what I hoped was rainwater. Poverty was one of the biggest factors leading to the Russian Revolution and many of the population here should be homeless and starving. While I did not currently see anyone sleeping on the street, it did not mean there weren't others close by.

Beyond the flickers of the solitary light, it was hard to make out where we were in the darkness. I waited for my eyes to adjust so I could detect a landmark of some kind, but before I could, Gryphon pulled me close, resting my back against his chest.

"I'm going to scout overhead," he breathed in my ear. "Arm yourself and wait here."

Nodding once, I snuck a glance back at him over my shoulder, ignoring the sharp beak and focusing on his eyes. They shone like jade beacons in a storm. I could feel a steady thrum of his magic and power emanating from him, but before I could say anything further, he shot into the sky with a flap of his mighty wings.

I pulled my jacket tighter around my body, reaching into an inside pocket located near my breast to withdraw a small knife Gryphon had insisted I bring for protection. We both felt it was too risky for me to have any other weapons since there would likely be people on the edge of desperation all too willing to attack me to get them. I pressed my body flat against the wall behind me, taking another few steps back into the shadows. The eerie quiet reminded me of the moments before Gryphon first appeared, walking out of a glowing portal and scaring the life out of me at my lab in New York. So much had changed in such a short amount of time. I doubted I would ever be the same after all this.

Survive this first, Mirielle, I chided myself.

Every so often I glanced into the skies above to try and detect a trace of Gryphon's location, but I might as well have been wearing a blindfold for all I could see. The moon was barely visible, just a faint sliver crescent to my left.

After several tense minutes, my muscles were too rigid as I stood on high alert and I slid down into a crouched position. I could hear Jimmy's voice echoing in my head not to compromise my vulnerability like that, but my nerves were suddenly too strung out to care. While I had been in martial arts training of some kind for most of my life, I had never actually been in a situation like this where it was literally life or death. Fighting Gryphon when he first appeared didn't really count since I was thrust in that situation without warning. Now, I consciously chose to return to a time period marked with unrest, violent reform, and war knowing the potential consequences. I did not even speak the language, so even if someone were to come upon me, I had no way to communicate with them beyond hand gestures. A load of good that would do me.

Right at that moment, Gryphon descended silently in front of me, his eyes widening in alarm.

My face must have the subtitles on again, I thought.

Before he could even ask, I held up a hand and insisted, "I'm okay. Just anxious."

His face morphed into one of concern as he grasped my hand and pulled me upright. "This is why I didn't want you to come," he reminded me. "How can I help?"

It struck me how different his response was now compared to when I first met him. Although Gryphon constantly reminded me that time worked differently in Aeternitas, it felt as though several months had passed, and during that time his entire demeanor had changed. Yes, he was still a bit of a hothead, but his anger didn't last nearly as long as before. He tended to correct the behavior on his own, too, or at least listened to my responses afterward. Apologies were starting to become more frequent and easier for him to express. Now, here we were in a dangerous situation where the old Gryphon might have snapped and immediately sent me back to the castle, but instead I was met with understanding. It made my heart flutter...not that I had time to dwell on that at the moment.

"I'll be fine." I shook my head firmly, squashing my anxiety as best I could. "The only way to conquer your fear is to face it, right?" My joke was half-hearted, and the skeptical look on his face showed me that he could tell, but he stayed quiet, giving me the chance to change my mind.

After a pause, he nodded and wrapped an arm around my torso. "The Kremlin wall is about half a mile east of here."

Cloaking me with his wing, he pulled me towards the farthest recesses of the alley, away from the light. When it became so dark I couldn't even see my hand in front of my face, I couldn't help but whisper, "Do you have night vision or something?"

I felt his body shake as he contained his chuckle. "Glad to see some skills still impress you," he replied in a low voice.

He steered us down another dark alley behind the shops. More doors and windows were boarded up along this route, and a dog could be heard growling in the distance far behind us. I tried to crane my head to note the dog's location, but Gryphon told me not to bother. "He's not going to get us," he said.

We emerged at the end of a long row of buildings that opened up into a wider square. A few men in dirty, ill-fitting uniforms stood like sentries across from us next to a wooden door that must lead into the Kremlin itself, because a long wall extended into the darkness on both sides. In the daytime, the wall would be a rusty red color, but now everything was cloaked in varying shades of black. The men leaned against the wall casually, smoking cigarettes and chatting amiably. None of them so much as looked in our direction, but I found myself drawing closer to Gryphon, overly cautious due to the Berdan rifles next to them.

Gryphon also retreated a few steps and drew his wing in front of me to shield me from sight. "They weren't here a moment ago. They must have just come through that door."

"So then what do we do now?" I asked, my voice barely a whisper.

His knuckles cracked ominously as he clenched his fists tightly in front of him. "We need a distraction so I can take them out," he explained.

Before he could finish, I was already shaking my head. "No, absolutely not." One of his eyebrows rose, questioning my answer, so I rolled my eyes and elaborated. "They haven't done anything wrong. We're not hurting someone unless there is no other option."

Gryphon looked at me wistfully for a breath before nodding. "Just know that no such mercy will be granted to you if you are captured."

The warning lacing his words made me shiver, but I held firm to my decision. Plus, I was worried about doing anything that would trigger a problem with time since Gryphon's explanation on time travel didn't exactly give me warm and fuzzy feelings. Maybe I would come to regret the decision, maybe not, but for now we needed to backtrack and find another way into the Kremlin.

"There's another doorway I saw about a half a mile or so to the right. Let's go back the way we came and see what we can find," Gryphon offered. Tension radiated from his body and I felt a small stab of guilt for making him worry so much about me.

We retreated backwards with our eyes focused on the sentries outside the door. That's definitely why we didn't notice the guards behind us until I felt the cold muzzle of a gun at the back of my head and heard the distinct click of a bullet being chambered.

CHAPTER 30

Compassion is Powerful

Faster than I would have thought possible, Gryphon whirled around and grabbed the muzzle of the pistol pointed at my head, bending it upward at a 90 degree angle. His right arm swung out simultaneously to strike another guard on the side of his head, but a third man behind the first two was already screaming for help. I could hear the guards from the Kremlin door running towards us, shouting orders at others in Russian.

Gryphon engaged all three of the guards behind us in a fight, disabling their other weapons in a similar manner to the first, where they would all remain inoperable no matter where they fell. I could see the fear and alarm in their eyes as they tried to comprehend his beast-like form. Talons were flying as he sliced at any point of their bodies he could reach, all of them crying out in pain. His wings tucked in tight against his body, shielding his back from the bullets that now began to shoot down the alley.

Gunfire!

My brain registered the sound, but my body didn't react in

time, and before I had time to duck, a white-hot pain seared through my abdomen. I felt the blood soak down my side, though it was hard to see in the dark light. Slumping back against the wall, I quickly sank to the ground.

"MIRIELLE!" Gryphon's roar should have frightened everyone, but by that time, more guards had arrived on each side of the alley. They all had guns pointed at us.

I could sense him reaching to his magic to lash out at the men surrounding us. Shakily, I reached the hand not clutching my side up towards his. My vision was starting to blur around the edges and it was next to impossible not to succumb to the fatigue wanting to envelope me. If he released all of his magic now, he would be useless for probably days, and I was no longer in a state to defend us.

"Don't hurt them," I whispered to Gryphon. "Please don't hurt them."

He crouched down in front of me, wrapping his wings around us. "I have to get you out of here! I can only heal you in Aeternitas!" Gryphon was frantic as he pressed both his hands to the wound in my side, his hands quickly filling with more of my blood.

Before he could say anything else, multiple pairs of hands grasped him by the wings, arms, and neck, pulling him away from me. I felt more hands snatching my arms, attempting to haul me off the ground. Unable to take the pain anymore, I let my eyelids droop as the blackness swallowed me under.

The first thing I registered upon waking was how frigid the temperature was. My breath came out in distinct white puffs above my face and my extremities were too stiff to move properly. The rough rock underneath me certainly didn't help as it was nearly ice cold to my touch.

Blinking away the blurry edges of my vision, I slowly turned my head to the right. I was lying on the ground inside another cell. *I'm sure imprisoned a lot for someone who's never committed a crime,* I thought wryly. The biggest difference between this cell and the one in Aeternitas was the guard in a threadbare overcoat standing outside the metal grate. When he saw my eyes were open, he yelled out in Russian to someone beyond my line of sight.

I figured this was my sign to sit up, but the pain radiating down my side quickly snuffed out that idea. As stiff as my fingers felt, I was able to gingerly brush them across a large bandage wrapped around my midsection. It must have been the reminder my brain needed because suddenly searing pain was all I could feel. My head was throbbing and there was a dull ache constantly radiating from where the bullet made contact.

A man in a furry black hat and long gray coat rapped on the grate with his knuckles. His eyes were dark and colder than the air in the room, making an involuntary shiver ripple down my spine. I couldn't see his hair, but he sported a beard long enough to tuck into his pants. Power surged from him. I had a feeling he was the one in charge.

"Where's Gryphon?" I asked. My voice was raspier than I expected, like I smoked a pack a day.

"I ask question. You answer," the man replied in a thick accent.

My snort was more of a reaction to the image of a mafia hitman his accent conjured than what he actually said. I hadn't really expected an answer.

Turning my head upward, I focused instead on sitting upright.

I had to use the wall along my left side to pull my torso off the ground. The room spun temporarily, but I managed to sit up enough to lean against the wall and get more of my bearings. My wrists were bound by thick rope to metal hoops on the wall and the movement made the abrasive material burn against my skin.

The Russian man kept his eyes on me with a calculated look that made my blood run cold. "Name?" he demanded.

Gryphon and I had agreed in all our planning that it would be better for me to use a pseudonym in case anything was ever written down about someone encountering me. If a historical text ever contained the name Mirielle, it would be far more memorable than a simple name, which is what I offered now. "Mary."

The man nodded. "Comrade Nikonovich," he identified himself. "I am in charge here." He began to pace in front of the cell door, looking at me out of the corner of his eye. "You broke curfew, Mary."

Inwardly I rolled my eyes, but outwardly I merely glared at him. "I've been known to do that a time or two. Where's Gryphon?"

"Your monster?" Nikonovich countered. "He uncooperative." The curl of the man's lips indicated how much he enjoyed Gryphon's defiance.

As if on cue, a cry of pain echoed down the chamber. It was too distant to tell if it was Gryphon, but my mind pictured a hundred different images of ways they could be brutalizing him. There was no way of knowing if he had attempted to use any magic, but if he had, he could be weak and vulnerable. And they were bound to notice that he never died, no matter how they tortured him. Somehow a sense told me he was in trouble, like I suddenly had ESP. It was a direct connection to him that told me he was in terrible pain. It was gut wrenching, and I felt an overwhelming need to get to him. I had to make sure he was okay, to protect him the way he had been trying to protect me all this time.

My glare was enough to at least give the comrade pause. His self-satisfied smirk dropped for a moment before he shook his head and began pacing in front of the cell door again.

"Clearly you are American spy, so I give you one chance to tell me what you want. Then I cause much pain."

He doesn't know any better, I reminded myself before I snorted derisively. It wouldn't do me any good to argue because the Russian Revolution was already unfolding. By the end of this year, the entire country would be reconfigured by the Communist party and rebranded as the USSR, the Union of Soviet Socialist Republics. It would remain such until the early 1990's. It was actually the regime that forced Mr. Cooper to flee Armenia and emigrate to the United States.

"I am not a spy," I replied, hoping my voice sounded more confident than I felt. "I am an American who is sympathetic to your cause and came to learn more about socialist reform." It was a lie that slipped out easily enough at the moment, though I had no idea if anything of the kind had ever happened at that time. I was playing with fire, but at that moment, it seemed the safest option if it got me out of this cell and closer to Gryphon.

Nikonovich's burly eyebrows scrunched together as he considered my explanation. His dark eyes did not give a single thought away, but I tried to maintain eye contact and avoid blinking just the same. After several tense seconds, he revealed a sinister smile that made my heart drop to the pit of my stomach.

He barked an order to another guard I could not see and the rough clanking of cold metal hitting cold metal rattled through the chamber. Two men in black fur coats entered the room holding long rifles. I scrambled to stand, but Comrade Nikonovich snapped another order and before I could move, I was being assaulted by the ends of both rifles. One man sent a sharp kick into my stomach, and it was all I could do to curl up in the fetal position, using my arms to shield my face and head as best they could. My vision blurred as the butt of a rifle hit the exact spot where the bullet had penetrated my abdomen, razor sharp pain shocking my system.

"No more!" the Comrade commanded. Blood filled my mouth and my right eye was swelling shut from where I had been struck, but I sat up enough to spit the blood in his direction. *Fuck him.*

He responded by giving me another evil smile.

"Fix answer for next time," he said in broken English.

Once the echoes of the guards' footsteps died down the hallway, I allowed myself to stretch out and assess the damage. My entire right side was bruised and I suspected my ulna was fractured. Gingerly, I braced my left arm around the bandage on my torso and pulled it back in disgust. My entire arm was soaked with blood. I was too scared to look down.

"Gryphon!" I whispered before once again allowing the darkness to swallow me whole.

CHAPTER 31

Priority #1

GRYPHON

My head snapped up abruptly, like an invisible puppet master pulled on my strings. I had the overwhelming sense that Mirielle was suffering and in grave danger. Cold water dripped down my face from where the Russian guards had held my head in a metal tub full of water. That was before they tried to take a saw to my wings, but after they used a torch against my skin. Now my hands were strung up above me as I dangled a few feet off the ground in a windowless room. There was a drain in the center of the floor that was rimmed in rust colored stains that I knew came from blood. I shuddered to think of how many people had caused those stains in this room before me.

Without a clock or hourglass, it was hard to determine how long I had been locked inside this chamber, but I was desperate to find Mirielle. She needed proper medical care for the gunshot wound to her abdomen or she could die, which was a reality I refused to accept. Although she had asked me not to use my magic to hurt any of our jailers, in truth, my rage boiled so strongly that I was afraid unleashing it would mean the death of every living creature in a ten mile radius. My imagination ran wild with unbidden memories of her clasping her tiny hands over the gaping hole in her side, causing the bile to rise in my throat after my stomach had long since emptied its contents.

The image kept my mind sharp and focused during the humans' so-called torture sessions; they were more of an annoyance than anything. While I still experienced pain and discomfort, my regenerative capabilities were strong enough that the burns on my flesh healed within minutes and my lungs returned to normal function before they hauled the wash basin from the room. I was too concerned with leaving this place to find her to care much about what the humans attempted to do to me. It was unusual for my powers to be so strong, but that was an issue to examine after I safely returned Mirielle to Aeternitas.

Without warning the door to the chamber burst open with a loud bang and a slew of guards entered and pointed their guns at me. A taller man with a furry black hat entered next and stopped right in front of the door, behind the line of firearms.

He barked an order at the guards in Russian, probably assuming I could not understand him. "Do not fire! We need him!" The man then switched to broken English to address me. "I spoke to girl."

Flames erupted in my gut. If that man had harmed a hair on Mirielle's head, I would ensure that not only was his death slow and painful, but he would spend all of eternity having his body broken repeatedly.

"What you after?" the man continued.

I merely glared at him, envisioning all the different ways I could end his life. Unless I had the chance to do it 100 times over, I doubt it would bring me enough satisfaction to ease my anger.

He smirked. "Where you from?"

My teeth ground against the restraint I felt for not snapping the chains from my wrists and cracking the man's skull into the cement behind him. "I will tell you nothing until I see the girl," I replied in clear Russian.

The man leered at me, baring yellow-stained teeth, only showing a brief moment of shock that I could speak his language. "I am Comrade Nikonovich. I make rules," he snapped.

My magic was curling so strongly in my fingertips right now that they began to ache. Self-preservation was kicking in, and my body's natural instinct to use my powers in defense was going to make me act. I feigned as though I was merely trying to crack my neck while rotating my head in a circle, but in reality, I wanted to ensure there wasn't a jade green glow emanating from between my hands.

The iron cuffs around my wrists, however, were starting to grow warm from the heat my magic gave off. *That* was definitely something they were bound to notice.

"Take me to the girl," I repeated, gritting my teeth as I prepared to break free from the cuffs.

Comrade Nikonovich ignored me and instead issued another order to the guards. "Two of you will remain here to watch him. The rest, come with me."

Two would be far easier to subdue. Perhaps luck was on my side for the moment.

As the guards filed out behind their leader, I pushed my wrists closer together to maintain the façade. The iron was all but gone in between my wrists; I had mere moments to act. The door slammed loudly and stomping feet echoed down the hall to the left. My body sprang into action, dropping me to the floor where I landed on the balls of my feet, wings tucked in tightly against my back.

Both guards immediately opened fire, but their arms were shaking with such fear that their aim was barely accurate enough to hit the wall behind me. Swiftly, I crossed the room to grab each of their heads in one of my hands and shoved them together. There was a loud crunch from their skulls cracking against one another before they crumpled into a heap on the floor. Hopefully I struck them hard enough that they would not remember much.

Millenia's worth of training taught me how to be deft and silent on my feet. Wrenching the door open, I found a long stone corridor branching in both directions. Only a single lantern hung to my left at the juncture of a turn. There were no other guards and no other doors. Since the comrade's retreating form had echoed to the left, I went to the right.

The hall melted into darkness. I could feel periodic drips of water staining the walls as I ran my fingers along to keep myself on course. The air smelled earthy, a sign that we were subterranean, and although there was the occasional turn or door, I saw no other signs of life. Every door I tried was locked. After several minutes of wandering, it was entirely possible that I walked in a giant circle. There was no way to get my bearings.

At long last a set of stone stairs ascended to a small landing with a door. This door was a darker, more polished wood than the others I had seen, which gave me hope that it would lead some-where meaningful whereby I had access to escape.

I emerged in a narrow courtyard. Judging by the fiery orange light casting a haze over everything, the sun was setting, though I did not know if only one day had passed or ten. Across the way a guard began shouting at me, raising a hand to signal me to stop, but he had no sooner taken two steps than I was airborne, my wings flapping quickly.

When I was in the human world, my wings typically had an

iridescent lining that offered a sort of camouflage to the human eye whenever I was actually in flight. Mirielle had compared it to the inside of a conch seashell. As soon as my wings took me high enough to pass the top of the building, concealment took over and I knew the guard could no longer see me.

From this vantage point it was easy to ascertain that I had been housed at the Kremlin Armory, the building where all the weapons and ammunition were held. Mirielle had suspected the revolutionary forces would have a stockpile of guns there as they attempted to arm citizens on their side in Russia's civil war. It was a dangerous place to be, with most of their forces comprising of militia rather than a designated army. I needed to find better cover immediately.

Now, though, I found my heart sparring with my mind. One desperately wanted to find Mirielle and get her back to my realm where my healing powers could address her gunshot wound. I refused to acknowledge that I might only find her corpse. A nagging voice in the back of my mind (that sounded an awful lot like Mirielle's, truth be told) insisted that this was the perfect opportunity for me to locate the lost Faberge eggs. The Patriarch Palace, where she believed they were being kept, was in my peripheral vision on the right.

So what comes first? I thought humorlessly. *My miracle or the egg?*

CHAPTER 32

Necessary Evil

GRYPHON

It was an outrageous question, and I burned with shame for even considering it. Mirielle came first. She would *always* come first. I began to circle the walls of the Kremlin, attempting to dig into the sensation in the core of my being telling me Mirielle was on the verge of death. It was the strangest feeling; like I was connected to her on some sort of spiritual level.

There were only one or two guards posted outside the doorways in and out of the Kremlin and in front of buildings that must house people or things of importance. They would not spare manpower to protect empty, worthless buildings. As I flew above, a congregation of guards in front of the Patriarch Palace caught my attention. There were far more there than anywhere else, and all of their gazes were locked skyward, rifles already pointed upward. Comrade Nikonovich only knew of my desire to return to Mirielle, not the egg, so that had to be where they were keeping her.

I grinned. *Sometimes humans make things too easy.*

Rising higher, my wings flapped harder to gain several feet in height before I abruptly dove at a 45 degree angle, barreling towards the guards. My momentum built as I hurtled closer and I threw my weight to the right so that my body began rotating like a torpedo into the guards. They were all clustered so close together that once I was in their presence, I knocked them all down like dominoes. A few tried to get back up, but some well-placed blows to their heads incapacitated them. After only a few minutes, I stood panting in the center of what looked like fallen human bowling pins.

It was too risky to go through that entrance because the likelihood of there being more guards just across the threshold was high. Instead I flew up to the second story and glanced through the windows to find an empty room that might provide better access. On the back side of the building, a darkened balcony held promise.

Landing gently on the ledge, I tucked my legs underneath me to tumble across the floor of the balcony, then righted myself with my back against the wall next to the doorway. I paused a moment to listen for the sounds of life inside but heard nothing. Stealing a peek in the glass of the door, all I observed was darkness. My hand grasped the door handle and I sent power through my fingertips to melt the locking mechanism inside so the door would open. Mirielle's presence felt stronger; I knew she was here somewhere.

The room inside was a cluster of more human junk. It had never ceased to amaze me the way humans clung to objects and accumulated possessions beyond their own needs. My parents were much the same, insisting on enormous rooms in the castle to be filled with things serving no purpose beyond the servants having more to clean. This room was storage of some kind, judging by the large number of wooden crates stacked haphazardly. I could only just make out the outline of another door on the other side of the room.

Walking through the maze, I could hear guards shouting

outside the interior door. Their footsteps were heading away from my location and as the sound faded, I opened the door a fraction to glance in the hallway. Empty.

I kept my back along the wall and crept slowly down the length of the hallway, allowing my sense of Mirielle to guide me. No other guards materialized. They must have discovered the damage out front and all gone to investigate further. A staircase led me down to the first floor near the front door, and my suspicions were confirmed when I heard them arguing about what had happened in Russian. One guard snapped an order to notify Nikonovich, which hastened my speed.

Where are you, Miracle?

I closed my eyes and urged my feelings for her to come to the forefront, blocking out all other senses momentarily. It was urging me downward, subterranean again, but I could not see another staircase. Going through several antechambers, I stopped abruptly inside a human church. I vaguely remembered Mirielle's explanation that the palace was actually a church and not a traditional palace like that of Aeternitas, but in that moment I had been too distracted by the way her bangs fell into her eyes and the happiness they radiated to really pay proper attention to what she said.

Human churches tended to make the hairs on the back of my neck stand up. Religion was an entirely human custom, and no matter how many times I watched the mortals pray to their deities, it never prevented or stopped any destruction or harm from happening. So many deaths occurred on the premise that it was what a particular god or goddess wanted, yet nothing ever prospered or changed. It made my lip curl in disgust.

This particular church was far too ostentatious for my taste. There were large panels of Jesus Christ as well as murals on the upper part of the walls depicting him with his disciples. Gold framed nearly every surface, making the room glow even in the dim light from an assortment of candles around the room. There were wooden pews that looked far too uncomfortable to sit in, but perhaps that made it easier for the humans to focus on their prayers. Torture devices could sometimes bring about intense concentration.

An alarm bell went off in the recesses of my mind on alert for Mirielle that she was in serious trouble. It drew my attention swiftly to the left, where an altar with a few gold candlesticks was pressed against a wall. As I stepped closer, a cold current of air assaulted my face, making me notice the faint crack along the left side where the altar did not quite meet the wall. It was there to conceal a passageway.

Cramped stone stairs led down to a stone hallway identical to the one from which I escaped. The temperature dropped substantially, and although I did not feel the cold, I worried for how the frigid air would affect Mirielle. My sense of her was growing, but so was my trepidation that I was walking into a trap. I longed to feel the comfort of my sword at my back, long since stolen from by the Russian guards. The talons my fingers sported were deadly enough but my sword was my weapon of choice.

The narrow hall widened enough to accommodate two people and a torch bracketed to the wall produced ominously flickering light amongst the shadows. The air smelled like decay, which sent a shiver down my spine far more than the icy air. A whimper came from a grated cell door to my right.

"Mirielle!" I whispered in relief.

However, the sight in the cell once I darted to the door made my stomach drop. Comrade Nikonovich was holding a barely conscious Mirielle against his chest, a small handgun pointed to her temple. Blood soaked her clothing from the waist down, and the right side of her face was bruised and swollen.

Fury pounded through my veins and I felt my magic surge to greet it like an old friend.

"One move and girl dies," Nikonovich taunted me. He pressed the barrel harder into her head as if to prove his power. Another whimper escaped Mirielle's mouth.

It was the whimper that did me in. My power roared in response and sent an emerald green ball of fire through the iron of the cell door, directly into Comrade Nikonovich's face. He screamed in pain, clutching his face as the skin sizzled and popped in the heat. The weapon was immediately forgotten, discarded to the floor a few feet away.

Mirielle dropped, too, crumpling to the ground with a thud. She did not stir and a wave of panic washed over me. I sent another blast of power to obliterate the rest of the door, swiping my talons across the comrade's exposed jugular, barely registering the enjoyment when his blood gurgled.

I raced over to her and dropped to my knees. Turning her so that her body was laying properly on her back, I felt a faint pulse along her wrist and assessed the damage. Her facial lacerations would have to wait. The gunshot wound was the real threat, killing her slowly. I doubted any kind of healer here had removed the bullet. We needed to return to Aeternitas immediately, but first we had to find our way back to the mirror's portal. Despite how strong my magic felt at the moment, I would never risk her safety by trying to teleport now.

"Miracle," I whispered, completely uncaring of how my voice caught in my throat that threatened to swell close. "I'm taking you home. It's going to be alright."

As gently as I could, I slid my arms under her knees and

behind her back, standing up so that she rested in my arms. She stirred enough to bring her forehead against my neck. I thought I heard the faint sound of my name leave her lips, but I couldn't be sure.

Returning to the balcony upstairs was a race against time. As we emerged in the cathedral, a guard that had to be no older than twelve shouted at me in Russian to stop, but all I had to do was snarl at him to send him running from the room. Nearing the front door, I could hear more of them coming to storm the palace in an ambush. I darted up the stairs and down the hallway to the storage room with the balcony. If I could get us in the air, it would be easier to locate the mirror's portal.

Mirielle rustled against my neck as soon as I entered the dark room with the balcony. This time I heard her command to stop and abruptly skidded on my heels. Her eyes were open, but barely, and she squinted towards the farthest corner of the room.

I followed her line of sight and noted a twinkle of light coming from something inside one of the crates. There was a small beam of light from a streetlamp outside filtering in through the door's window that caught the item perfectly to illuminate it in the dark space.

"Get closer," she mumbled.

I let out an exasperated sigh, but wove through the teetering crates to the corner. It wasn't like I could ever deny her anything.

There, resplendent in jeweled glory, was a crate full of Faberge eggs. The largest one cradled in the middle exactly matched Mirielle's description of the Hen with Sapphire Pendant. The gold twinkled ominously in the light as though mocking our plight.

"Take them," Mirielle muttered. Her words were laced with

pain, whether from her battered jaw or her gunshot wound, I could not be sure.

"You'll have to hold them…" I hedged. It was insanity to snatch these now with her barely clinging to life and guards right on our heels. I could already hear their loud stomps up the stairs and calls to check all the rooms and alcoves. "We need to leave NOW."

She nodded. "Just put me on your back. I can hold on."

"Never," I breathed, infuriated with the idea. It would be too risky in the best of circumstances to fly with her on my back.

Mirielle reared her head back to look at me, fully opening her left eye. "We came here to save your people, Gryphon," she said. "It can't be for nothing. We are taking the eggs."

The shouting from the guards was growing louder. They were closing in on us. We had mere moments. "Fuck the eggs, Mirielle!" I burst out in an angry whisper. "I need you to *live*."

Her smile, even as bloody and jagged as it was with her injuries, was like a balm straight to my heart. All my fears and agitation slipped away. I found myself gripping her tighter against my body, resting my forehead against hers. "I've got the eggs," she whispered. "You just hold on to me."

"Forever," I countered.

She jerked her legs down out of my arms and leaned forward to tightly wrap her arms around the crate. I hated the loss of pressure against her abdomen, but I knew her steely resolve too well to refuse her. She clutched the crate to her chest and I swept my arm under her knees again so she was cradled in my arms again. The crate was heavy, adding a lot of extra weight that would greatly slow us down, but I knew Mirielle would not leave without them.

We had just reached the outside door when the door behind us burst open, three guards pointing their guns inside. "FIRE!" one thundered at the sight of us.

A spray of bullets hit my wings that had instantly folded against my back to protect me. I kicked through the outside door, sending wood splinters flying. Mirielle ducked her face into my chest to escape the debris and I launched myself over the balcony. Several other guards stood below, rifles pointed in the sky towards us, and opened fire.

I redirected my efforts upward, my wings beating madly to propel us skyward. We rose well over thirty feet, and it wasn't enough. I roared in pain as a bullet nicked my left bicep.

"Are you hurt?!" I yelled to Mirielle.

"No!" she screamed. "Go! Go!"

The pain and wrath from the bullet hitting my skin sent a surge of magic through me so powerful stars burst in front of my eyes. I felt it shoot out of my body and heard the cries of agony below as it hit the guards. My magic had never felt so strong, not even before the curse.

That must be why it took me a moment to register there was no longer any weight in my arms. I looked down in horror to see Mirielle's ashen face locked in a silent scream as she plummeted towards the ground below. She still clutched the crate to her chest, holding on for dear life in the free fall.

There wasn't a moment to lose. I pointed my hand, palm out, at her and used my magic to open my own portal just beneath her. She pelted down through the greenish-gold smoke and collapsed onto my bed back in Aeternitas. The wind leaving her body on impact was the last sound I heard before I crash-landed onto the stone floor in my bedchamber, my voice hoarse and terrified as I bellowed for Darda.

CHAPTER 33

A Loss

GRYPHON

It had been the equivalent of eight days since Mirielle and I crash landed through the portal and still she slumbered. After Darda arrived, she guided me on how to best clean Mirielle's gunshot wound, but neither of us knew the best way to get the bullet out of her body. There was no exit wound, so I knew it was lodged somewhere internally and leaving it would only increase her chances of dying. Darda immediately went to the castle staff and located someone who had experience with these types of injuries.

That was how Mateo the butcher's knife wound up in my bed chamber, along with about a dozen or so more of Mirielle's closest friends who were now frantic with worry. In another life that would have ignited my temper, but now, with her very life thread hanging in the balance, I did not register the intrusion. Her beloved Mr. Cooper, Anastasia, Wade, and Ambrose were never more than an arm's length away, and I knew that if she woke —*when* she woke—she would want to see them so I permitted them to remain.

Mateo had been a Spanish soldier in their Civil War, although he could not remember all of it, and had survived a similar gunshot wound. He provided instructions in Spanish to clean the entry point of the bullet with soap and warm water along with the instruments I would be using. Blood was everywhere, saturating the mattress and bedding, which he felt was a sign that the bullet may have nicked an artery. I knew I would be able to heal it as long as I found the bullet first, but he advised there was no way to locate it without going in blind.

At that point, Wade made an offhand comment that he thought there were medical devices now that could locate a bullet inside a body, but he had no idea why he knew that. His memory didn't expand enough to tell me what it was called so I could return to the human world and retrieve one. It frustrated me to feel so clueless about the mortal world. I should have recruited a healer of some kind after Mirielle's last injury!

Bracing myself, I placed a firm hand on the flat plane of Mirielle's abdomen and used a pair of long tweezer-like forceps to push into the hole in her side. I felt grateful she had blacked out because I could not imagine the agony she would be in if I attempted this while she was awake. The wound was approximately four inches above her hip bone, so Mateo said I should not hit bone right away. Therefore, when I probed the device further into her wound, with more blood gurgling out in the process, and struck something harder, it gave me pause. He advised me to gently clamp the hard thing in question and see if it would move. It took me three tries to use the forceps properly given how unfamiliar I was with such an object, but on the last attempt, I felt the hard spot move. Success!

As quickly as I could, I withdrew the forceps and held up their contents for Mateo to examine. Based on what he could remember, he thought the bullet was complete, meaning there were no other fragments to retrieve. He admitted that he did not recognize the type of bullet or know much about weaponry, though.

I could practically feel the life force draining from Mirielle's body now that the bullet had been dislodged. There was more blood gushing out now and Darda barked an order for me to apply lots of pressure with the bandages she retrieved. With both my hands placed over the wound, bearing down on the gauze beneath my fingers, I called upon my own healing powers like I had before and projected them into Mirielle. I pictured her alive and well, smiling at me from her worktable, her bright red bangs falling into eyes filled with mirth. In my vision she had decided to stay with me in Aeternitas, and we were both ready to celebrate her decision.

The truth before me was far different. Mirielle's skin was so pale that she resembled a corpse, and her breathing was harsh and shallow. She had lost so much blood...how much damage could a human body take?

My powers felt stronger than they ever had before the curse. Despite using them for their regenerative capabilities now, I did not feel fatigued or weakened. I felt Darda's scrutiny in the background, making me wonder idly if my eyes were glowing gold again like Mirielle always pointed out to me, but after several minutes of willing my magic to heal her, I withdrew my hands to assess the situation. The blood flow had finally stopped and the bullet hole had closed, albeit with a rough, jagged scar. Mirielle remained as pale as ever, though her breathing had improved.

"There's nothing to do now but wait, dearie," Darda gently guided me. Her presence melted around me like a comforting blanket.

Her words moved me to break down into sobs, emotions of fear and despair no longer at bay. She had spoken to me like a mother consoling her child, not like a servant to her master, and it was exactly what I needed. I barely noticed her ushering the others out into the antechamber, but could not stop myself from uttering my deepest fear out loud. "What if I lose her?"

Darda returned and it was like she placed a loving hand on my shoulder, just as she had when I was a lad. "We never lose the ones we love," she whispered softly.

That only made me cry harder because she was right. I loved Mirielle, and the thought of her light leaving this world was an immeasurable pain. My miracle needed to live up to her name and return to us.

In the days that had passed since, Mirielle remained asleep, just like her recovery after the Elemental attack, only this time I could not see any improvements as the days wore on. Color never returned to her skin, she remained cold to my touch despite the warm fire and fur blankets Darda provided, and her breathing remained shallow. Her pulse was weak, but it was there, so my caretaker continued to remind me to have faith that my magic would heal her.

I could barely bring myself to leave her side. The rest of the castle occupants took turns sitting with us, talking to Mirielle as if she were awake and wanted to know the latest reports on the restoration work in the warehouse. She never stirred. They all became disheartened after the first few days, probably thinking I could not hear their whispered arguments in the antechamber outside my room about whether or not she would wake, but I tuned them out as best I could. Whenever it happened, I would lean forward from my bedside chair and gently stroke her head.

"Don't listen to them, Miracle," I would say. "Come home to us. To me."

Food no longer held any appeal and days went by before Darda threatened to imprison me in the tower if I did not eat something. Sleep evaded me like the sunlight outside Aeternitas for I was too fearful of missing the moment when her beautiful eyes opened. I wanted to be the first thing she saw when she awoke, mostly to save my own sanity and know it was real.

As one day bled into the next that bled into the next, I began to devolve into crying fits again. It seemed like such a cruel twist of Fate to bring someone as important as Mirielle into my life only to tragically lose her so soon. I needed more *time*. Ironic, given our location. Darda offered gentle reassurance, but I could tell that she worried about me just as much as Mirielle. I had never been so attached to someone and did not know how to navigate the feeling of grief...even losing my parents to the curse hadn't registered with me emotionally like this. I was becoming a shell of who I used to be, but all of it paled in comparison to Mirielle's suffering.

Regret must be the deadliest of emotions because it ate me alive. I regretted leaving Mirielle alone in that alleyway. I regretted not shielding her sooner to prevent the bullet from hurting her. I regretted not using my magic as soon as they all converged on us, her compassionate heart be damned. Truth be told, I regretted taking her to the Kremlin in the first place. My common sense must have lost a fight with my cock because my need to impress her had allowed me to risk her safety with that single decision. And now...

The only thing I couldn't bring myself to regret was having Mirielle here in Aeternitas. She opened my eyes to so many things. The quality of not only my life, but my staff's life and the other castle inhabitants affected by my mother's curse had significantly changed for the better. I finally knew how it felt to have the respect and admiration of my subjects, and the sense of hope it renewed for a future in Aeternitas was a debt I could never repay. Mirielle had permanently changed this realm—permanently changed me—whether she meant to or not.

"Please open your eyes, Mirielle," I quietly urged her once more. A hot tear rolled down my cheek, landing on her cold hand clutched in my own. "Please come back to me."

CHAPTER 34

Dream or Nightmare?

MIRIELLE

A tingling sensation began to build in my toes and my fingers, but it hurt too much to move anything. My entire body felt as though it was crushed by a meteor, patched back together too quickly, then decimated again. It was safer in the black void where I had escaped and currently resided in. Although I could vaguely register soft voices whispering in my vicinity, they were as light as an echo of the wind. I was content right where I was, even if I had no idea *where* that was.

Somewhere in the recesses of my mind, a tiny voice reminded me that Gryphon was injured, too, and while I wanted to check on him, I wasn't quite ready to leave this place. It might be dark, but it was oddly comforting. So much so that I began to wonder if I had been here before. There was an almost smoky, sepia-tinted filter on my surroundings, which was absurd because there was nothing around me. A cloaked figure was approaching me out of the darkest shadows, their face mostly obscured by the hood. They stopped too far away for me to discern any visible features through the smoke.

"You must take the journal, Mirielle," a feminine voice said. *A familiar voice...*

I tried to shake my head because I had no idea what journal the voice meant, but it was still too painful to move.

"His journal will tell you everything! You must take it!" the voice commanded again.

The cloaked figure faded back into the shadows and the smoke began to dissipate. I was left in the black abyss, alone once more. It seemed like a good time to rest.

It could have been seconds that passed or it could have been years. When I started to feel more aware again, I noticed the tingling sensation was not as strong as before. Movement no longer seemed so daunting, although it felt exhausting. I tried to move my fingers to test my abilities and a warm hand clasped mine.

"Mirielle!" Gryphon cried out. Only it sounded muffled, like I heard the remnants of his voice at the bottom of a well. I tried to flutter my eyes open, to see him and reassure him that I was here, but my eyelids did not want to cooperate. Wrenching them open would hurt too much, I decided, and instead let my hand go limp in his. It was better to go back to sleep. Yes, sleep felt better than anything.

The next time my consciousness returned, I was fully aware of all my extremities. While everything was sore, it was not altogether painful. More like the kind of muscle fatigue you felt after a really good workout. *That* I was all too familiar with, thanks to Jimmy. Give me the right recovery drink and I would be up in no time.

Ever so slowly, I opened my eyes, first taking in the room through my lashes. I was back in Gryphon's bedroom, nestled into warm blankets on his bed, while Gryphon himself was sitting in a chair beside me. His head was resting on the edge of the mattress next to me, his hand still firmly clutching my own.

My heart wanted to melt at his tenderness. I squeezed his palm gently, not wanting to startle him, but at least let him know I was awake.

He jumped as if electrocuted, eyes darting frantically to search my face. The smile he offered when his eyes met mine could have powered the sun. It was dazzling, and for what felt like the millionth time, I was blown away by his spectacular beauty. His molten eyes were green, but quickly morphing into gold, and I wanted to quiver at their intensity.

"Hey," I mumbled lamely. My voice didn't sound like my own, too gruff and raspy, a sure sign that I hadn't used it in a while. "What happened?"

Gryphon continued to smile at me, both of his hands clasped tightly around my own. He remained seated in the chair, but a solitary tear rolled down his cheek as he gazed at me. "I healed you," he finally said.

I started to nod, but stopped when my neck all but screamed in protest. "How long was I asleep?"

At this, Gryphon's face fell and he became somber. He reached up to tenderly brush his palm against my cheek. "You have been sleeping for almost three weeks," he sighed.

Three weeks?! I couldn't really remember what happened. Random, sporadic images came to mind without any sense of recognition, but it was like trying to catch smoke with a net. I couldn't hold onto anything for more than a moment.

"No wonder I'm hungry," I joked halfheartedly because I didn't know what to say.

He let out a watery laugh. "I'll have Cook make you something, but first I have to let everyone know you are awake or Emil might choke me."

My eyebrows rose in surprise. "Has Mr. Cooper been here?"

Gryphon nodded. "All of your friends have taken turns sitting with you. You are the most beloved resident of Aeternitas, it seems."

Right on cue, Mr. Cooper and Anastasia entered along with Darda. I smiled as warmly as I could at both of them.

Anastasia cried out, "She lives!" making all of us laugh.

Gryphon shifted so that he was sitting on the edge of the mattress next to me and helped me sit up a little more, propping the pillows up behind me. Everyone began filling me in on the progress of the timeline in the warehouse. Apparently, Ambrose had been overseeing everything in my absence, but he was surly when giving daily assignments, which was causing some ill will to roll his way. Anastasia had us all in stitches again when she gave a near spot on impression of Ambrose's rough voice barking out, "Now, now!" as he was fond of saying.

My friends had been there for around 30 minutes when it dawned on me that Gryphon still sat next to me on the mattress, one hand clutching mine. He was engaging with Mr. Cooper and Anastasia more than I had ever seen him do before, but there was an edge to his posture and an undercurrent to the tone of his voice that made me wish to be alone with him again. I had thought there was relief in his eyes earlier...had I been wrong? What was upsetting him?

"Oh my god, we didn't break the curse!" I suddenly burst out.

Gryphon's head turned sharply in my direction. Darda must have recognized something in his expression because she quickly mumbled an excuse and the three others left the room immediately. When the door shut firmly behind them Gryphon rose and crossed to the middle of the room, facing me with the same resolute stance that I had come to recognize as a sign of the old Gryphon.

"The Faberge eggs have been added to my collection," he explained, "but no, they did not trigger anything in regard to the curse. It was all for naught." His jaw clenched at that admission and shame washed over me.

"I'm so sorry, Gryphon," I whispered, willing myself not to cry. "I really thought one of those would be the treasure. Here, let's go look at my notes..." I flung the blankets off and tried to swing my legs over the side of the bed.

He was at my side in two seconds. "You'll do no such thing!" Gryphon snapped. "Return to that bed at once!" Two firm hands grasped my shoulders and shoved me back down.

Guilt was overriding my common sense because I knew all too well not to push him, but for some reason my body chose violence and I stood back up, meeting him chest to chest. "I have work to do! MOVE!"

I attempted to sidestep him as an arm with the force of iron clamped around my waist and pressed me onto the mattress again. It was too hard against my gunshot wound, the sudden twist of pain making me hesitate to fight back. That was all the opportunity Gryphon needed to wrestle my legs back onto the bed so I was laying down like before. When I tried to sit back up, he moved to straddle me, using both his arms to pin my wrists above my head.

"We have to fix this, Gryphon!" I yelled, straining as much as I could to break his hold on my wrists. "I have to break the curse!"

He only applied more force and locked his knees around my thighs. "Keep fighting me, Mirielle, and I shall take great pleasure in tying you to my bed!"

My mouth dropped open with an audible pop. One glance down told me that he was enjoying this position a little too much. All of my sass disappeared in an instant, replaced by panic and lust. Panic because as much as I wanted him to be my first, it would still be my first time. Lust because hello—he was chiseled to perfection and as gorgeous as a god.

"You...we're..." I stuttered. My mouth had gone dry and I found it difficult to form coherent sentences. Gryphon adjusted his weight so that he no longer pinned my wrists down and instead laid on the bed beside me. His entire body pressed alongside me, one leg intertwined between mine, and pulled my hands down to hold against my chest. We gazed at one another, and I felt something stir in my chest.

"The only thing you have to do is rest, Miracle," Gryphon said. The hand not holding my hands against my chest began faintly grazing my cheek.

Tears began to well in my eyes as I started to register the ramifications of what he was saying. "But the curse," I squeaked out. "Mr. Cooper...Wade...what about my friends?" I didn't want to cry, but it was hard to hold back the floodgates.

Gryphon pulled me into his chest, resting his chin on my head as he held me. "You were wonderful, Mirielle," he replied. "No one could have done more."

I refused to accept the comfort he offered. My mind whirled like a rolodex as I tried to mentally go through my notes and the timeline in the warehouse. There were still so many places we could look! We just needed more time—and time was frozen here, so why couldn't we keep searching?

"Gryphon?" I drew back from him so I could look him in the eye for my next question. All the time we had spent together meant I had learned Gryphon's body language, and I felt pretty confident that I had picked up on his cues when he was trying to hide something from me. "How do you know that time is running out if there is no such thing as time in Aeternitas?"

Instead of changing the subject or ignoring me as I had anticipated, he smirked at me. "Ever the scientist," he murmured, brushing my bangs away from my eyes. "There is nothing but time in Aeternitas. But come. If anyone has earned the right to know the truth, it is you."

He extracted himself from my limbs before helping me to stand. The movement didn't hurt, but he continued to fuss and insisted on placing an arm around my shoulders to support me. He guided me through the bedroom and onto the enormous stone terrace. Sensing my hesitation in the doorway, Gryphon gave me a small smile of encouragement and squeezed my shoulders in reassurance. He would never let me fall again.

The terrace stretched most of the length of the West wing. After all of my time in Gryphon's rooms, I knew that his private office and living area also spilled onto the same balcony. I had never ventured out further than the door before, but now that we were outside, I realized that this balcony was far larger than mine. It stretched so far out from the castle that it looked like it ended in a black void. The same dense fog surrounded us, yet I had the sense that we were in a place of great importance. A gut feeling told me this place was significant, though I had no idea why.

As Gryphon guided me closer to the edge of the terrace where I could no longer see any landscape beyond the fog my nerves demanded me to stop. We were pushing our luck that I wouldn't have a panic attack.

Gryphon let go of my shoulders to approach the short stone wall. With a wave of his hand a blood red rose encased in a crystal globe hovered in the air in front of him. The rose was wilting, with only two petals clinging for life on the stem. Petals previously shed cluttered the bottom of the globe and as I looked at it, I noticed an emerald green glow, similar to the light Gryphon produced with his portals.

"This is the rose my mother held when she cast her curse," Gryphon explained. His focus remained on the flower before us. "As it has bloomed and wilted, so, too, have the residents of Aeternitas. I suspect we only have enough time for the last petal to fall."

My heart broke at his tone for I could hear the despair yielding to resignation. Gryphon was trying to accept his fate, knowing there was not enough time left for him to make another attempt in the human world. I had failed him. I had failed them all.

"Gryphon," I choked out, my voice catching on his name, "I'm so sorry!" Tears began to stream down my face, too strong for me to hold back. "This is all my fault!"

I tried to raise my hands to my face to cover what was escalating into ugly sobs of anguish but in a moment, I felt Gryphon's callused hands gently pull mine down. He yanked me into his strong arms, holding me tightly against his chest, one hand wrapping around my waist while the other cupped the back of my head. His heart beat the same steady rhythm I had grown accustomed to in all my nights curled up against his chest and it was that sound that soothed me. He held me for several long moments, giving me the time I needed to compose myself.

"You have done nothing for which there is blame," murmured Gryphon. "That is a burden I, and I alone, must carry."

I shook my head fiercely into his chest, not caring that I was probably wiping snot and tears down the front of his shirt. "Stop talking about yourself like that!"

He pulled back enough to see my face, gently posing his knuckles under my chin to force me to look up at him. His eyes were so golden they were almost glowing. "It is difficult to have a single regret about my actions, the curse, or any of it, when they all led me here to you," Gryphon admitted.

It was my undoing. The musical cadence of his voice coupled with the most romantic sentiment I had ever heard made my resolve disintegrate. My lips sought his with a spark to ignite my entire body. His arms tightened around my waist while mine wound around his neck, determined to keep Gryphon as close as physically possible. My skin may as well have erupted in flames and when I broke away in order to breathe, he merely redirected his attentions to my neck. The friction from my nightgown against my erect nipples was spiking my desire higher until I could no longer bear the heat.

I took two steps back from him, leaving him panting, with another noticeable bulge in his pants. Smiling coyly, I reached up to untie the light string fastening the top of my nightgown, extracting one arm and then the other, before letting the entire garment pool at my ankles. My eyes remained fastened on his, the hungry glint in his expression making me feel more confident than ever. I wanted this. Wanted him.

To his credit, Gryphon never once raked his eyes down my naked form. The sexy smirk I loved was back, though, and his labored breathing told me just how hard he was restraining himself. "Mirielle, I do not wish to hurt you," he whispered.

I shook my head. "I'm not in any pain."

"Bodily discomfort is not the only source of anguish you might experience. I cannot keep denying myself this pleasure," Gryphon warned me. "If you consent, I shall take you to my bed and there will be no stopping what is to come."

My heart fluttered and despite how badly I wanted this, my cheeks flushed at his words. Slowly I stepped forward until I could press my body against his and wrap my arms around his neck again.

"Make me your miracle," I murmured before crushing my lips to his once more.

CHAPTER 35

The Oath

GRYPHON

Mirielle's naked form before me was the ultimate test of Fate, and I wanted nothing more than to bind myself to her completely. She was exquisite, her skin pink with desire, long red hair cascading over one shoulder. I loved the way her bangs always fell slightly into her eyes as if they wanted to shield her from the pain of the world. And her body… my crown be damned, my father's displeasure at our union was such a trivial price to pay in comparison to tasting all her muscular curves. Lust had completely overtaken my body and I no longer cared whether her feelings might be compromised. I had to claim her, once and for all.

In my excitement, I nibbled at her lower lip and she squealed in delight. There was a frightened anticipation in her eyes, like she knew I might ruin her and wanted to take that chance. I ran my hands over her bottom, moaning in ecstasy at how they filled both hands, before pulling her thighs apart to circle around my waist. My clothes were preventing me from feeling the wet heat at her core and needed to be disposed of immediately. But first, I crossed back into my bed chamber, setting her on the bed so I could remain between her thighs.

I trailed kisses along her jaw and down her neck as she fumbled with the strings tying my shirt. It took longer than I expected and a quick glance revealed why—her hands were shaking so much that the strings kept slipping through her fingers. Sense finally intervened and I backed a few paces away, training my eyes on her face because one look at her glorious body and I would be done for.

"Mirielle, we don't have to do this," I said.

She wrapped her arms around her body so I could no longer see the tremor in her hands. "No, I want to!" she insisted. "It's just first time jitters. Didn't you have those?"

Sadly, I shook my head. "No, darling, for I was certain of my decision...a decision lust, alcohol, and poor judgment made *for* me."

I loved the way her nose scrunched up as she considered my words. Oh, but I loved everything about this woman.

"Are you saying you regret your first time?"

Her question made me smile. It was always in absolutes with her. Ever the scientist, needing definitive answers and proof. I crossed back over to her and gently pulled her arms away so that I might take her hands in mine.

Staring deeply into her eyes, succumbing to the electric connection I always felt when I got lost in their myriad of colors, I replied honestly, "I'm saying the perfect partner is worth the wait. There is no rush, Miracle. I have nothing but time."

I could tell my words moved her by the way they softened. A small smile tugged at her lips and I leaned my forehead against hers. She had no idea how long I would wait for her to be ready.

"How about a bath instead?" I suggested.

We both laughed as she helped me undress in the bathroom for she was not used to the small buttons on my breech-like pants. By then some of my erection had lessened, but I noticed the way she sighed with longing as she snuck a glance. Steam began to fill the room from the hot water, along with the scent of roses, and I stepped into the water, turning back to hold my hand out for hers.

The water felt incredible, soothing some of the tension along my spine. It had been such a long few weeks as we waited for Mirielle to return to us, and now the day's events were catching up to me. Forcing Mirielle to give me her body left a foul taste in my mouth, something I could never bring myself to do no matter how badly I desired her, and I was reminded of my former life where whore-houses were a frequent nightly haunt. "Everyone has needs" had been my logic then, but I was filled with shame at the thought of Mirielle knowing such details about my past. There were always easy women willing to couple with the prince of Aeternitas and none of them had a single name or detail that stuck out in my mind now. Intimacy in any form felt different now that I knew what it meant to respect my partner. I craved her bliss more than my own release.

Mirielle emerged from underneath the water, hair wet and pushed away from her face. She pointed to a bottle on the opposite side of the bathing pool and asked, "Care to help me clean up?" Her smile was so sincere, so trusting, that it made my heart skip a beat.

I tugged her to me through the water and tried to keep my thoughts innocent as her breasts pressed against my chest. "Anything you need," I whispered.

We moved to the bench along the side of the bathing pool and she settled between my legs, her back to my front. My cock nestled firmly against her lower back and I tasted blood from how hard I bit my lip in longing. I massaged the soap through her hair, trying to be as gentle as possible in case it brought on any pain. She claimed to feel fine, but this was a woman who brushed off a gunshot wound to her abdomen. Acting stronger than she felt was her superpower.

After rinsing the suds from her long hair, Mirielle leaned back against my chest and practically purred with contentment. I wrapped my arms around her waist to keep her close, breathing in her fresh, rosy scent like a man obsessed. It seemed only natural, with my chin resting on her shoulder, to turn and lightly kiss her cheek. However, Mirielle must have had a similar thought because her head turned at the same moment and our lips found one another again.

This kiss did not leave a trace of fear in her eyes, merely the same echo of ravenous hunger that overwhelmed me. Ever so slowly I grazed one hand up her abdomen, tracing along the bottom curve of one breast, before circling one finger around her budding nipple. The tremble I detected was one of a woman feeling the heat of passion. Her coy smirk spurred me further.

"Should you wish to stop, merely say the word," I reminded her quietly.

Her response was another kiss, deeper this time, as one of her hands guided my unoccupied hand down to the apex of her thighs. She spread her knees wider, granting me easier access, and I moaned into her mouth as my fingers slid into her heat. I arched one finger inside her, my thumb circling her clit.

Our kiss deepened as our tongues clashed and I introduced a second finger. Her muscles clenched around me in response. Wanting to make her body explode with pleasure, I picked up the pace on her clit, moving my other hand to pinch hard on her swollen nipple. She gasped and rolled her hips forward, her core locking my fingers in a vice grip as she rode out her orgasm.

Her eyes were round as saucers when I extracted my fingers from her wet center and stuck them both in my mouth to suck her sweet juices off them. She tasted like the perfect combination of sin and salvation. It didn't matter that my fingers were tainted with her bathwater. I would drink that, too, at this point. If it had anything to do with Mirielle Townsend, I wanted it, plain and simple.

"Gryphon." She exhaled my name slowly as if she was still riding her wave of pleasure by saying it out loud.

I kissed her lightly on the lips and stood up, exiting the bathing pool in one swift movement. The castle staff kept a basket full of Mirielle's preferred fluffy drying sheets in this room at all times now and I plucked one up to wrap around my waist. This time was about her and her pleasure only, and I feared that if she saw the physical reaction my body had to the sound of my name on her lips, she would feel obligated to reciprocate.

"Come," I commanded, holding one hand out to her again like when she entered the bathing pool. "You must rest."

Mirielle blinked rapidly and her mouth popped open in a round O. "That's it?" she sputtered. "You just...do the stuff...and now I sleep?!"

It took every ounce of restraint I had to hold back the proud grin fighting to dawn my face. "There is no rush, Miracle," I reminded her. "Your body might still be recovering and I do not want to be the reason you experience pain."

She rolled her eyes and ignored my hand, swatting it out of the way like an annoying fly as she climbed the stairs and exited the pool. Her pink Sherpa bathrobe appeared on the counter, freshly laundered, and she tugged that on after hastily drying herself.

"Just go, then!" Mirielle snapped.

Angering her had not been my intention. I swung her around to face me, tilting her chin up to look at me as she stubbornly trained her eyes on the floor. "Is the lady not satisfied?" I asked.

Mirielle huffed. "In some ways, but why can't we finish what we started?"

This time I couldn't stop the smirk from crossing my face. "I already tasted how you finished, Miracle."

Her cheeks flushed as red as a rose. "That's not what I meant."

I nodded. "I know what you meant. I also know that I sensed hesitation earlier, and if you are going to give yourself to me, it will only occur when there is no shadow of doubt clouding your mind."

Hazel eyes darted to mine, equal parts embarrassed and relieved. No matter how she might try to deny it, I was certain that she still felt trepidation at the thought of sex. And it was not enough to me that she offered her body out of a lust-filled daze that she would later come to regret. If it happened—when it happened—I needed to know that she gave me everything, which was what she would receive from me in return.

Gently, I brushed her wet hair out of her face and kissed her forehead. "I am going to check in with Darda and the others. Get some rest," I instructed.

Mirielle sighed and I felt all the fight leave her. She nodded and retreated into the bedroom. I requested a change of clothing that immediately appeared on the counter before me. When I crossed out into the main room, a quick glance over my shoulder assured me that Mirielle was curled up in our bed again under a pile of blankets.

As the door shut behind me, I stopped abruptly. *Our bed.*

I quite liked the way that sounded.

CHAPTER 36

An Unwelcome Intrusion

As soon as the door shut behind Gryphon, I sat upright in bed. There was something off about his behavior that I couldn't quite place. Was he disappointed in me? Angry with me? His signals were so hot and cold that it left me confused as to where we stood. I had fallen in love...had he fallen in resignation?

My thoughts were too chaotic to sleep and I really didn't feel any more pain. The hot bath had soaked some of the stiffness out of my joints—and I'm sure the orgasm didn't hurt—so I found myself with restless energy that needed to be diverted. I crossed into Gryphon's private office, hoping he still had some of my notes at his desk. Whenever I had a problem with an artifact at work, I always went back to the very beginning to retrace my steps. If the Faberge eggs weren't going to break the curse, there had to be something else I missed. Plus, I had not turned into a piece of furniture. That meant I had to be the human meant to help him. That alone gave me hope that we could find the other piece of the puzzle.

Rummaging around through all the clutter, I mentally scolded Gryphon for being such a slob. All of my maps, lists, sketches, and notes were out of order, hastily thrown in seemingly random piles on the desk. As I rounded the corner, my knee slammed into a drawer that was partially left open.

"Fuck!" I snarled, hobbling into the chair and massaging my kneecap.

Using my other foot, I tried to push the drawer shut, but something sticking out prevented it from closing all the way. Upon closer inspection, it looked like Gryphon's journal.

"The journal..." I muttered to myself. An echo of a voice reminded me how important the journal was. It contained something we needed, maybe? Gryphon had been writing in the thing every evening since I had relocated to his private rooms, and I knew it was important to him. Based on casual conversations, he had been writing in it for a long time. It was the same leather-bound brown journal that had the missing corner of parchment that led Gryphon to my lab in New York.

As I pulled the journal from the drawer, I considered the outcome. Gryphon had never allowed me to touch the thing before. He insisted its contents were for his eyes only and I always imagined it was something akin to a diary. It would be a betrayal of his trust to read it.

But I *really* wanted to.

BOOM!

Something sounding like a bomb going off erupted in the castle behind me. I sprang to my feet, instantly alert. The last time something like this happened it was an Elemental attack—did they come back for round two?

The same caterwauling alarm went off as it had then, only louder. Maybe it was closer now that I was in Gryphon's rooms. I rushed into the bathroom and barked out, "Fighting clothes-NOW!" and was instantly gratified with the same black stretch type leggings and top as before. The shirt this time around was more of a crop top with a lower neckline than I would prefer and I cursed Gryphon's ridiculous requests under my breath as I changed.

There wasn't enough time to do anything with my hair as more sounds echoed through the rooms. The ground was shaking beneath my feet. I needed to find Gryphon.

I sprinted out into the hallway before skidding on my heels to see parts of the castle wall were breaking off. There were gaping holes in the stone and wind howled through the openings. A ripple went through the floor, sending me to my knees on the floor.

Darda came around the corner, gliding faster than I had ever seen before. "Get back into the room, dearie!" she yelled. "He's coming! He's coming!"

"What about you?" I asked. I finally pulled myself upright, but the ground only started to shake harder. Some of the stones were beginning to crumble. "What the hell is going on?!"

Darda's comforting presence washed over me, the calm amidst the storm, like always. "I have my job and you have yours," she replied. "Just go! Now!"

I stumbled back into the antechamber of Gryphon's private rooms and found more destruction. One of the double doors leading into his bedroom was knocked off its hinges, but I could not move either door to open. The office would have to do.

Inside his office, books were rattling off the shelves and cascading down on the floor. The alarm went off again, the loudest I had ever heard thus far. This room must have been the source. I made my way over to the desk, Gryphon's journal still on top, as best I could with the floor's trembling. A jade green light on the terrace caught my eye, and as I squinted into the fog, it almost looked like the rose's globe was back. But that was impossible. Gryphon told me only he could summon it; no one else was even supposed to know he had it.

A resounding crack brought down a large chunk of the ceiling right in front of the doorway, thereby blocking me from the only exit. A small hole had been carved out in the door, but it would never be wide enough for a body to crawl through. Smoke from falling debris was starting to permeate the air in the room, making me cough and wheeze. I was desperate to know what was happening and where all of my friends were. I needed them to be safe. And Gryphon—where was he?

"MIRIELLE!" he screamed through the hole in the door. I could just make out the worried lines etched across his beautiful face. His skin was white as a ghost, with a sheen of sweat, and the green of his eyes had darkened until they were nearly black.

"Gryphon, what the fuck is going on?" I shrieked back. "It's like the castle is falling apart!"

At that moment, another rippling wave trembled through the floor and large chunks fell away in the space between the door and me. I was truly trapped. My heart started hammering in my chest as panic set in.

"I have to send you back, Mirielle," Gryphon yelled. "It's the only way to keep you safe!"

"What?" I screamed. I could barely hear him over the sound of smashing stone.

"Our time has run out," he cried out, louder so I could better hear him. "You will always be my miracle!"

My mind finally snapped because suddenly the world was in slow motion. I shot to my feet, one hand stretched towards him as if I had the power to ward off what was to come, the other hand gripping onto the desk for dear life. A powerful blast of Gryphon's magic seared through me, kicking me back into a glowing portal he opened behind me. I felt the same free fall as I had every other time, but this one was different. My eyes stayed trained on Gryphon's face, tears streaming down his cheeks, his eyes morphing to a glowing gold until the green loop of the portal tightened and closed between us. Life returned to a normal speed as I landed on my back on a plush surface.

"Miri!" Someone called to my left.

I couldn't answer because I was too dumbstruck by what had just happened. Gryphon was in trouble, he needed me. And as I tried to get my bearings, I realized my hand was clenched around Gryphon's leather journal, my fingers so tight and tense that I might have broken them. Sounds started to filter in around me as I sensed someone approaching; the familiar noises of New York City bustling in the background. Gryphon sent me home.

So why did it no longer feel that way?

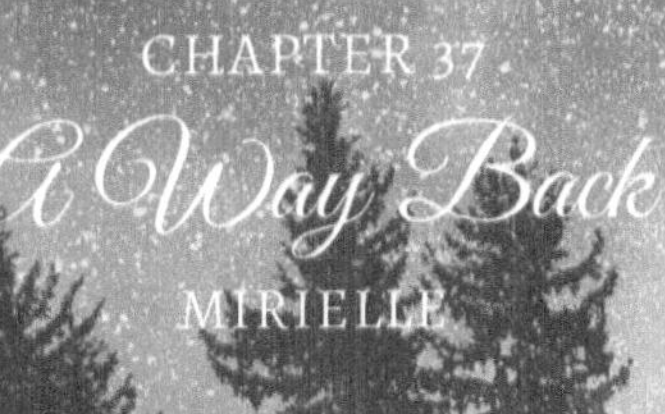

MIRIELLE

It was the last thing in the world I expected to see, but Barrett Collins' face hovered over mine. He kept repeating my name and shaking my shoulders like he was trying to rouse me from sleep when I was very clearly looking him in the eye. His expression mirrored the worry I had last seen etched on Gryphon's face and my mood darkened at the comparison.

I swatted at him impatiently. "Barrett, you can see that I'm fine!" Sitting upright, I recognized the rough brick wall to my right and the creamy down comforter. We were in my apartment. Specifically, we were in my loft bedroom in my apartment. "How on earth did you get in here?"

A look of annoyance flashed across his face. "How about we start with where the fuck you've been, huh? You've had me freaking out!"

Rolling my eyes, I pulled my legs around him and got off my bed, where he remained seated. I crossed over to the small mirror above my only dresser and noted the large bags under my eyes.

Otherwise my appearance looked the same, though I desperately needed to run a brush through my unruly hair.

"Okay, and where did you get that getup? How did you get back here?"

I turned just in time to see Barrett appreciatively taking in my backside and glanced down to realize I still had on the stretchy black leggings and crop top the bathroom had given me when I thought I would be entering a fight with an Elemental. "Get your mind out of the gutter, Barrett," I sighed as I headed down the spiral staircase that led into my kitchen area.

Although Gryphon had promised me food, our side activities had sort of gotten in the way and I realized how hungry I still felt. Rummaging through my fridge, I found lots of fresh fruits, vegetables, and Greek yogurt that I definitely didn't buy. Turning around, my extended island that fit two barstools and also served as my only dining area in the apartment was covered with papers, including a map of the city that had jarring red X's in a few places.

Barrett came down the spiral staircase and stopped, leaning against the wrought iron rail and crossing his arms across his chest. He was wearing loose jeans and a navy Henley shirt, but his detective's badge still gleamed at his hip. There was a leather holster setup around his shoulders that held a Glock 22 on each side.

You only know that thanks to Jimmy, who is stuck under an attack at Aeternitas.

I scowled at the direction my thoughts had turned. That would be my third order of business, right after I got some food in my stomach and figured out why Barrett frickin' Collins was in my apartment.

"Why are you here?" I snapped, pushing aside all of the healthy stuff for a box of leftover dumplings I knew were in there somewhere. Except...I couldn't find them. "Did you throw away all my food, too?!"

He had the audacity to snort. "I did you a favor. Some of that shit looked like it graduated high school with us."

So today would finally be the day I committed murder in cold blood. "Barrett, for the last fucking time, what are you doing here?!"

Barrett let out an exasperated huff and stepped forward, leaning over the island and placing both his hands down to brace himself as he yelled back, "I've been here waiting on your sorry ass, that's what! You've been gone for three days, Miri!"

"Don't call me that," I muttered automatically as I tried to comprehend what he was saying. All of those months in Aeternitas had been the equivalent of three days here in New York?

It was Barrett's turn to roll his eyes at me. "Yes, let's get into the semantics of your name when I've been scouring every inch of the city looking for you after I watched some new fucking Marvel super villain walk into a glowing circle with half your lab equipment! This is so typical of you, Miri!" He smacked the counter to emphasize his point, making me jump in alarm.

His words, though dripping with sarcasm, brought me up short. "You saw Gryphon?"

Barrett glared at me. "Don't dignify that thing with a name. It was a monster."

This was the same old Barrett who had made my life a living nightmare all through high school. Other people's opinions didn't matter and no one deserved respect unless *he* said the person had earned it—and his standards were ridiculously unreasonable. He was cocky and arrogant and needed to get out of my apartment immediately!

"Okay, show's over, Barrett. I'm gonna need you to get the fuck out now," I ground out through clenched teeth. "People's lives are at stake and I have a lot to do!"

He crossed his arms over his chest again, his face resolute. "Saving lives is kind of my job now. If you need that kind of help, I'm staying."

"Ugh!" I threw my hands up in frustration. "I can't even think straight until I get some food in my stomach!"

Slamming cupboards open I scrounged around for a can of soup that I dumped into a bowl before tossing it in the microwave. Barrett came around next to me and began pulling fruit out of the fridge, then setting it on the counter behind us. There was a cutting board and long knife already out on the tiny workspace and a fancy blender now graced the counter on the other side of the refrigerator.

"I'm making a smoothie. Do you want one?" Barrett asked. His voice still held an edge of irritation, but I could tell he was trying to offer a shaky truce.

Unfortunately for my life-long grudge, a smoothie sounded divine. "Only if it's blueberry banana. That's my favorite," I replied, equally as gruff with him. One smoothie was not going to get him off the hook.

As we settled in across from one another on the barstools, he tried to casually ask, "So who's this Gryphon guy?"

I snorted into my soup. "Oh no, stalker, we're starting with you," I said. "How did you get into my apartment?"

He shrugged. "Showed the supe my badge and said I was investigating a missing person's case on ya. He let me right in."

My building supervisor was an older Asian man heavily into Buddhism named Mr. Yeung. Even without identifying me as a missing person, Mr. Yeung would have cooperated with Barrett's flashy badge and gun.

"I am not a missing person," I reminded him.

Barrett paused from biting into a banana. "Nobody knew where you were, Miri," he said, his steely blue eyes boring into mine. "Sounds like a missing person to me."

The look he pierced me with was unsettling and only increased my longing for Gryphon.

"You wouldn't believe a word of it, even if I told you." I hastily began rinsing dishes out in the sink and loading them into the small dishwasher. "Why would you even look for me? I've made it very clear how I feel about you."

At this, Barrett's shoulders slumped and he turned his attention back to his banana. "I know you've got it all wrong about me."

"Sure I do." I stomped back up the stairs to find a hair tie and shoved Gryphon's journal into a messenger bag. There had to be some clue as to how I could get back to Aeternitas inside. Mr. Cooper was still there, and they all needed me. If Gryphon fought another battle against the Elementals I honestly didn't know if he could recover. The rose suddenly appearing on the balcony made me question some things, too, but if the journal was all I had for now, it was time to go back to my lab and examine some things.

Barrett followed me, not bothering to hide how his eyes raked my entire body. "I sure hope you're not planning on heading out in that," he commented.

"I don't have time to change," I called over my shoulder as I swept past him, my hair now secured in a ponytail.

His loud footsteps echoed hot on my heels as I sped towards the front door. "Miri, you can NOT go out in that! This is New York frickin City!"

I rounded on him, not expecting him to be quite so close. He didn't back down, but stood nose to nose with me, glaring down at me, chest heaving.

"Barrett, there is nothing wrong with what I'm wearing. And even if there was, you're nobody to me. You don't get to tell me what to wear."

He let out a frustrated sigh. "I'm just trying to protect you!"

That made me laugh. "'Protect me?!' You have been the bane of my existence since I was thirteen-years-old!"

His entire body stiffened. There was fury in his eyes and I automatically retreated another step away from him. He stepped back, too, like we both needed the space from one another, placing his hands on his hips and diverting his attention to the floor.

"Miri, I have been in love with you since the second grade," he said after a moment.

Initially I didn't think I heard him correctly. That was impossible. "I didn't even know you in second grade," I sputtered.

Barrett snorted, then rolled his eyes. "We were both in Mrs. McMahon's class at PS 291. One day when our class was outside playing, a bigger kid in another class pushed me down. I scraped up my back pretty bad. You came to my side, held my hand, and told me it was okay to cry if it hurt. You said you wouldn't tell anybody because everybody needs one special person in their life."

If he had told me he crash landed here from another planet, I would not have been as surprised as I was by this revelation. I remembered that day perfectly. The temperature was just starting to give way to spring after a particularly brutal winter. My mom hadn't gotten me a winter coat and I had been sick a lot. Mr. Cooper had been nursing me to the best of his ability when my mom wasn't around—which was often—and the line about everyone needing one special person had come from his mouth the night before when I tried to thank him.

On the playground there had been a wiry little boy with a face full of freckles who tried to play a game with some of the older kids from a higher grade. They made fun of him, shoving him hard onto the cement. With the still melting ice in patches on the ground, the poor little boy slid a bit and had some road rash. I remembered the entire exchange now that Barrett brought it up, but it wasn't like it had become a core memory for me. Until now, I didn't even remember the little boy as Barrett.

"But you didn't start going to school with me until sixth grade," I countered lamely.

He shook his head. "No, I returned to New York City for sixth grade. The summer between second and third was when my mom's addiction issues got really bad, so my grandparents came up from Florida and took me. Once I started acting out too much down there, they sent me back. Which was why I acted out in the first place. I wanted to come back up here to you."

This didn't make any sense. Barrett Collins, the asshole bully of my younger years, who had tormented me mercilessly until I graduated, was actually what...infatuated with me?

"Then why did you become such a giant dick to me?" I asked incredulously. "You made me miserable."

Barrett had the good grace to look sheepish. "I came back expecting you to have missed me just as much as I missed you. You didn't even remember me, and I took it hard. But then I also got so mad when there were any other guys who tried to give you attention. I tried to do good things to get you to notice me at first. Why do you think I was always in the library in middle school? I read every book I saw you read in hopes that you'd ask me a question and I could impress you with my answer. But none of that ever mattered. So I started doing stupid shit instead," he finished.

My mouth hung open in shock as random memories came back. He *had* spent way too much time in the library. It always drove me crazy that I couldn't have a quiet place to study there because he would come up and bother me. He used to snatch books out of my hand or insist that whatever table I used was already his spot, forcing me to move. Then he would do the same thing at the next table, and the next, until I left.

"Barrett, some of our exchanges in high school were downright terrifying. You acted like a goddamn predator," I reminded him.

He nodded in agreement. "Yeah, I was a dumbass then. I can readily admit that. I didn't know how to treat a girl the right way. Especially a girl like you! Still don't, obviously." He snorted as he looked down at his hands awkwardly clasped in front of him, embarrassment preventing him from looking at me.

"Barrett..." I started, unsure of what to say. I needed some time to process all of what he said, but ultimately, I knew my heart belonged to Gryphon. Nothing Barrett said mattered.

"Look," started Barrett, "you don't have to say anything now. I'm not expecting you to feel the same, but I'm hoping you'll give me a chance to start over with you. Hell, the only reason I responded to the call about Mr. Cooper is because I was afraid you'd been there with him and got hurt, too. Everything I do is for you, Miri."

The blue of his eyes somehow became lighter as he gazed at me with a look I now recognized as hope. It was the same sort of look Gryphon had on his face when we were discussing the missing treasure. That comparison made me clamp my mouth shut on the admission that I already loved someone else. I didn't have it in me to hurt Barrett like that.

"Okay," I breathed, smiling at him. "But only if you call me 'Mirielle.'"

A cheeky grin broke out across his face. "Deal."

He crossed over to my coat rack and grabbed one of my winter coats. "At least put this on. It's been snowing," he said. I could tell he was trying to change the subject and save both of us from the embarrassment of continuing our conversation. "Now where are we going?"

I slipped the coat on and made to leave my apartment. "*I* am going to my lab," I corrected him. "You can go wherever you need to."

"No dice," he replied. "You just randomly disappeared for three days, somehow magically appeared in your bedroom in an outfit that has me seeing stars, and you're defending some freak who looks like a hawk." Barrett had already thrown on his own leather coat and slammed the door behind us.

Powerwalking out into the bustling city street, I hoped to lose him, but he managed to keep himself at my side. We made it four blocks in huffy silence before I finally stopped short and said, "Barrett, you can't help me with this! You wouldn't even believe me if I told you."

Instead of arguing with me, Barrett took one step closer so that he was nose to nose with me again. His icy blue eyes were flirtatious as he replied, "Everyone needs one special person, right?"

His words coupled with the intense way he challenged me sent a shiver down my spine, but it wasn't one of fear. It was something else entirely that I didn't have the time to examine. I had to find a way back to Aeternitas.

"Fine," I lamented, "But you are gonna think I'm crazy."

He laughed out loud. "Mirielle, I've *always* known you were crazy. That's old news."

As we made our way through the city that was now flushed with snow, I tried to give him a basic rundown of what happened to me after I found the parchment piece in Mr. Cooper's apartment. Thankfully, Barrett didn't ask any questions, though his facial expressions told me he didn't believe a single thing I said.

The fact that he didn't stop or insist I was insane made me hope he was willing to keep an open mind.

My lab was marked off with police caution tape when we arrived. Barrett rubbed the back of his neck and tried to look apologetic when I shot him a look of pure venom, but it hardly mattered now. Nothing had been touched since Barrett's last encounter here with Gryphon, which he had described to me after I was done loosely explaining my travels to and from Aeternitas. My colleagues at the museum must have a target on my back by now; there was no way this hadn't interfered with their work.

Inside the room was much the same as always. Several pieces of equipment used for restoration were now missing, still occupying the makeshift workstation I had created at the warehouse in Aeternitas. I eagerly rushed over to my worktable, flipping on the overhead light so I could examine the journal. It had to be thousands of years old and despite seeing Gryphon write in it every night, there couldn't be more than 200 pages inside.

I hung my coat on the back of my chair as Barrett slid into the chair across from me. "So now what?" he asked.

"Now I figure out a way to get back to Aeternitas," I said simply.

"And you think this old piece of junk is gonna open up a magic portal so you can do that?" It was hard to miss the sarcasm and disdain dripping from his voice.

"It certainly has before," I countered with a smirk.

He rolled his eyes at me but didn't comment any further. It looked like he was biting the inside of his cheek as he mulled over his thoughts.

The journal looked completely ordinary, something I could pick up at a Barnes and Noble any day of the week. The paper was a heavier vellum than what we used in the United States for paper, but given what I knew of Aeternitas, that wasn't altogether surprising. There were markings inside that did not resemble any language I recognized, but Gryphon had mentioned once that he wrote in the "language of the ages." I had laughed at the time.

What caught my interest now was that there were so many pages that were still blank. Despite his constant scribbling, it looked like this journal had barely been used.

"Grab a pen for me, will you?" I asked Barrett.

He pulled one out of his coat pocket and handed it to me. "You really come prepared, huh, Miri?"

"You're doing it again," I said through clenched teeth, keeping my eyes trained on the journal.

"Doing what?"

"Being a jackass."

That silenced him and we both returned to staring at the journal. I had no idea if my experiment would work and I sincerely hoped I didn't damage his journal, but if it meant I could return to Gryphon, I would try anything.

Using the pen, I flipped to a blank page and wrote,

Hello, this is Mirielle.

I gasped out loud as the ink disappeared. That was how Gryphon managed to write so much on the same pages. Barrett merely raised his eyebrows at me without comment.

"Oh, shut up," I muttered. "This is exciting."

Picking up the pen again, I wrote,

What can you tell me about Gryphon, the crown prince of Aeternitas?

Barrett, leaning forward to see what I was doing, snorted derisively. "Of course he's a fucking prince," he griped.

The ink disappeared and a written response came, so I ignored him. The journal simply wrote back,

Everything.

I squealed in delight. "This is it!" I cried happily to Barrett.

"Whoopee," he drawled, twirling a finger in the air in his sarcasm. He dropped back down into the seat across from me, leaning back to prop his ankles on the table. "Even I know Harry Potter was better off leaving the diary alone."

Too motivated to let his shitty attitude deter me, I ignored him and settled down to examine the journal more closely. I wrote back a response asking it to show me.

Several entries appeared, some in the untidy scrawl of a young child. These were Gryphon's memories. On the one hand, I hated to invade his privacy, but on the other, desperate times called for desperate measures. I was a speed reader, but there was a lot to comb through.

"This might take a while," I warned Barrett.

The look he gave me was equal parts pensive as it was searing. "I'm not going anywhere, Miri," Barrett said. "If you're here, I'm here."

That statement was far too loaded for me to address, but I filed a mental note to return to it if I was unsuccessful with the journal today. It was time to read.

All I do is disappoint my parents, young Gryphon wrote. Father came to observe my sword lesson today. He yelled at Captain Champlaigne because I wasn't moving fast enough. It was my first time with a real sword and I was so excited to show Father, but I know I let him down. I shall work twice as hard tomorrow.

Father and Mother are fighting again. Father screamed that he would banish her from our kingdom. I didn't know he could do such a thing. Father said if I ever grow up to be like her, he'll banish me, too. Mother was crying, but Darda stopped me from going after her. I hate it when Mother cries. Darda always tells me that people say mean things when they're angry, and that Father would never really banish me, but I'm not so sure.

Lessons are becoming more grueling now. I don't know why I need to study so much. It's not like any of it matters when my destiny has already been decided for me. My mother acts as if my behavior is abominable, yet I know for a fact my father visits brothels more often than I. She would hate to see how many women occupy his bed most nights. Maybe I should tell her so she forgets my indiscretions… it's not like their fights are foreign to me. I have long accepted that I will die alone. A better end than theirs, I'm afraid.

Their quarrels will be the death of us all. The rafters quake with the sounds of their screams. If this is what my future holds, I want no part in it. The bottom of a bottle of mead offers far more promise than an eternity of their constant bickering. Good thing our mead cellar will never run out.

Tears ran freely down my face as I continued to read. All the passages were the same, a history of Gryphon's misery, loneliness, and despair over his future. They grew worse after the curse and he spun further into his spiral of self-loathing. He blamed himself for everything each time an attempt failed. But he never gave up. As much as he expressed hatred for what he had done and what had become of his kingdom, Gryphon continued searching for redemption.

No, I realized. *He was looking for something else entirely.*

Rolling my shoulders to prepare myself for whatever came next, I wrote,

I need to know how to return to Aeternitas. Gryphon needs my help.

Only a second went by before the journal's reply appeared.

No, he needs YOU.

The sentiment echoed similar declarations I had heard from Darda and Gryphon about me being the one to break the curse, but it felt far more significant coming from a magical journal that reminded me of Tom Riddle's diary. I proceeded to write a few different requests to be allowed entry back to Aeternitas to no avail. The journal did not open a portal and nothing more appeared on the pages.

Clearly, I was missing something. I repeated the words out loud with different vocal inflections on the four words, though that was pointless since the emphasis was obviously on the capitalized word. It was like the answer was right in front of me, but too blurry to see.

Barrett grew annoyed with me in seconds. "How many times are you gonna say that, Miri?"

I actually stomped my foot I was so irritated. "For the last time, it's Mirielle!" I burst out. "I *hate* being called Miri!"

He had the audacity to grin cheekily at me, his tongue just barely poking out between his white teeth. "I know. That's why I do it. It gets your attention."

"There are other ways to do that, you know," I said pointedly.

Barrett smirked. "None that get the rise out of you that I like."

His flirting was going to be a huge problem if I could make it back to Aeternitas. Gryphon would mutilate him. "You do realize that Gryphon and I are...we're..."

"Do you love him?" Barrett asked, the shock evident in his voice.

That one simple question was all it took for me to finally connect the dots. Hastily, I grabbed Gryphon's journal and scribbled a response that I hoped might fit the bill. The ink faded into the paper immediately and then the eerie quiet I recognized blanketed the room.

"Yes!" I jumped in place, pumping both fists in the air like a cheerleader while Barrett leapt to his feet, eyes scanning the area while one hand posed over his gun in the holster. All of the lights flickered out as an emerald glow hovered ten feet in front of me. The glowing light expanded, stretching to an oval tall enough for Barrett and myself to walk through. I could just barely make out the castle's grand entrance way through the portal, hazy with smoke and dotted with rubble.

I moved to run through the portal, but Barrett's hand clamped down around my wrist. "I'm coming with you!" he yelled.

"It's going to be dangerous!" I argued. "You don't know the castle like I do!"

He shook his head fiercely and pinned me with a glare. "I'm not letting you go in alone!"

His hand slid from my wrist into my hand, weaving his fingers through mine. Accepting the inevitable, I lunged forward, Barrett half a step behind.

CHAPTER 38

Battle Weary

GRYPHON

ending Mirielle back to the human realm was torture of the acutest kind. As soon as the portal closed behind her, I regretted my decision, but I was too weak by that point to go after her. Ultimately, she would be safer in her beloved New York City anyway and her safety was paramount to me. The alarm sounded because the rose was down to its final wilting petal. My mother's curse would finally be complete, damning every inhabitant of my castle. If I wasn't feeling so fatigued from its effects, I would be wallowing in my grief and shame.

The walls of the castle continued to disintegrate with pieces of falling debris every few feet. Flooring crumbled as I stepped further into the antechamber of my private rooms. I needed to check on Darda and the others and at least try to keep them safe. For Mirielle's sake I hoped to preserve all of the belongings in the warehouse. Although she would never see it again, my broken heart yearned to bring her joy one last time.

At the crossroads down to the main staircase, I found Darda huddled with a few of the members of Mirielle's beauty entourage

"Master, what is happening?" one of the hairbrushes asked.

"Quickly, into the warehouse. I am going to seal the door behind everyone. Hopefully it will be enough to keep everyone safe." I ushered them all forward, but Darda didn't budge.

"Sire, you'll never survive if the castle falls," Darda stated incredulously. "Why are you protecting us instead of saving yourself?"

It hurt to hear the shock in her voice. I knew I had always taken my staff for granted in the past, and although I was no longer afforded the time to repent for it, I hoped I had made some strides since Mirielle whisked her way into everybody's hearts. I certainly no longer felt like the same person.

"Because some things are more important. You all have become more important to me." I gulped, too fraught to say more. "Come," I instructed, "we'll gather the others as we go. Darda, go to the kitchens and collect everyone you can."

Darda apparated to the kitchens instantly, barely giving me time to register her wave of approval washing over me. The beauty products huddled close to me as I raced down the hall. We rounded a corner and found the floor had fallen away, creating a gap more than fifteen feet long. My wings unfurled, though there was no luster anymore in the feathers. I felt too weak. Without pausing to think, I scooped all of the brushes and curling wand into my chest and flew over the opening.

A large chunk of the ceiling caved at that moment, striking one of my already weakened wings, and I went tumbling down. We crash-landed with a skidded stop a floor below. All of the beauty products were screaming and I could feel blood on the left side of my face. I didn't want to alarm them any more than I already had, but it hurt. A lot. I almost felt too faint to stand.

"Master, we'll get help!" one of them cried. "Stay here!"

Another alarm went off, this one from the front gate. It was the alarm signaling an attack. The Elementals had arrived.

I groaned, in agony or frustration I no longer knew. "Curse the stars, they must have a spy amongst us!" Ignoring the way my vision swam in front of me, I clambered to my feet and swiped my bicep along the side of my face, smearing the blood more than actually stopping it. "Get everyone to the warehouse! I have to meet the guards!"

Or what's left of them, the unhelpful voice in my head reminded me.

Shaking out my wings to assess the damage, I only hesitated for a moment before taking off through the hole we had fallen in. I soared through several holes in higher floors of the castle until I emerged over the West wing to look towards the castle gate to the left. There were several large patches of fire visible from even my vantage point, making my heart drop in my chest. One of them looked to be in the direction of the kitchens. I had no way of knowing how many people Darda had wrangled up yet. Even her magic had limits.

"Emil!" I cried out. Mirielle would never forgive me if I lost him. Circling around one of the towers, I looked for the closest opening in a wall nearest the kitchens. Slick sweat coated my body, pain still radiating from the wound to my head. Normally by now my regenerative properties had already healed injuries. Perhaps I had misjudged my mother's fondness for me; perhaps I was turning mortal.

The idea pulled at my heartstrings as Mirielle's image came to mind.

Just as I passed through the threshold into the castle, my wings gave one last tremulous shudder before dropping limp down my back. I could feel their magic leaving my body like a visceral well.

They folded into my back, using the last dreg of magic as concealment, and the sense of their presence left my body.

It was the wrong time to mourn, so I sprinted down the hall towards the commotion. Flames met me at the end of the hall, extending out into Anastasia's beloved courtyard. All of her beautiful flowers were charred black. As I rounded the corner towards the kitchens, Darda came into view in front of the kitchen door. Smoke billowed out from inside, and my heart dropped into my stomach as I realized Emil hovered next to her, covered in black soot.

"He wouldn't leave until we got the others out, my lord," Darda explained.

Emil coughed. "Where's Mirielle?" he demanded between fits.

Even without his memories of their past, Mirielle's dear Mr. Cooper continued to protect her. Families truly were made, not born.

"She is safe," I assured him. "You must go to the warehouse. The castle is under attack."

"Your wings, my lord," Darda started, "have they...?"

I nodded. "They are no longer operational."

She didn't say a word, but transported Emil and I to the warehouse entrance. Others were inside with Ambrose shouting orders and trying to restore some semblance of organization to the chaos inside. All of the castle staff were yelling, and several rushed forward upon my arrival to pepper me with questions. Even though I could not see Wade's expression, I sensed his fear as I noticed him hovering near the front. Mirielle had revealed to me that she believed Wade to be a missing teen from New York City, and although I could not recall precisely where I had crossed paths with him, her assessment came fresh in my mind.

It was why I looked at him to say, "It will all be well. Everyone stay inside. Darda is in charge, with Ambrose second in command."

Emil joined the others, which I now saw included the beauty products I had abandoned earlier. There were hundreds of objects inside, but from what I could tell from the doorway, the warehouse itself remained intact. It was a room that was not originally part of the castle and therefore made of a different kind of magic. My suspicions were correct, that it would withstand the culmination of the curse, it seemed.

Darda hesitated in the doorway before turning back to face me. "You don't have to sacrifice yourself, my lord."

Despite the loud crash I heard behind me, far too close for comfort, I offered my nursemaid a soft smile. "You have been a most loyal companion, Darda," I said. "I'm sorry that I did not tell you sooner how much I appreciate it."

For once she was at a loss for words. "My lord..."

As awkward as it was, I wrapped my arms as best I could around the writing desk, kneeling down on one knee to do so. "Gryphon," I corrected her. "My name is Gryphon."

My nursemaid's sadness enveloped me in a suffocating cocoon. In it I felt her sorrow, her gratitude, and her overwhelming love. A love I had always taken for granted and ignored, pushing it away in favor of my own self destructive hatred. Although I had failed to save her, she at least needed to know how much she meant to me.

"I love you," I whispered with one final squeeze before turning on my heel and rushing towards the fray.

The Elementals were definitely on the offense, their *Saxum* warriors swinging huge lassos of boulders above their heads only to launch them into the remaining guards of Aeternitas. Guards who, I was sorry to see, were struggling to move. Their movements were no longer that of fluid soldiers accustomed to wielding swords and battle axes, but instead reminded me of young toddlers in leading strings learning to run and balance themselves. Every swing of their weapons was choppy and I noticed more than one fail to parry or block incoming blows.

Their water creatures, a race known as the *Imber* force, flanked the *Saxum*'s backs, sending pelting waves of salt water into any group of guards totaling more than three. It was brutal to watch, though I very much doubted my aid would make a difference in my current state. Still, I would never allow Aeternitas to go down without a fight.

Vulcan, king of the Elementals and my uncle on my mother's side, strode through the front door like he owned the place. There was a swagger in his steps as if he was certain of his victory that made my blood boil. My father had never permitted him here because he strongly disagreed with Vulcan's violent—and often bloody—ambition. Which was ironic considering my father's own path of destruction.

"GRYPHON!" Vulcan roared from the middle of the foyer.

All the fighting paused as I stepped up to the top of the stairs, glaring down at my uncle. I had only met him twice, and both times had been unpleasant. His black, beady eyes gleamed as he took me in now just as they had back then—a predator appraising what he considered to be easy prey.

Underestimating me would be his folly. Darkening my doorstep again would be his demise.

"Nephew," he greeted me with a pompous wave of his hand. "You seem to be under construction."

I remained at the top of the stairs, unwilling to yield to his mundane commentary. His tricks were useless against me, even weak as I felt. This was my realm and these were my people. I may not have saved them, but I would fight to the bitter end to defend them.

"Rumor has it your subjects are due for new leadership," Vulcan continued.

As if to emphasize his point, some of the plaster collapsed from the wall to his right.

"You are not welcome here," I replied, my voice laced with venomous warning.

My uncle extended his arms out, looking around at the haggard guards watching warily. "And who is going to stop me?"

Bright emerald green sparks illuminated several feet in front of him at the base of the stairs. My heart stopped and time froze as Mirielle stepped through a barely materialized portal, followed by the man I recognized from her lab, Bennett or something.

She did not look up to me or do anything to get the bearings of her surroundings. My impressive little miracle raised her hand above her head, instantly summoning Stellarum, the sword of Aeternitas, while staring King Vulcan down. She moved into a battle stance, her form perfect as soon as her fingers closed around the hilt.

"Me," she declared fiercely.

CHAPTER 39

Fight for Aeternitas

I could feel Gryphon's eyes burning holes in the back of my head as I faced off against whoever this was. He had a crown on his head of jagged rock that featured symbols of the four elements on it, making me conclude he was the king of the Elementals. Gryphon had mentioned once in passing that their king was technically his uncle, but I could not see any family resemblance as the king's angry face glared at me. Scars marked his cheeks and his cold eyes shone like the darkest flint of obsidian; his greasy gray hair brushed away from his face.

The man sneered at me. "And who, pray tell, is Aeternitas' champion? A woman, at that!"

"Whoa, Miri! Don't you think you should let someone who knows what they're doing fight this guy?" Barrett called out. He hovered anxiously behind me along a row of Aeternitas guards and Elemental warriors who had all formed a circle around us to watch.

Although I was terrified somewhere in the back of my mind, right now all I could focus on was my deep desire to wipe the condescension off Vulcan's miserable face. To me he embodied every bully I had ever had, every villain I had ever read about, and every misogynistic, abusive asshole my mother let into our lives. He reminded me of how weak and helpless I had become at the Kremlin despite all of my combat training, how I ended up as another damsel in distress cliche. Fear wasn't going to compromise my abilities this time. I might be David squaring up against Goliath, but he was going to second guess himself the next time he faced off against a woman.

Instead of answering him, I smirked. Drawing up my sword, I made to swing towards his shoulder, making him move to parry, then feinted at the last second and brought my sword down hard against his shin.

The Elemental king roared in pain, taking two steps back before raising a hand, palm up in my direction. I recognized it as the same move Gryphon used whenever he was about to cast powerful magic and made to dive out of the way when I felt a warm body line up next to mine.

"Oh, she knows," Gryphon said proudly to Barrett. He stood next to me, his arm raised in the same pose as the king's, only Gryphon looked down at me with eyes filled with warmth. They were trying to morph into gold, but kept fading to a dull green, which couldn't be a promising sign. Blood caked one side of his face and the arm on that side had splotches of road rash. The Elemental king looked to be fighting against Gryphon's bond over his movements, his face contorted in fury.

Gryphon wasn't healing.

"You have to get upstairs!" I demanded.

"Not a chance," he replied smoothly. "Let's show them how it's done."

Gryphon reached behind his back, summoning his own sword.

That was the signal for all hell to break loose. Pandemonium reigned as all the warriors on both sides attacked one another. The king broke free of Gryphon's restraints and disappeared into the crowd. Clashes of swords upon stone echoed as more castle rubble fell from the ceiling. Before I could chase after the Elementals' leader, a water fighter like the one from my previous battle stormed towards me. It was all I could do to block his blow, Gryphon at my back fighting god knew how many.

A loud bang behind me filled the foyer with the smoke of a firearm, making me turn in alarm to Barrett aiming one of his Glock 22's at an Elemental creature made of boulders. Although the bullet blew a small chunk of rock off the rock man's torso, it succeeded more at royally pissing the thing off. He bellowed something in a language I could not understand and swung at Barrett, who ducked just in time. The enormous boulder-shaped appendage slammed into the staircase banister, causing a crack to ripple its way up the stairs before ultimately splitting the marble into pieces.

"Barrett!" I shouted. I had no idea if he could even hear me above the din in the room, but he was going to be killed if he used a weapon like that against these things. "No guns!"

"You brought a cowboy to an Aeternitas battle?" Gryphon grunted over his shoulder to me.

I rolled my eyes. "Now's not the time to start comparing dick size, Gryphon!"

Fire warriors poured through the doorway, lighting the beautiful tapestry above the door in a white hot blaze. It hurt to see the hourglass emblem of Aeternitas disintegrate into ash. They outnumbered us three to one, and even with my limited weapons training, I could tell the Aeternitas' guard was moving sluggishly. We needed to retreat to safety.

My heart stopped as Gryphon's jagged cry came from behind me. Whipping my body around, I turned just in time to catch his body before it crashed to the ground. There was a dagger made of stone protruding from his chest.

"Barrett!" I screamed. "Help me!"

Barrett was at my side a moment later. "Holy shit!" he yelled when he saw Gryphon's wound. Blood was everywhere and Gryphon was growing paler by the second. He told me that his mother would never take his immortality away, but right now I wasn't so sure. "I thought you told me this guy was a warrior or some shit? Doesn't he know not to get stabbed?"

"You need to get him upstairs! Get him into his own room and lock the doors!" I ordered.

Gryphon moaned as he slumped further against me. "No!" he groaned. "I will not leave you again!"

I kissed him lightly on the forehead, then looked directly into his eyes. "I'm not going anywhere."

His eyes finally morphed into gold as he smiled faintly. "Be safe, Miracle."

Smirking, I gave a half-hearted laugh. "Always."

Barrett came around to Gryphon's other side and pulled Gryphon's arm around his neck, supporting as much of Gryphon's weight as he could. They shuffled awkwardly towards the stairs, Aeternitas guards blocking every Elemental who tried to approach. My eyes followed them until I saw them go down the hallway, completely away from the fighting, but no matter how strong the urge was to nurse Gryphon, I knew I needed to find Vulcan and end this thing once and for all.

Instantly three water warriors lunged towards me, making me barrel roll away. I sprang to my feet right in front of a fire creature, who kicked towards me, narrowly missing my torso. My sword met his arm and sparks showered us both. Our fight became a whirlwind as I panted to keep up with his fast pace. My limbs were aching, but I couldn't think about that right now.

Another water fighter sloshed towards me, the shelled blade of his sword dragging menacingly across the marble as he stalked me. The fire creature was trying to push me backward, no doubt meaning to box me in so they could both overpower me. As they closed in on me, I made a split second decision that would either be incredibly bold or incredibly stupid. In one fluid movement, my sword was tucked in against my chest and I rolled like a child on the floor towards the water thing. The momentum knocked the creature into the fire warrior, and the ear piercing scream from the water warrior's mouth reminded me of the velociraptor cries in *Jurassic Park* while the fire soldier's flames were doused, causing him to disintegrate into smoke. Clearly these things were not meant to touch one another.

Aeternitas guards were beginning to fall as more of the Elemental fighters poured through the door. Most of the foyer was now on fire, elevating the temperature far beyond what was comfortable. The only reason I hadn't succumbed to smoke inhalation were all the holes in the floor, walls, and ceiling from the castle crumbling. I looked around desperately for an idea on how to beat them because I did not return just to see my home fall.

My home. As soon as the words rolled through my head, a wave of peace washed over me. This *was* home. Here with all my friends, Mr. Cooper...Gryphon. I felt a sense of belonging here that I had never experienced anywhere else before. Home wasn't a place, it was a feeling, and my home needed protection.

Stellarum began to glow brighter in my hand. It was vibrating with power, making my whole arm tremble. Some unknown instinct told me to raise the sword straight above my head, point towards the ceiling. Beams of what looked like starlight shot out, striking all of the Elementals within a ten foot radius. They all screamed as they fell, great cries of agony, and evaporated into mist. The beams began to grow in length and in number, and I had to add my other hand to keep Stellarum upright. Aeternitas guards paused, awestruck at what my sword was doing.

No, not my sword, I thought. *The sword of Aeternitas.*

One by one, the starlight pivoted around the room until most of the Elementals realized they were the targets and began racing for the door. The Aeternitas guards settled into formation behind me and the light from Stellarum only grew stronger. My teeth were rattling in my head as I held onto the hilt for dear life.

"No, you idiots! Go after her! Get that sword!" The Elemental king had been uncovered as his army made a mad scramble to escape Stellarum's beams. None of them listened, and instead he was caught up in the fray exiting through a gaping hole near the door when the starlight managed to extend far enough to hit the mass exodus of warriors at the front.

The guards began to cheer behind me as the last of the Elemental warriors escaped, two instantly bursting into mist as Stellarum's power caught them. The light died down and my arms gave out, and I dropped to my knees as the rest of my body followed suit. Exhaustion like I had never known threatened to overpower me, but all it took was one simple question from a guard and I was sprinting back up the stairs.

"My lady, where is the crown prince?"

A great shuddering groan rang through the castle as the stonework began to really fall in earnest. Running up to Gryphon's room was like playing Frogger; I had to watch my footwork just as much as the sky overhead to dodge falling debris. Loud crashing told me it was the entire castle falling. Just as I rounded the corner to go down the hall leading to Gryphon's rooms, the walls on both sides began caving in. My lungs threatened to burst as I spurred myself faster, the rubble of the walls nipping at my heels.

I wasn't going to make it. The doorway to Gryphon's private rooms was getting closer, but the walls were crashing in around me faster than I could clear them. Without pausing to think of how ridiculous it was, my hand whipped Stellarum out from its scabbard at my hip and held it above my head, blade edge horizontal to the floor. The same starlight beams appeared, destroying the rocks right before they fell on me.

As I closed in on the last few feet, I somersaulted myself into the doorway, only missing the last of the rubble by a millisecond. Stellarum clattered to my side, drawing my attention away from the bruises and cuts I could feel forming along my arms and back. Holes littered my outfit, which was now a sooty gray from all the smoke and debris flying everywhere. I wanted to lean against the door for a few minutes to catch my breath, but there simply wasn't *time.*

"I'm coming Gryphon!" I screamed before standing up and shoving open the door just enough to slip into the antechamber.

CHAPTER 40

The Curse

GRYPHON

"**I** am telling you, we have to go back and save her!" I roared again at the pompous prick Mirielle brought with her. Just his cocky American attitude alone grated my nerves. "She will be killed!"

The man rolled his eyes. "Weren't you the one downstairs who said she knew how to fight the ugly guy? I promised her I would listen to her once we got here and I'm doing that, no matter what!" He angrily shoved me back down on the bed by the shoulders where I had attempted for what felt like the dozenth time to get up.

Mirielle came back for me and now I would never get to see her again. How she had managed to return flummoxed me, but that hardly mattered now. The castle was quaking as it fell apart, the rubble raining down on the terrace outside my window. The rose's orb glowed neon green, visible now to everyone at the curse's final culmination. I desperately hoped the magic of the warehouse would hold and keep everyone safe inside. None of them deserved to die because of my failure, even if I couldn't return them to their natural forms.

Fatigue was holding me hostage. The wounds to my head, arm, and chest had not healed, although Mirielle's friend had somewhat staunched the bleeding. He had torn up some of the bedding to create a makeshift sling around my shoulder to cover my stab wound.

"Can't you at least go to her?" I gritted through my teeth. "She needs someone!"

The man gave a bitter laugh as he held onto the bed post at the foot of the bed during a particularly powerful tremor. "Mirielle has always needed me, she just doesn't realize that yet."

Hearing this was the equivalent of swallowing glass. Before I could argue his point, Mirielle herself caught my attention...*as she dodged falling rock on the terrace to get to the rose!*

"MIRIELLE!" I bellowed. Seeing her in danger like that reinvigorated me because my own injuries paled in comparison. I leapt from bed right as the American tried to push me back in it. "Oh no," I countered. "Not this time, cowboy." One quick punch to his jaw was all it took to overpower him and I set my sights on my miracle.

She had barely made it halfway across the terrace. That far out eliminated the threat of falling debris, however the bright emerald light from the orb was blinding and creating a tornado of wind. Both her arms were blocking her face as she tried to power through the magic.

Whether it was the sight of her struggle or the last fleeting remnants of my power leaving my body for good, I managed to dash through the falling castle stone without getting hit. It was like the rocks themselves wanted me to find my way to her. The distance between us lessened, but the light and force from the rose's orb was overpowering. My good arm was up in front of my face trying to block out the blinding light. I could just barely make out the last crimson petal on the stem.

The wind circling from the rose's orb felt strong enough to rip holes in the clothing on my body as I closed the gap to her. I tried to pull her back to me, yanking on the waist of her pants. "Mirielle, this is too dangerous!" I yelled towards her. The wind whipping around us carried my voice away instantly. "It's too late now!"

She shook her head as fat tears rolled down her beautiful face. "No, it isn't! I can save you!"

"What?!" I cried. How could she possibly believe that?

Her red hair flew around us in a whirlwind as she turned to face me and brought both her hands to my face. There was so much warmth and happiness radiating from her eyes that I couldn't help wrapping my arms around her waist to draw her closer. Even in the most chaotic moment I had ever experienced, she was stunningly beautiful and my sense of calm. I wanted nothing more than to hold her, so if it was going to end like this, my existence would close on a note of pure bliss.

"Don't you get it?" Mirielle yelled, her hands forcing me to gaze into her eyes. "You've had the missing item all along, Gryphon! It's love!"

Although the power radiating from the orb was growing so strong I could feel the tingle of my skin as it started to burn, everything was drowned out in that moment. The light, the wind, the castle...it all fell away. There was only Mirielle, with her fiery spirit, fierce compassion, and never ending grace. Her epiphany rang true in my heart, yet I hardly dared myself to hope. My entire world rested on her answer to my next question.

"What are you saying?" I roared over the chaos.

The smile that lit up her face would stand out in my mind for the rest of eternity as the single most spectacular sight in all that had been and all that was yet to come. "I'm saying, I love you!"

Her hands wound into my hair and drew my lips to hers.

Our kiss sparked something inside, something that would forever change me. *She loved me.* Nothing else mattered. In that moment, all sense of time, of my family's expectations, of my duty to Aeternitas disappeared. *She loved me.* And what's more, I loved her. A love so pure and true that I realized even if I had to live a mortal life in the human realm, I would do so gladly with her. Anything without her would merely be a survival, and damn it, now that I knew how glorious it was to feel her lips against mine, to see her eyes shining like stars, I wanted to live. *She loved me.*

I beamed down at her. "Mirielle Townsend, I love you, for now and all of eternity."

Gold sparks showered over us as the wind stopped howling. The orb containing my mother's cursed rose shattered, revealing a perfectly formed blooming scarlet flower. Pieces of the orb began to spread through the air around us in an emerald green haze. It mixed with the golden sparks and spread further, coating the terrace as it edged towards the castle. Chunks of debris flew back to their original place as the magical wave from the orb repaired all of the damage. The gold sparks rained down from the highest tower, replacing missing tiles along the roof as well as returning the decorative flourishes along the windows and seams to their former glory. The Aeternitas castle of my childhood was emerging right before my eyes.

In my arms, Mirielle giggled, then laughed outright. Her laugh was infectious and I couldn't help but join her before drawing her lips to mine once more.

A woman cleared her throat loudly behind and a voice I never thought I would hear again said, "Well, well. I hope I'm not inter-rupting anything."

I spun on my heel, holding Mirielle's hand tightly in my own. "Mother."

The Next Step

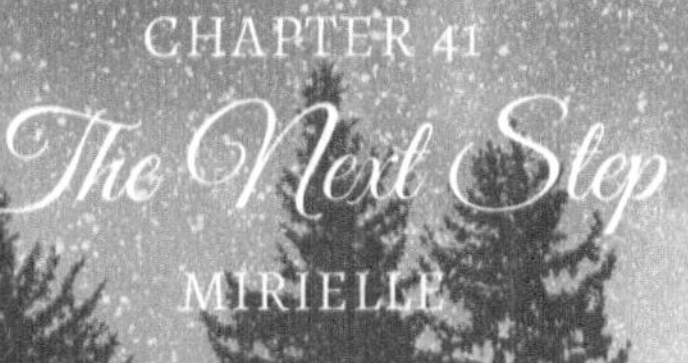

Mother?! The woman standing before us was wearing an emerald green dress and had on a black cloak with the hood down. A wild mass of golden blonde curls tumbled down her shoulders, identical in color to Gryphon's wild mane. There was nothing threatening or frightening in her posture, but I had the innate thought that this was not a woman to be trifled with. She oozed confidence and power, and there was something about her voice that I recognized...

"You're the one who visited me in my dreams!" I burst out.

Gryphon looked at me in alarm, but the woman smiled warmly. It changed all of her features, making her appear as a kind and loving motherly figure.

"Oh, Mirielle, how I've longed to meet you," she said, opening her arms for a hug.

I moved to give her one, but Gryphon pulled me back, my hand still clutched in his. "What's the meaning of this?" he demanded coldly, glaring down his nose at her.

She sighed and had the wherewithal to look contrite. "You must be so angry with me, Gryphon, dear," his mother replied.

Gryphon didn't say anything, but his jaw wasn't clenched like it usually was when he was angry. His body remained loose and at ease, all of his wounds now healed and the blood gone, although the makeshift tourniquet was still present.

I sensed Barrett come up behind us. "Yo, everything inside is all nice again and shit," he exclaimed. "Who is this?" He stopped just a few steps to my left, pointing towards the queen.

Gryphon's mother smiled at him. "You both can call me Gaia," she explained. "I am Gryphon's mother."

"Who has been gone for millennia," Gryphon inserted quietly. There was still no anger in his tone; he sounded more reproachful than anything else.

It was the reproach that made me realize what was going on. Gryphon wasn't angry. He was hurt. His mother had cast her wicked curse and then abandoned him.

"There's much to explain, my dear," she began, drawing a few steps closer to him. She reached out her hand and after a very tense pause, Gryphon took it. "I'm so sorry for the pain I caused you. All I wanted to do was help you." Tears brimmed in her eyes as she gazed at her only son.

Slowly, I withdrew my hand from Gryphon's and took a step backward, hoping to allow them to share a private moment. Although he glanced back at me, Gryphon didn't comment.

"I was so scared that you were adopting all of your father's bitterness and ambition that you would miss out on the true beauty that life holds. We kept you too isolated...you never had a chance to see what you were missing out on," Gaia explained.

Barrett shuffled uncomfortably next to me. I knew he was

thinking of his own mother and his unhappy childhood spent in the shadow of her drug addiction.

"You always hated Father," Gryphon countered. "This was just a way to get back at us both!"

Gaia shook her head fiercely. "No!" she corrected. "I love your father and the joy it always brought me was overshadowed by his constant battles and bickering with my brother. I wanted you to know love, to know joy...I wanted you to experience everything you've only just begun to experience with Mirielle." Both of their heads swiveled towards me and my cheeks flushed with embarrassment. "Love is what makes life worth living, Gryphon," she said. "And you deserve that just as much as your father, even if he was too stubborn to see it. I couldn't find any other way to make you understand."

My heart melted at hearing my suspicions confirmed. After reading the entries in Gryphon's journal, I knew he never felt any love from his parents. His father's cold, calculating demeanor had rubbed off on him too much, and Gaia was right—Gryphon deserved to be loved. Although her methods were drastic, she acted as a mother determined to give her child the best would act when faced with impossible odds.

Tentatively, hoping to give Gryphon time to collect the many thoughts that were no doubt rumbling inside his head, I stepped forward to offer my own hug to Gaia. She beamed at me and embraced me with all the love and warmth I had always wanted from my own mother. Her happiness in meeting me and seeing her son again felt genuine, and I hoped that in spite of how angry he must feel, Gryphon didn't let his rage fly off the handle again now that opportunity presented a second chance.

When I pulled away from her embrace to look at Gryphon, his eyes were still wary, but soft. There was no hint of the violent hostility he was prone to suffering. And he surprised all of us when his next move was to hug Gaia himself.

"I missed you so much, Mother," he whispered into her hair.

Happy sobs choked me as I watched Gryphon transform in front of me. He was no longer the beastly spoiled prince gambling his life away, but stood before us as a man who had faced his demons and come out stronger on the other side. I was so proud of him that I could barely contain my joy.

Giggling through my tears, I asked, "Is there room for one more?"

Both of them laughed and pulled me into their embrace. The three of us were all sniffling and clinging to one another, lost in the rapture of the moment. Hope blossomed like I had never known in that moment.

"Now isn't that a pretty picture!" Darda's voice came from behind us.

I pulled away, incredulous as I looked at Darda in the flesh for the first time. She was just as I had pictured in my head, an older woman with gray hair piled in a haphazard bun on top of her head and face full of wise wrinkles. Her eyes sparkled as she took us in, her hands in fists on her broad hips.

"I told you I'd take care of him, dearie," Darda said to Gaia.

Gaia laughed. "And you did a marvelous job, as always."

"Wait, you knew?!" Gryphon asked.

Darda snorted. "Raised him since he was a babe and still, he doubts me! Of course I knew. Yer ma wasn't gonna leave you completely stranded, now was she?"

Gaia smiled sheepishly. "Darda just wanted the same things for you," she offered.

"Now, there's plenty of time for all that," Darda interjected when Gryphon opened his mouth in retort. "Young miss Mirielle has some business to see to first."

"What...?" My voice trailed off as my beloved Mr. Cooper walked onto the terrace in his usual tan sweater, brown slacks, and loafer combo. He looked exactly the same as he had my entire life; no worse for wear after everything we had experienced.

"Mirielle, my darling girl, what's it take to get a hug around here?" he quipped.

My heart had to be bursting by now. *He remembered me.* I didn't even try to hold back the sobs as I hurtled myself into his arms, nearly knocking over the both of us. I let myself cry on his shoulder as I inhaled his familiar scent of tobacco and peppermint, too overcome with happiness that the curse had not permanently taken him from me. He enveloped me in the same hug that had comforted me for as far back as I could remember and I gave a silent prayer of gratitude that I hadn't lost him.

"Everyone is already down there planning a party, so how about we get ready?" Darda called.

"A party?" Barrett repeated. "We just watched a castle piece itself back together and you wanna hit the dance floor?"

"It's what we do here, sonny," Darda replied smartly. She crossed her arms over her chest as if ready to challenge him.

"I mean, I could use a shot of whiskey right about now." He shrugged, offering me a smirk that I couldn't help but return. He *had* saved Gryphon's life, after all.

Gryphon snorted derisively. "Oh, we have something much stronger than that, mortal."

After Darda ushered Barrett to his own room to freshen up and Gaia smothered Gryphon and I with more hugs and cheek kisses before she swept off to her own suite of rooms in the castle, we were finally left alone. Mr. Cooper had long since joined the others down in the kitchens, promising to whip up something special for me personally. I could barely contain my joy and wondered idly if I might start levitating in my happiness.

I was soaking in the bathing pool with fragrant bubbles all around me when Gryphon entered the room. He had personally gone down to check the guards of Aeternitas and thank them for their service to his realm. My suggestion of bestowing each of them with a medal of honor had been gleefully accepted, with Gaia offering to create something temporary until the Aeternitas goldsmiths could forge something more permanent for them to wear on their uniforms.

His eyes had become permanently transformed to the liquid gold color that I now recognized as what it was—love. They seemed to glow now as he observed me in the bath, a smile of peace and contentment etched across his handsome face. Slowly, while maintaining eye contact with me, he undressed from his shirt and pants, pausing slightly before removing his underwear and exposing his erect cock. He never touched himself, only gazed at me, but the intimate moment made my knees quake.

The water rippled as he climbed down the stairs on the opposite end of the bathing pool, languidly moving through the bubbles and foam until his chest was pressed against mine. He brushed my wet hair back from my face as he commented happily, "Love suits you, Miracle. You are glowing."

I wrapped my arms around his neck, using my body's weightless state in the water to help pull me up a little higher, then bound my legs around his waist. Gryphon responded quickly by grabbing both of my ass cheeks to press my wet heat closer. The head of his cock just barely rubbed at my entrance, and this time around, I felt no hesitation or flutter of fear. My body wanted to commit itself to Gryphon just as much as my soul already had.

Kissing him lightly, I leaned my forehead against his. "I love you," I whispered.

He sighed happily. "Say it again," he breathed.

I smiled. "I love you."

Gryphon's lips became more urgent as they traced their way along my neck, up to my jaw, and back to my lips. "As I love you."

My hips began to grind against him as his fingers gripped my ass hard enough to bruise. His cock felt like a steel rod at my entrance, gently parting my folds. I tried to push myself down, but his hold on me tightened. Gryphon pulled his head back to gaze at me quizzically.

"Are you certain?" he asked incredulously.

A blush creeped up my cheeks, his golden eyes smoldering. I nodded. "I am."

Steam billowed around us, but that wasn't what made my skin feel like fire. Gryphon's gold irises swirled with intensity and there was a very pregnant pause before he let go of me, pulling my arms from his neck and taking a few steps backwards.

"No," he stated firmly.

My heart pounded in my ears as embarrassment washed over me. How could he say no at this point? After everything that had just happened?

"No..." I repeated slowly as my mind tried to process the situation.

Gryphon shook his head. "Marry me first," he said.

CHAPTER 42

Time to Celebrate

Before I had a chance to form a coherent response to Gryphon's startling request, a loud bang echoed from the bedroom and Darda's cheerful voice called out, "I hope you're both decent and not being wee devils, now!"

She peeked her head into the bathroom and instantly withdrew. "You could've warned a lass!"

Even I recognized that my laugh sounded fake and too high pitched. Darda's entrance was the perfect excuse to buy myself some time because I couldn't believe what Gryphon had just said. If he had offered to give me my own set of wings it would have been equally surprising. Marriage was never something I wanted, nor was it something I was prepared to consider now. There was too much yet to settle before we could broach that subject.

Clambering out of the bath, I hastily grabbed a fluffy bathing sheet and wrapped it tightly around myself, letting my wet hair soak down my back. I joined Darda out in the bedroom only to find her with a few other companions.

"I thought you might want to meet the team that's kept you

looking so beautiful, dearie. Not that you need much help in that department," Darda added with a wink. She gestured towards a short black woman with magnificent curves and beaded locs. Her makeup was flashy and glamorous, and I felt a twinge of envy at her skill with eyeliner.

"I'm Rita," she said, embracing me fiercely. There were tears in her eyes as she pulled away. "Thank you for what you've done," she whispered.

"This is Pamela," Darda said and the next woman stepped forward to hug me. She was an older woman with the kind of olive skin tone that made it impossible to guess her nationality. Her thick gray hair was piled into an elaborate bun on top of her head and there were wrinkles around her eyes as she smiled at me.

"It's such a pleasure to really *meet* you!" Pamela said emphatically. She placed a gentle kiss on my cheek before returning to Rita's side.

"That must make me Vogue!" A tall transwoman with perfect cheekbones bent down to do the European cheek kiss greeting. She wore a long black dress and heeled boots that I would have broken my neck wearing.

"You're the genius behind all my clothes!" I cried out.

She beamed. "That's me, darling, and don't you ever forget it!" Vogue winked before conspiratorially pulling me in close to whisper, "And wait until you see what I have for tonight's ball!"

I chuckled. It was so fulfilling to see them in their human forms. They were not at all what I was expecting, but somehow their physical features matched their personalities perfectly. "Do you normally live here in Aeternitas?"

All three nodded.

"We came to help you get ready!" squealed Rita.

Suddenly, Vogue stiffened, nudging the others, and the three of them bowed deeply. Darda sank into a curtsy as well. Glancing behind my back, I noticed Gryphon had entered the room, fully clothed in a simple tunic shirt and black pants. He gave a curt nod to them before offering me a small smile and exiting the room.

I hoped his surliness had to do with fatigue and stress from the events of the day rather than my lack of response. Had he noticed?

"Come on, ladies, let's do this!" Vogue swung both arms around Rita and Pamela's shoulders to escort them to the bathroom. "Darda, don't let her see the gown yet!" she called over her shoulder.

When I turned back to Darda, her brown eyes were filled with warmth. She was a few inches shorter than me, but I swore in that moment I felt dwarfed by her energy. A gentle hand grasped mine tightly and the same sense of calm enveloped me as it always had around Darda.

"It's a lot to take in, my dear," she said kindly. "Don't let it overwhelm you."

The same fake laugh as before slipped out. "Meeting everyone isn't the overwhelming part."

Darda nodded like she understood. "Then let's just focus on tonight, shall we?"

We walked into the bathroom still hand in hand before the glam squad pounced on me. Even now with Rita and Pamela in their human forms, they talked over one another and answered each other when one posed a question to me. Vogue helped them with my eye makeup, a shimmery gold ombre design that darkened at the outer corners of my eyes. She carefully applied the boldest wing I had ever seen in eyeliner that contained gold sparkles.

All of them described normal life in Aeternitas now that their memories were restored. They were delighted to see all of their friends again and informed me that celebrations would take place throughout the entire kingdom, not just the palace. Everyone was eager to celebrate the end of the curse, the return of the queen, and the beginning of a new era in Aeternitas. Hope clung to the atmosphere like a new molecule. It was easy to see how happy they were here.

I realized not everyone would feel the same way. Many of the people affected by the curse were humans who belonged back on Earth and now that their memories were restored, they were probably just as eager to get home to their loved ones. My obligation wasn't just to save them from the curse, but to send them back where they belong, I decided. If I was going to do it for Mr. Cooper, it was only fair that I help everyone else.

"Darda," I began, "how hard will it be to send everyone home?"

She had been helping them weave a strand of gold chain through the big curls Pamela created, and caught my gaze in the mirror at my question.

"I don't rightly know," admitted Darda. "That sounds like a question better posed to the queen."

I nodded, already formulating a plan of attack in my head. I generally found it was easier to approach someone of authority with a proposed solution rather than just a problem. It was how I always started conversations with my supervisor at the museum, so it should be an appropriate tactic with a mythical queen.

It took far longer than I would have anticipated to curl all of my hair, then use the gold thread woven through to pull the curls away from my face. When all three stylists were satisfied with their handiwork, Vogue instructed me to close my eyes so they could lead me by the hand into the bedroom for my gown. We all giggled as I stumbled through the doorway, my excitement taking hold.

My breath caught in my chest when they finally permitted me to open my eyes. The same velvet mannequin from my old room now stood in front of me with the most spectacular dress I had ever seen. A strapless bodice that glittered with gold flecks melted down into a full skirt of tulle and chiffon, also in gold. A slit divided the front of the skirt that rose high enough to toe the line of indecency. The color perfectly matched the sun as though even the gown wanted to indicate the dawn of a new epoch in Aeternitas. Vogue swiftly turned around the mannequin to display the open back where chains of the gold flecks crisscrossed in an elaborate pattern down past my waist.

"A dress fit for royalty," commented a voice behind me.

I spun quickly to find Gaia resplendent in a dress that perfectly matched the emerald green of her eyes. A large gold and emerald crown stood on her head, marking her every inch the queen I imagined her to be. Her curls were somewhat tamed into an elegant knot at the back of her head. She nodded once to Darda and the others, who hastily exited the room.

"I just wanted to take a moment to properly thank you," Gaia said once the door closed behind them. She took both my hands in her own and gave them a gentle squeeze. Her eyes radiated the same intensity as her son's. "What you did for my kingdom is a debt I will never be able to repay, but what you did for my son is more than any mother could ask for."

Her words made me flush, embarrassment running through me in droves. "It was only what everyone deserved," I offered. "Especially Gryphon."

She smiled. It was just as dazzling as his. "Do not lose faith in him, for I have no doubt that he will test you."

Apprehension sidled into my gut. I wondered if she somehow

knew he had proposed to me and I had not yet given an answer. Allowing another empty laugh to fill the silence, I nodded weakly.

Gaia placed a soft hand on my cheek, a brief caress that held more love and kindness than I ever received from my own mother, and turned to leave. When she reached the door, she turned back, tilting her head to the side as she surveyed the dress and me. With a snap of her fingers, the gown was on, clinging to me like a second skin, gold heels sparking on my feet.

"Own how gorgeous you are, Mirielle." Gaia gave me a small wave and swept from the room, greeting Barrett as he hovered on the threshold outside.

Barrett's wolf whistle when the door closed behind him made me flush with embarrassment again. "Damn, Miri, you're a knockout!"

I rolled my eyes but couldn't help crossing over to the full length mirror propped against the opposite wall. I barely recognized the glowing woman looking back at me. My glam squad deserved an award.

"Thank you," I whispered.

Barrett came closer and gently titled my face up to look at him. "Are you alright?" Concern was evident in his features as he assessed my expression. "You look tense."

It was like the floodgates opened. "I'm completely overwhelmed right now. There's so much to do to get everybody home. I can't just leave them here! And then there's all that history to contend with. All those artifacts should be preserved and given to a museum."

He nodded. "Then that's what we'll do," he said simply.

I let out an exasperated sigh. "It's not that easy, Barrett!"

"Nobody ever said it was, Miri. But we both know you won't

stop until everyone is safe. You care too much." It alarmed me how well he knew where my thoughts had scattered.

"I'll need to start right away, but I don't even know where to begin."

"We'll figure it out." Barrett shrugged as if it was no big deal.

I snorted. "*We'll* figure it out?"

His steel blue eyes held mine and he slowly placed a hand on my waist to draw me closer. Heat, from his body or mine, was filtering through my dress until a small trickle of sweat traced its way down between my breasts. A red flag waved somewhere in the back of my mind to warn me that Barrett was too close, but I was mesmerized, drawn to the connection I felt radiating through my skin.

"You're my special person, Mirielle," Barrett murmured. "Where you go, I go."

I gulped as a shiver raced down my spine. "Barrett, I...I..." Words failed me as his eyes continued to bore into mine. His other hand now curled into my hair, his broad palm warm and soothing against my cheek. Dark brown hair fell across his eye as he leaned closer and reality snapped into place.

"We can't, Barrett." I pulled away from his hold, turning my back to hide the tears I could feel forming. Tears of guilt or tears of relief, I could not tell.

He huffed in annoyance. "Why? Because of some pompous prince?! He's not right for you, Mirielle!"

The bossy attitude turned my sass back on. "You have no idea what's right for me!" I snapped, my fists resting on my hips in challenge as I whirled on him.

Barrett smirked, though a coldness settled in his features. "I know you. I know you better than you know yourself."

I shook my head, throwing my hands up in exasperation. "He

asked me to marry him!" Half mad with Barrett's arrogance, half lightened to admit it out loud, I dared him to challenge me further. Some part of me wanted the fight, the fire, to work out some of the anxious energy that clouded me since Gryphon's revelation. There was no way I could fight him in the way I needed while in a ball gown, however, and I made to move past him to the door.

A strong arm caught me around the waist as Barrett spun me around to face him. "You don't even believe in marriage!" he countered.

My jaw dropped before I remembered I didn't want to give him the satisfaction of winning. "Who told you that?"

Barrett's face was grim. "No one had to tell me. As an addict's kid, I don't believe in it either. Happy ever after's are different when you live in the real world."

I was dumbstruck at how accurate his assessment was. That was exactly why I had never wanted that kind of commitment. Marriage had never appealed to me...and Barrett understood why.

Things will be different with Gryphon, the voice in my head insisted.

"No," I argued. "You're wrong! I love Gryphon!" The tears were starting to flow and I tried not to ruin Vogue's work on my eyes as I swiped at them.

"Miri, love is just the foundation," Barrett said. "You need more than that to build the house."

Although his tone was harsh, his eyes indicated sincerity. His statement weighed heavily on me as I withdrew from his arm. "Enjoy the party," I whispered.

Barrett's words continued to echo in my head even as Mr. Cooper twirled me around on the dance floor. Gryphon and I barely had a moment together once I arrived downstairs in the great hall with all of his newly returned subjects swarming the crown prince and their beloved queen. He stopped to chat with every person, smiling cheerfully and shaking their hands, forsaking the stiff formality I expected him to embody. Happiness was changing him and he didn't even realize it.

That was not to say that I wasn't bombarded with just as many hugs and introductions. There was so much joy saturating the air that I could practically taste it. It clung to all of the interactions as long lost friends and family members embraced one another, and it was hard for me to hold back tears. The more I observed happy reunions, the more I choked up.

My heart sank a little as Wade arrived and confirmed my suspicions that he was just a young teen. His dirty blonde hair was artfully messy and he wore a Youngblood t-shirt. "My-my!" he grinned before pulling me into a hug. "Isn't this crazy? Yo, I can't wait to tell my friends back home!"

"No!" Although Gryphon had never said otherwise, I sincerely doubted anyone was permitted to speak of Aeternitas in the human world. For all I knew, though, there could be a spell of some kind that would wipe everyone's memories when they returned home. It was yet another question for me to catalog for later when I discussed everything with Gaia.

"Where is home for you?" Mr. Cooper asked him.

Wade shrugged. "I lived with my aunt in Queens, but she works three jobs. I kinda just do my own thing."

Mr. Cooper glanced at me with raised eyebrows and I knew exactly what he was about to say. "When we go back, you will live with me. Mirielle and I are your family now."

I didn't think a smile could spread that wide. Wade bounced on the balls of his feet as if hardly daring to believe it. "Really? I can?"

Mr. Cooper hooked an arm around his shoulders before throwing the other one around mine. "Of course. But your studies come first in my house!"

"Trust me," I warned in a laugh, "he means it!"

And so the night went on. Ambrose turned out to be Ambrose Bierce, the famous writer and journalist believed to have disappeared around 1913. The piano who led the band during the first grand ball was none other than famed orchestra conductor Glenn Miller. His plane was considered missing in action during World War II. It turned out that several of the people I knew to be lost historical figures were actually taken in Gryphon's quest to find the person referenced in the curse.

My anger rose just as instantaneously as it had when I first saw the warehouse, though I was able to calm myself down rather than find Gryphon in the crowd and call him every name in the book like I wanted. It greatly soured my mood to realize all of the people who had been caught in the crossfire of this curse. So many lives were forever changed. There had to be a way to make it right.

I needed to talk to Gryphon. Surely now that the curse was broken, we could return everyone home and give them a chance to lead the lives they should have had. He had to understand now what it felt like to have a loved one. As I circled in a lap around the ball room, however, he was alone on the outskirts and appeared deeply lost in contemplation.

CHAPTER 43

Yet to Come

GRYPHON

Mirielle looked lovelier than ever as I gazed at her across the room. Moments after my proposal, her glamour squad had interrupted us, along with Darda, who immediately barked at me to leave the room so they could get her ready. There was lots of hugging and crying as Mirielle got to meet each of them in their true human form, so I had acquiesced, instead going to my study to dress for the party there. She was resplendent now in a gold ball gown that made her look every inch the trophy I imagined her to be.

I knew I had startled her with my sudden marriage proposal, which was the only reason I had not pressed upon the fact that she had not yet given me an answer. It was not planned for me to say it, but the moment felt so right, and the thought of her finally giving her body over to me as my wife was too tantalizing to ignore. Even now, hours later with the celebration in full swing around us, I found irrevocable pleasure in imagining her in a sparkling gown and the Aeternitas crown, seated on a throne beside me.

Convincing my father to approve of our union would be another matter entirely, but I felt so invigorated by love and success that I convinced myself it was a worry for another day.

"Happiness suits you, my lord," Darda commented as she sidled up next to me. It was so similar to my previous conversation with Mirielle that I could not help but laugh out loud.

"Must I remind you that my name is Gryphon," I replied instead, earning Darda's warm smile in response. I embraced her in what must have been my thousandth hug of the evening, having gone through a reception of sorts with all of my subjects upon our arrival in the ballroom.

Darda jutted her chin in Mirielle's direction where my miracle laughed and chatted with Ambrose and Wade. "Take care of her," advised Darda. "That's one woman you don't let get away."

I smiled jovially. "Oh, I don't intend for any such thing. In fact, I asked Mirielle to marry me."

The smile slipping from my nursemaid's face confused me, but she quickly masked it with pride. "A wedding in the castle would certainly be something special," she offered. Darda gently squeezed my hand before melting back into the crowd.

What looked like the entire kingdom had gathered in the ballroom and the relief and delight was palpable in the air. Friends and family members had been reuniting all evening, giving me an overwhelming sense of accomplishment. My mother's curse had been effective for I never would have considered something so intangible as the missing puzzle piece, but seeing the tears of joy on my subjects' faces as they thanked me was humbling. Aeternitas would now enter its golden age with a fresh beginning. I vowed to rule them as a different kind of prince. Someone worthy of Mirielle's love who embodied her compassion.

Mirielle's so-called friend sauntered over to me, exuding a cocky swagger I did not like. Barrett's admiration for her was written all over his face, and although she had assured me that she no longer regarded him as her childhood bully but a friend, the way his eyes continued to roam over her body made him public enemy number one in my book. A lock of his dark brown hair fell just into his eyes as he leaned against the wall behind me, crossing one ankle over the other. Someone had provided him freshly laundered clothing from Aeternitas, but he managed to wear the shirt tight enough to show off his toned muscles, which oddly threatened me. His size was nothing compared to mine, but I could not shake the jealousy that he had known Mirielle for most of her life.

"I suppose we never did formally meet," he said casually, holding out a hand. "I'm Barrett."

My back stiffened as I gripped his hand in a firm shake. "I know who you are," I replied tersely.

He grinned at me like my words amused him. "Miri told you about me?"

I gritted my teeth at the absurd nickname. Why did Americans find the need to shorten everything? "Yes, Mirielle mentioned what a pest you can be."

Barrett's grin only widened. "Seems like you don't like me very much."

Turning to fully face him, I made no attempt to stop the warning lacing my tone. "I don't like anyone who wants what I have." I crossed my arms over my chest, itching to call for my sword. No doubt Mirielle would frown upon challenging him to a proper fight, though.

The venom in my voice didn't deter him. "Doesn't really seem like you have her, though, does it?" Barrett nodded towards Mirielle, who was now on the dance floor with Emil.

Anger simmered just beneath the surface at his insinuation. "On the contrary," I countered. "I proposed to Mirielle only hours ago."

"And she said yes?"

His arrogant reminder that Mirielle hadn't actually given me an answer rankled me deeply, but I didn't want to give him the satisfaction of knowing that. Choosing to ignore his comment, I turned on my heel, calling over my shoulder, "Enjoy the party."

"She'll never say yes to you," he countered loudly.

Barrett's irksome comments succeeded in dampening my high spirits. I wandered onto the balcony, lost in thought. Even the sight of my realm without that infernal fog could not break the darkness swirling inside my head. Stars finally winked down at us cheerily, the occasional shooting star crossing the sky in a myriad of colors. The sky here resembled that of the Northern Lights on Earth, bright colors painting their way across the vast void. Bonfires from the village beyond the castle walls dotted the landscape where more of my subjects celebrated. With a jolt, I realized I had never fully explained to Mirielle what Aeternitas encompassed, or my role in all of it.

As if reading my thoughts, my mother's voice came from behind me. "Dwelling on the future or the past, my dear?"

I turned to offer her a stiff smile over my shoulder before facing the village again. "I have much to explain about our realm if I am to build a future with Mirielle."

She walked up beside me, standing shoulder to shoulder. "And is this a future you can only see in Aeternitas?"

Snorting, I shook my head. "My duty to this kingdom has been drilled into my head since birth. I will not forget my place again."

From the corner of my eye, I could see my mother nod. "But is that the life you want?"

"What are you saying, Mother?" My back felt ramrod straight with tension from the turn this conversation was taking. "Have I not proven everything I am willing to do for this realm?"

Mother smiled lovingly at me, caressing my cheek with a warm hand. Her eyes were the same glowing emerald mine had been before love altered me permanently. "You have nothing to prove, my dear, but everything to consider. Your fate is no longer your own if you wish to include her."

Her words gave me pause, yet when I tried to reflect on that, she focused on adjusting the medals on my jacket. "I am so proud of the man you have become. You have shown tremendous strength and honor, for which we are all grateful. Enjoy this moment...I fear there is far worse yet to come."

She gave me one last smile before slipping back through into the ballroom. Music filtered out, reminding me of the joy inside, but it was a joy I no longer felt. Her words confused me more than they reassured me, and now I had another worry to add to the list. A long conversation with Mirielle needed to happen as soon as possible, but if I was being honest with myself, somewhere deep inside I doubted what her choice would be.

I was so lost in my ruminations that I did not hear when Mirielle approached. Her arms wrapped around my waist from behind as she pressed her forehead between my shoulder blades.

"You have a habit of escaping parties thrown in your honor," she scolded me.

Her teasing was enough to draw a smile to my lips. Pulling her around to face me, seeing the light twinkling in her eyes made me feel like the luckiest being in the world. I kissed her firmly on the mouth, my hand tangling in the long curls trailing down her back. My wings threatened to expand behind me as I fought the urge to take off into the night sky with her in my arms.

She giggled as she pulled away from our kiss. "Now isn't the time to start something you can't finish! Everybody's in there waiting for us!"

I sighed, willing my dick to cooperate and not give all of our friends an intimate show.

"You know," Mirielle said pensively, "we need to return everyone to their real homes. Everyone you've taken has a life back home waiting for them."

Mirielle was right, though it would be a massive undertaking. For more reasons than she realized.

"And everything in the warehouse needs to go back," she said. Sensing the argument on the verge of my tongue, she placed a hand over my mouth. "None of those things belong to you, Gryphon."

Squeezing her waist, I earned another giggle and her hand dropped from my mouth. "They actually do belong to me, and I am the only one who can keep them safe from human destruction."

She rolled her eyes at me. "Not all humans are destructive," Mirielle countered.

I snorted. I knew better than anyone the toll human nature exacted on her world. All that treasure needed to stay in that warehouse if it had any hope of preservation. Convincing her of that was unlikely, however, and I wanted to continue to bask in the light of the moment. Mirielle was glowing with love and excitement.

All I wanted was to keep that happiness on her face, but I knew she would have misgivings about what I needed to tell her.

"Miracle, do you remember when you tried to ask me about Aeternitas? And how my life used to be?"

She smiled and nodded. "You told me you couldn't tell me

much because of the curse. If this is your invitation to let me ask my questions, we'll be here until Doomsday."

In spite of myself, a shaky laugh escaped. "I know we will be, but there is something I must tell you. Aeternitas serves a purpose for your world as well. My mother, my father, and I all make the human realm possible."

Mirielle pulled back slightly, wariness streaking across her face. "Meaning...?"

"Aeternitas is what you could call a final resting place. All of the people you can see in that village behind you, and in other villages around the castle, are here for a reason."

Confusion settled in and I could practically feel the gears turning in her head as she tried to analyze my explanation. It was flimsy at best, but I was suddenly fearful of her reaction now that she was to learn the truth.

"'Final resting place' sounds like an afterlife," she said incredulously. "Like you're saying—"

"This is where souls come after death," I finished for her.

Mirielle's arms dropped from my waist and she took several steps backward until she bumped into the balcony railing. Her mouth hung open in shock. "Is everyone here dead?" she asked tearfully.

"Oh no, my love!" I was startled by the conclusion her mind had drawn. "You do not *have* to die to come to Aeternitas but *when* every soul on Earth dies, this is where they come." I paused because this would be the part that would be the scariest revelation of all. "This is where *I* bring the souls who have passed on."

Her eyes grew round as saucers and she gripped the railing for support. "You bring them? That sounds like a nightmare! Like you're the Grim Reaper or something."

Flinching at the high octave her voice had taken on in her fear,

I nodded. "That is one of many names the humans have created for me, yes."

A feather could have knocked her over in that moment. Tears filled her eyes and one trailed down her cheek as she jutted her chin behind me. "And your mother? Who is she, then?"

I glanced over my shoulder to see my mother laughing gayly with the captain of the guard, an Aeternitas soldier named Meritus. My jaw clenched at Mirielle's reaction. "Some would call her 'Mother Nature.'"

The incredulous laugh that escaped from her mouth was reminiscent of Mirielle's time locked in the tower. She shook her head, wrapping her arms around herself as she tried to hold herself together, not that I could blame her. I knew how outlandish it must sound to a human.

"Your mother is responsible for the weather!" she laughed, higher pitched and scarier than normal.

I shrugged. "And the changing of the seasons."

"Oh, of course!" Mirielle's hysterics continued. "How could I forget that?! Especially after you told me how all the seasons exist here!"

"Mirielle..." My patience was wearing thin with her theatrics. Yes, she had every right to be shocked, but given all she had already seen and experienced in my realm, could this really be the straw that broke the camel's back?

"And you!" Another maniacal laugh. "You want me to marry you and what—rule over it all?!" It was hard to tell if she was laughing or crying as she doubled over, clutching her side and struggling to breathe.

That's what this was about. Her disbelief was founded more in my proposal than anything else I told her.

"No, Miracle," I tried to console her, crossing over to rub her back and bring her upright. "I am not the king, nor will I ever be."

Mirielle sniffled, wiping the back of her hand across her nose. She had been crying. "Your father is the king," she clarified in a whisper. When I nodded, she added, "Your father who you said won't like me."

At her statement, the sky darkened and thunderous black clouds of smoke rolled overhead. There was a tiny point of bright blue light in the center that was growing larger by the second as strong winds blew leaves off the trees and knocked us back towards the doorway.

Mirielle had fallen in the power of the wind gust and struggled to right herself as I pulled her off the ground. The smoke was furling in great waves as though angry, sending a shiver of trepidation down my spine. Out of instinct, my magic transformed my clothing into the body armor I preferred for battle and my wings unfurled behind us, their luminescence fully restored with the rest of my powers.

Barrett, Emil, and a few other trickled out next to us, the shock and fear mixed on all their faces as they watched the darkness coming our way. My mother pushed through the wall of onlookers and took a few steps in front of me.

She turned back to me, an apology frozen on her features. "Gryphon," she yelled. "You were not the only one freed from the curse."

My hands turned to fists and an angry fire worked through my veins. I knew exactly what her warning meant.

Mirielle looked between us both, her hair whipping around her as the gusts blew stronger. "Who does she mean? What is happening?"

"My father is coming," I yelled over the gale.

She grabbed onto my arm as she looked fearfully up at the darkening sky. "And who is he?"

"Our real enemy!" my mother called.

Mirielle looked at me, clearly still confused.

"The enemy of us all," I explained. "My father is here. Or as you mortals know him, Father Time."

The End

Acknowledgments

Writing something like this is much harder than I would have anticipated because I feel like there are so many people to thank. Epoch comes into the world already surrounded with a team of love and support, and for that, I could not be more grateful. This has been a labor of love on so many counts.

To my editor Lea, another B&N cohort, you are the absolute best. I loved getting to work with you on Epoch and how you helped me bring these characters to life. You molded me into a better writer, which is more than any decent author can ask for. An editor like you is worth your weight in gold!

To my artist Arianna, my B&N hire buddy, you really did the damn thing! How you were able to take the images from my mind and turn them into beautiful artwork for readers to enjoy, I will never understand, but I am so grateful you could. You are beyond talented and deserve all the recognition!

So much gratitude for my found family for their continued support. My friends are the absolute best. To my Tennessee favorites, you are treasured. Ohio may be where I live, but y'all made Clarksville my true home. Kat, I will never stop thanking you for pushing me to go after my dreams. It's so scary but so worth it.

To my Ohio family, from the bottom of my heart, thank you. You have all sacrificed so much time and energy to be a part of this craziness. I know there were times when you questioned my sanity (hell, I did, too!), but now that we are on the other side of the madness, I hope you can see how it paid off. Thank you, Corey, for serving as my model for Barrett. Thank you, Mom, for the ridiculous level of promotion. Thank you to my bonus mom, Cheryl, for never failing to pick me back up when I needed it most. This book is a reflection of all of you. May it make you proud.

My deepest thanks to all of the Samantha Gail Starlets I have met along the way. My Booktok Book Club peeps deserve a special shout out because y'all helped me see how much my book can connect with readers. It meant more to me than I could ever say. Thank you times infinity!

And lastly, to the three most spectacular sons I could ever imagine, this is all because of you. Jack, Tristan, and Cael, you make me want to be a better person because I can't believe I have the honor of being your mom. Don't ever give up on what you want. If I've taught you nothing else in life, I consider that a success. I love you all so much.

-SG

About the Author

Samantha Gail is a former Probation Parole Officer who supervised sex offenders before deciding she needed more happily ever after's. Her work falls into multiple genres, primarily thriller, fantasy, and romance. She currently resides in Ohio and writes when she's not spending time with her three children and three furbabies.